D0313022

REFRACTION

NAOMI HUGHES

PAGE STREET
PUBLISHING CO.

PAGE STREET
PUBLISHING CO.

For the One who believed in me

when all I could see were the shadows

CHAPTER ONE

THE COPS START TAILING ME ON BANYAN LANE. I should be worried about the contraband sewn into the bill of my baseball cap, but all I can think about is whether or not I remembered to lock my loft before I left this morning.

"Marty Callahan," calls one of the officers in an easy voice, like I'm an old friend he's spotted at a party. But his eyes are trained on me like I'm a dangerous animal, and whatever Cisco Island is nowadays, it's definitely no party.

I give the cops a faux-surprised grin and a middle-finger wave—carefully measuring the amount of disrespect in the gesture, enough to seem normal for me but not enough to piss them off more than necessary—then speed up a little.

I did lock the loft, I'm sure of it. I can almost hear the way that final, biggest dead bolt clunked heavily when I slid it into place, can almost feel how the rusted padlock flaked in my hand when I pulled the key out. But the need to go back and check just in case tugs at me anyway, even though I should be way more worried about the two jokers behind me.

"We're talking to you, Callahan," says another voice. It's the other officer, the younger one. He sounds a lot less casual than his partner. Which probably means he intends to stop me, pat me down, do a "random" search for the dangerous illegal goods they suspect—but haven't yet managed to prove—I sell. Any other day, that would be no problem for me. I haven't moved any goods in weeks. But today, the desperation got a little too strong, and I managed to convince myself the heat had died down enough for me to venture back out. A decision I'm cursing myself for now.

There's a small crowd ahead of me, weaving in and out of the early-afternoon shadows cast by the gnarled trees that line this street. The islanders must be headed to the ration dispensary for weekly distribution. Maybe I can merge with them, buy myself some time while I figure out an escape route. I step off the sidewalk and onto the cracked asphalt of the road.

"Told you he'd rabbit," mutters the younger officer to his partner. They're a bit closer now, near enough for me to hear the viciousness in his voice. He *wants* me to run. He wants to be the one to catch me. I glance at him again, a little longer this time, taking his measure. He's maybe twenty-five, with a curly mop of bright ginger hair and bright green eyes that are much more expressive than he probably wants them to be. I bet he's the type who would've worn mirrored sunglasses to hide his fear back before they outlawed glasses.

It's not a good thing, him being afraid of me. Scared is dangerous. Scared makes mistakes, and mistakes get people killed.

My mind skitters back to my potentially unlocked loft. The key is in my pocket, I remember. If I was still using the same system as I used to have a while back (left pocket for keys to doors that were currently locked, right for ones that were unlocked), I'd be more sure that I hadn't accidentally left my home wide open and vulnerable. But I abandoned that key system over a year ago. And, I force myself to remember, it never really worked in the first place anyway.

"Easy," says the older cop to his partner. I can see sweat beading on his umber skin from here, but he doesn't move to wipe it away, keeping his gaze on me. At his side, Ginger is practically vibrating with the need to give chase.

I reach the back of the crowd and start weaving between the people. I breathe shallowly. I'll never get used to this smell: unwashed bodies and barely contained terror. It's everywhere on this godforsaken island, ever since the aliens knocked out our power—and therefore the town's desalination plant—last year during the Fracture. No one except the mayor and her lackeys can afford to waste precious fresh water on a shower now, and no one goes to the beaches unless they have to.

When I reach the middle of the crowd, I glance around, trying to map out an escape. Banyan trees line either side of the street here. Their knotty limbs spread overhead, twisting together in a canopy that looks like a thousand interlocking fingers, while thick prop roots dangle down and burrow into the ground. If you look hard at some of the trunks, you can still spot the original tree that's been long since starved by the banyans that planted themselves in their crevices. This street used to be a big tourist attraction because of these trees, or so I've heard.

The locals call them strangler figs, my brother told me when we first moved here last summer. *I can see why the tourists like them so much. Either way, they're an invasive species.*

I shake off the memory and glance behind me again. Ginger and his partner are coming up through the crowd now, and there's no viable escape route that I can see. Trying to slip between all the prop roots will slow me down too much. There's a storm drain with a loose grate south of here that's served me well in the past, but the cops are between me and it.

My pulse kicks up a notch. The contraband in my hat is sewn into the brim, its shape hidden by a thin piece of paperboard, but there's still a chance they'll realize the weight of the cap is off and tear it apart to find out why. And if they finally get their proof of what I've been dealing in my little black-market niche . . .

Unthinking in my anxiety, I put a hand in my pocket and curl my fingers around my key. Its teeth bite into my palm: a pain as familiar as breathing. And just like that, the compulsion washes over me like a tidal wave—I need to go back to my loft *now*, have to be absolutely sure that the dead bolt is drawn and the padlock is secured and no one has broken in during the few hours I've been gone. The urge is overpowering, the way it used to be a few years back.

This is vital, it tells me. *This is a matter of life and death. You have to be absolutely certain everything is secure.*

I did lock the door. My loft is secure. I am ninety-nine percent sure of it.

That's not enough, it whispers. *One percent unsafe is still unsafe.*

And the thing is, I *know* that little voice is lying. I know exactly what's happening. My therapy made sure of that. But sometimes the urges still feel as inevitable, as absolutely, impossibly *necessary* as they used to. And sometimes I forget that trying to fight them only makes things worse. Like now, when I'm so focused on trying to logic my way out of my compulsions that I can't pay attention to the actual danger that's coming down the street behind me.

I need to take care of this, right now. I squeeze the key tighter, roll my neck, and take a deep breath. Then I tell my OCD: *Yeah, maybe I did leave everything unlocked, and maybe someone will break in and steal all my stuff. It's not impossible. Also, screw you.*

The compulsion ebbs, robbed of its fuel now that I'm accepting my fears instead of fighting them. I open my hand and release the key. Finally, I can focus on the actual, real-life trouble at my back instead of my own anxiety. I turn my head to look for the officers.

"When I give the signal, run," murmurs an unfamiliar voice about six inches from my right ear.

I startle. Some guy is walking right next to me—tall, brawny, with a superhero-esque square jaw and pretty-boy blond hair. He's around my age, maybe a year older. When he catches my flinch a glimmer of satisfaction sparks in his blue eyes.

I dislike him instantly.

He waits for me to ask the obvious questions: who is he, what's he doing, et cetera. "What's the signal?" I ask instead, belligerently.

Something that might someday have aspirations of becoming a smile flits around the corners of his mouth. "You'll know it when you see it."

I narrow my eyes and study him more closely. He looks a tiny bit familiar, but then nearly everyone does after more than a year of being stranded in a cut-off island city with the same three thousand other people. I'm pretty sure I've never talked to this guy before, though, which is why I'm suspicious that he apparently wants to help me. If he's a law-abiding citizen, he wouldn't offer to help anyone escape the cops. If he's *not* law-abiding, I would've made his acquaintance before now.

I wait for him to tell me what he wants. The cops get closer. Ginger is almost within grabbing distance, but he's having trouble navigating through the people behind us, who are huddled together and talking loudly.

Pretty Boy is still striding along next to me, smiling that annoying not-smile, silent. He can afford to wait. I can't. This whole conversation—if you can call it that—is a subtle tug-of-war, and he's going to win.

But if he really is willing to help me escape, that's a trade I have no choice but to take.

"And what do you want in return for helping me out?" I ask at last, in a low voice so Ginger won't overhear.

Pretty Boy doesn't acknowledge the point he's scored by making me speak first. "I know what you sell," he says instead, "and I want to buy."

"I don't know what you're talking about," I lie coolly— but my brain is moving racecar-fast, trying to figure out how he knows I'm a dealer. There are rumors about me, sure, but there're rumors about *everyone* in this tiny town. The only people who have actual reason to suspect me are the cops. He's too young to be one of them, and he doesn't look stupid enough to be a rat either. And all my current clients know better than to refer someone without asking me first.

But if he *is* a potential new customer and he's desperate enough to approach me in broad daylight with the cops barely a dozen feet away . . . I could make some real money off him.

No. This is the first day I've smuggled goods in weeks, and it's nearly gotten me caught already. I shouldn't push my luck. I should lie low, hide out, wait for the mayor and her cops to focus their efforts on another target.

Pretty Boy doesn't respond for a second. Then he says, "Not even if I've got information that can get you to your brother?"

I stumble to a stop. People push past me. Ginger is ten steps away and I don't care. *"What did you say?"* I demand, rounding on Pretty Boy.

"I'll trade it to you tonight," he murmurs quickly, "at the boardwalk, just before sunset." He glances at Ginger. "But you've got to get out of here first."

I grab his arm, hold him in place. "What's the information?" I hiss. The rest of the world is an unimportant blur of background noise.

He looks at my hand clenched around his arm and raises an eyebrow. My reaction has confirmed how important his information—whatever it is—is to me. I should backpedal. Should reestablish control of the conversation. In my line of work, the most vital rule is to never show your cards, and I've just handed him the whole deck.

I don't move. I wait for him to speak.

"I'll answer your question if you answer one of mine," he says.

"Out of the way!" yells Ginger behind us, speaking to the huddle of people between us and him. The older officer is hanging back, still between me and the storm drain.

"What question?" I demand.

Pretty Boy nods at the crowd. "Where are these people going?"

I stare at him. What the hell is he talking about? The crowd is going to the dispensary. Today is ration disbursement. But the tone in his voice is strangely dark, and there's something odd in his eyes, lurking behind that cool satisfaction.

I glance up the road. There's a fork ahead—right to the dispensary, left to the road leading to Valkyrie Bridge. And the crowd . . . the crowd is turning left. I stop breathing, because there's only one reason people go to Valkyrie Bridge.

Pretty Boy pushes my hand off his arm. "Go and see," he tells me in a low tone. "After you get away. *Then* decide if you want to do a deal with me."

Then Ginger is on us. He grabs my shoulder, straight-arms me out of the crowd. The smell of him washes over me: fresh and crisp with light chemical undertones. It takes me a minute to identify the scent as dryer sheets. An unimaginable luxury in a city where most of the generators ran out of juice long ago. "Don't make this harder than it has to be," he warns me, eyes tight and vicious.

"It's like you don't know me at all," I say with a careless grin even though my heart is thundering in my ears. Caught. I'm caught. As soon as he finds the contraband I'm dead, worse than dead—

Something moves in my peripheral vision. Pretty Boy is sauntering up behind Ginger. He taps the officer on the shoulder. Ginger turns, and Pretty Boy punches him in the face.

Ginger hits the ground like a sack of potatoes. I stare at Pretty Boy, startled—and, despite myself, a little bit impressed.

Pretty Boy turns to me. "In case it wasn't obvious, that was the signal," he states calmly. The older cop yells, having spotted his partner on the ground, and barrels toward us.

I turn and run.

The crowd is clamoring, confused. I dive into it again and use it for cover as I dart toward the storm drain. Pretty Boy is sprinting in the opposite direction, and the older cop is running after him. Ginger is hauling himself to his feet, his nose spurting blood down his freshly laundered shirt. "Elliott!" he yells after Pretty Boy, like it's a curse word.

Elliott. My newest would-be customer. Who the cops apparently know by name—and who claims to have information that can reunite me with my big brother.

I pry the grate up in one smooth movement and slide down into the damp darkness. No one yells or points me out to the cops or tries to follow me. A clean getaway, at least till the next time I risk smuggling goods to a client.

Tonight. At the boardwalk, at sunset. I shouldn't go. The risk is too high. Every time I make another deal, my name rises a little higher on the mayor's list of suspects. Plus I haven't had the chance to vet Elliott, don't know anything about him beyond his name and that he has an impressive left hook.

But I hesitate anyway as I lower the grate back into place overhead, my hands lingering on the bars, my gaze caught by the view of the northeastern horizon. My brother, Ty, is about three thousand miles in that direction. Some days I can feel him like a lodestone pulling me out over the open sea. Those are the days I stand on the beach and stare squinting into the distance, trying to fool myself into believing I could see London if I just looked hard enough.

Today all I can see on the horizon are towering gray storm clouds. They look ominous, but not as ominous as the Shatter Ring—Earth's new ring made up of huge, orbiting shards of reflective alien metal—gleaming above them.

I grimace and turn my back on the sight. Then I pause, looking at the tunnel around me. West of here, this drain eventually connects to the old phosphate mines that run beneath the whole island. They're my own private, abandoned, and mostly condemned rabbit warren. My loft—the old head miner's office—is smack in the middle. I could go home. Rest. Lie low, the way I ought to.

Or I could go east, to Valkyrie Bridge, and see what Elliott thinks I should see.

Dread stirs low in my gut. It weighs down my steps when I turn and start walking. I count grates as I go, but there's no need. I hear the gathered crowd at the bridge long before I reach it.

" . . . wish they would just execute them. It would be more humane . . ." one voice says nearby.

"I'm glad it's not humane," someone else cuts in. "I hope he suffers for *days* out there. The punishment fits the crime; that's the whole point."

"But he's a minor—"

"One less dealer in town," says the other voice angrily. "That's all I care about. There can't be but a handful of 'em left now for the shadowseekers to catch, and then we'll finally be safe."

I stop. Sunlight pours through the grate in front of me, its bars painting gridlines of shadow across my torso. The comforting darkness of the tunnel is all around me, and I want to crawl back into it, want to hide—from what these people are saying and from the scene that I'm now certain is unfolding above me.

But I need to see. I need to know for sure.

I creep closer. A strand of dark hair falls in my face, and I shove it away with shaking fingers. I plaster myself against the tunnel wall and then slowly lift my head just enough to peer out.

The road here is set into the side of a hill. Directly below, through the legs of the people in front of the grate and over the heads of the crowd lower down the hill, is Valkyrie Bridge.

Palm trees—long since stripped of their coconuts—frame it to either side, their fronds hanging low under the oppressive August humidity. The bridge's entrance is guarded by statues of the mythical warrior women it's named after, their wings draped with sharp-edged feathers, swords held aloft. A few feet behind their backs, bright yellow caution cones are spangled across the road—not that those are necessary to keep folks off the bridge.

Because just behind the cones, the fog starts.

It's a soft, gray nothingness that cocoons the railings, wraps gentle tendrils around the caution cones, swallows up the blocky supports entirely. That smoky haze goes all the way to the mainland. All the way across most of the world, far as anyone around here knows. On a clear day, you can look out over the sound and see it swathing the horizon where there used to be the distant hotels and condos of a normal Florida coastline. Nothing but the occasional ham radio signal from London and Singapore—the only other cities still out there—manages to get very far through it.

I stare grimly at the fog. I can smell it from here: something acrid and chemical on the breeze, almost like ozone. It makes me nervous to be this close to it. Not because it's dangerous. The fog itself is harmless.

It's what's *in* the fog that fuels my nightmares.

A woman's voice cuts through the crowd's nervous chatter. "No one wanted today to happen," she says, and everyone falls immediately silent.

Hate shoots through me like adrenaline, mingling with the dread in my gut until it forms something leaden and horrible. I trace the voice to its source. Blond hair tightly pulled back, eyes a blue so dark they're almost violet. She's wearing a crisp white blouse and a holstered gun. Her gaze sweeps the crowd like a scythe. Everyone freezes in place instantly.

My hands curl into fists. I've only seen her a few times and always at as much of a distance as I can manage, but I recognize Mayor Ackermann's voice from the radio broadcasts. There's a transmitter here today too—a chestlike box sitting at her feet, looking harmless with its rows of switches and dials, sending out her voice to the city she protects. City Hall keeps some working radios scattered across the island at well-guarded spots so everyone can have the chance to hear her warnings.

I search behind her for the person on the receiving end of today's punishment. There's a row of cops at her back, guns in their hands or tucked into their waistbands. Only about half of them wear uniforms. The police department must've finally run out of stock, which is no surprise with the way they've been recruiting. Too bad they haven't run out of weapons, too. I scan over the row, looking for whoever they're guarding.

I find him kneeling at the bridge's entrance, hands zip-tied behind his back, his skin gray and pulled taut over his cheekbones like he's already a corpse. Sam Garcia. I know him by reputation only. He is—was—the island's only other remaining dealer.

There can't be but a handful of 'em left now, that guy had said a minute ago. He was wrong. There isn't a handful of us. There's just me and Sam. As soon as the boy on that bridge meets his fate, I will be the only dealer on Cisco Island. Which means the shadowseekers—the rumored unit of special-ops officers who've hunted down all the other dealers—will have exactly one target left.

Me.

"But this is the message we must send to *anyone* who would endanger our city," the mayor continues. Her voice arcs over the crowd like lightning looking for something to burn.

Fear is roaring through my blood. I pity Sam, but I'm terri-fied for myself. After this, every shadowseeker, every beat cop, and every random self-righteous islander with a score to settle—which is most of them—will have all of their attention squarely focused on catching me. I've gotten as far as I have by lying low, by staying as far down the mayor's suspect list as possible. But how long will it take them to find me now that they have no one else to hunt?

"Sam Garcia's dealings have cost lives," the mayor goes on. Behind her, Sam is shuddering, hunched over on himself like he's trying not to scream.

They always scream. Whether it's a few steps into the fog or halfway across the bridge, they always scream.

"It's justice that it now costs his own."

Sometimes, days after an exile, the body will wash back up on shore. Mauled, gnawed till it's barely recognizable. That'll be Sam soon. And after that, me.

"Sam Garcia," Mayor Ackermann says, turning to look at him. He stays bowed over, shoulders straining with his hands tied behind him. "You are hereby exiled from Cisco Island. If you attempt to return, you will be shot."

He finally raises his head. "How about we just cut out the middleman and you shoot me now," he says. The words are meant to sound cocky, but they quaver too much and his voice cracks at the end. He genuinely wants her to kill him rather than face exile. I can't blame him.

The mayor's mouth tightens. "I can't allow that." I listen for any hint of sympathy, of humanity, but all I hear is iron.

She nods at the row of officers. Two of them grab Sam by the arms and start hauling him toward the fog. His eyes are wild. He's thinking about taking a run at the cops and forcing them to shoot him or going just a few feet into the fog and then jumping off the bridge and trying to swim back.

There's a chance Sam could escape, I tell myself. There's a chance *I* might be able to escape, when it's me up there.

I turn my back. I stumble into the darkness, hurrying away before the screaming can start.

I know now why Elliott wanted me to see this. It's a warning: I'm next. Soon the shadowseekers will find the proof they need to incriminate me. And when they do, it'll be me hog-tied in front of the fog, me asking to be shot.

Me facing the Beings.

I'll never get to Ty. All my hard work, my months of careful dealing, all for nothing. I've spent nearly a year saving up ration coupons for bribes and hunting for ways to get safely off the island, to an airport, to the London university where Ty is stranded. I heard rumors that the mayor had a helicopter, that there was a chance it could fly above the fog. I searched for its pilot. I thought I was getting close—just a few more weeks of deals, of chasing down leads—but there's no way I'll make any progress before I get arrested now.

I could hide out in my loft. Stick to the tunnels, never do another deal, use the ration coupons I have stockpiled to survive for a while longer.

But if I give up now, I'll never see Ty again.

I stop in the middle of the tunnel, a grim desperation stealing over me. I will not let this happen. I will *not* be arrested and exiled, with no supplies and no pilot, forced to face the Beings in the fog while my big brother, who has watched over me my whole life, is stuck half a world away.

I have one other option. Before, it was too much of a risk. Now, Elliott has made sure I understand that it's my last chance.

I check my watch. I've got maybe six hours till sunset.

Plenty of time to make some preparations.

CHAPTER TWO

I ARRIVE AT THE BOARDWALK TEN MINUTES LATE BY design. The sun is half set already, peeking through the brewing storm clouds, painting the fog-drowned horizon in pinks and oranges. I nod in satisfaction when I see the proof of my lateness and then search for a way to waste a few more minutes.

This place is all rotting wood and sagging buildings, complete with a rusted-out Ferris wheel at the far end. Closer to me are a few decrepit game booths. I pick one that has a back wall strung with dartboards and spend a leisurely minute plucking out all the darts before I pace back to the front of the booth and start throwing them.

Thwack. Thwack. Thwack. I don't pay any attention to whether or not I hit the targets. This isn't for fun; this is a power play, making Elliott wait and wonder while I dawdle. He gained the upper hand during our earlier meeting. I've got to put him in his place fast if I want this deal to go my way now. I need to remind him that I've got just as much leverage as he does—after all, he might be my best shot at getting out of this hellhole, but *I'm* the only person left who's still selling what he wants to buy.

My body tenses when I remember Sam being hauled toward the fog. That won't be me. I can't let it be me. *Thwack.* I throw the next dart so hard that the tip snaps off, the shaft clattering to the boardwalk below.

I take a deep breath, trying to center myself. I can't walk into this deal scared or it'll go south fast. I glance at the sun again to check its position—two-thirds of the way down now—and then wince. One of the massive, distant chunks of reflective metal in the Shatter Ring is catching the light just right to blind me. I narrow my eyes to slits, let myself glare at the ring. A sluggish sort of hatred stirs beneath my nervousness. These chunks of metal are what separated me from my brother. They're what caused the deadly fog that now covers the entire world—with the exceptions of London, Singapore, and for some unknown reason, one tiny island off the coast of Florida. Also known as . . . us.

No one knows exactly what happened during the event we now call the Fracture. The only thing we do know is that one random Tuesday in July of last year, a giant reflective oval appeared in the sky like a second moon. *Aliens* was everyone's first guess. And when we—or rather, the people in charge of the missile silos on the mainland—started shooting at it, we knew our guess was right.

But it wasn't a ship the aliens had sent us. It was a weapon.

When the missiles hit it, it broke apart into a thousand massive pieces. Those pieces formed the Shatter Ring. And then they ended life as we'd known it.

We call it the Fracture because a lot of things broke that day, thirteen months and some-odd days ago. The world was one of them.

I throw another dart, actually bothering to aim it this time, and hit square on the smallest bull's-eye. I feel better now, more focused. Anger is always better than fear.

A hand reaches through my line of vision and plucks the last dart from my hand. "Still playing games you can't win?" asks Elliott's voice. Having expected him to try to catch me off-guard again, I don't startle this time, and when I turn to look at him I smile at the annoyance in his eyes. Point, me.

"Who said I can't win?" I reply easily. "In fact, I think I've done well enough to earn a prize."

Moldy teddy bears and holey tourist-tastic T-shirts dangle from lines strung across the booth's ceiling. I sort through them until I come upon a small stuffed fox that looks only a little bedraggled. I grimace at the selection—foxes creep me out, with their too-canny eyes and their sharp little noses—but I stick it in my pocket anyway for the sake of irritating Elliott.

"You're late," he says. The annoyance in his eyes filters through to his voice. My smile grows and sharpens.

"I'm a busy guy," I tell him. "I just inherited all Sam Garcia's clients, after all."

It's not exactly true—many of Sam's buyers, and likely my own, too, will go to ground after today—but the comment hits its mark. Elliott turns without a word and strides across the boardwalk. "Are we doing this or what?" he demands over his shoulder.

I stroll after him, wearing a casual mask to hide the uncertainty that tumbles through my stomach at his words. Part of me still worries he might be inclined to rat me out afterward, but I've taken what precautions I can, and this deal is a gamble I have to make. It makes me feel only a little better to know that ratting me out would be as dangerous for him as for me. The mayor strictly enforces her zero-tolerance policy for anyone caught participating in deals like this, which means snitches are as likely to face exile as us dealers.

"Depends on what information you've got to trade," I reply.

He stops in front of a building—an arcade, judging by the tattered sign—and pulls its glass door open. He looks at me over his shoulder. "I know where the helicopter is and who pilots it," he answers. My heart does an elated somersault, and I do my best not to let it show on my face as he continues. "It's leaving tonight to see if they can find any salvageable supplies to bring back from the mainland; rations are getting low, and the mayor is desperate enough to finally authorize the use of fuel. I can get you a gun, can tell you where the chopper will leave from. You can stow away. Hijack it once it lifts off."

I follow him into the arcade, feeling like I'm in a dream. This is perfect. Almost *too* perfect. I stop in the doorway and glance inside—ancient claw games covered in grime, retro-cool dance games with their screens busted through. The air is stale. Dust motes hang suspended in the slanting beams of fading sunlight like flies stuck in honey. This place doesn't *look* like a trap, and Elliott doesn't seem to fit the profile of a snitch, but still . . .

"How did you know about my brother?" I ask, lingering in the doorway. A few people know I'm interested in finding the helicopter and its pilot, but I haven't told anyone the reason why. I prefer to keep people at a distance. Especially clients, and especially this jackass. It makes me more than a little nervous to know he knows so much about my personal life.

I thought I had my anxiety under control, but with that one worried thought, it starts to snowball. This whole meeting could go wrong in so many ways. There's a slideshow of horrific outcomes marching through my head right now, one after the other, ranging from the possible to the wildly unlikely: we could get caught, shot, exiled. The helicopter could be a lie, a trap. The entire rotted boardwalk could collapse beneath our feet right now and drown us in the ocean.

The anxiety gains strength. A compulsion rears its head: I want to tap this door frame to keep myself safe while I'm inside the arcade. Three times on the left, five on the right, at exactly shoulder height. Three and five are good numbers. One is okay too, but it won't keep me as safe as three and five would.

I go still, catching the train of thought, concerned that it took me a second to recognize it and that it came so quickly on the heels of my lock-checking compulsion earlier today. I worked so *hard* to get through therapy last year, before I moved to Cisco Island, before the Fracture happened. I went to war with my obsessive-compulsive disorder and I won. What does it mean that some of my old compulsions are flaring up again?

Nothing. It doesn't mean anything. I'm fine; I know that tapping this doorway wouldn't actually keep me any safer, that it's magical thinking, that my OCD is lying to me as always. I wait for the urge to pass. After a moment—a few beats too long—it finally does. I try to exult in the victory but can't quite banish my creeping worry.

Elliott is peering at me from across the room. He's said something, but I was too absorbed in my brief battle with the compulsion to hear it. I try to play it off with a grin and a shrug, as if pretending not to hear him is another power play of mine.

"Sorry, got distracted. Say that again?"

It works. He bites back a frown but repeats himself. "I said, I did my homework. After I tracked down enough rumors and confirmed you were a dealer, I talked to some people who knew your aunt. One of them mentioned that two boys came here last year to live with her and that the other one left again after just a few weeks."

Ah. That makes sense. Ty did stay for a while after he moved me here, in preparation for what was supposed to be his year of studying botany abroad.

Elliott is watching me carefully. His old veneer of cool satis-faction has replaced his annoyance. Whatever he says next, it'll be another attempt to throw me off-balance.

He proves me right. "They also told me that you haven't been back to your aunt's place, or to her grave, since she died," he says. "Though I guess I shouldn't be surprised. You don't strike me as the sentimental sort."

I don't bother responding to that. He's chosen the wrong tack; I barely knew Aunt Irene. She died of a wound that went septic hardly a month after the Fracture.

But he's not done. "Which was why I was so surprised when my guess about you wanting to get to your brother now turned out to be right. It seems pretty sentimental to me, trying to get across the world through the fog to someone who might not still be around."

"Don't talk about him like he's dead," I snap, suddenly sick of the back-and-forth. Knowing only one way to shut him up, I take off my hat, tear the brim's seam, and pull out the thing that's been hidden there all day.

It's a mirror. Tiny, backed with thin brown plastic, the hinges at the bottom broken from where it used to sit atop a makeup compact. Its reflective surface is covered with beige masking tape.

Elliott's eyes land on the mirror. He pales. I smile, feeling more than a little vicious. I don't think he's weak for being afraid of what I'm holding—everyone's scared of it, including me— but I'm happy to finally come out on top of this conversation.

Mirrors have been deadly for over a year now. Ever since the Fracture, looking at your own reflection has become an exercise in suicide. It took everyone a few days to figure it out at first, to start smashing their mirrors into powder or tossing them into the sea, but by then it was too late for the rest of the world.

Looking into a mirror creates the fog. In the fog lurk the Beings. Beings shred people, and often anything else they touch as well, to pieces. This is a chain of events that is particularly unfortunate when you have a giant ring of immense mirror shards orbiting over your head. No one is sure why the Shatter Ring didn't do to us what it did to the rest of the world. But although we may have been spared instant annihilation, we're still cut off from everything, and the mirrors we have down here on the ground are still plenty dangerous. Especially with more and more materials being added to the Reflectivity Index every day. The aliens—whoever they are, whatever they want—must be ramping up their attacks, because with every month that passes, stuff that is less and less reflective starts suddenly producing fog. Like glasses, for example. Which is fine with me. More goods to sell.

But sometimes, when I'm smuggling a load of newly too-reflective goods out through the tunnels beneath City Hall, I can't help but wonder how far it will end up going. When will soap bubbles be too reflective? When will everyone be required to get rid of their window glass? I think one day the ocean itself will be too still, reflect too much of the sky, and then it will be the end of us all.

I pull a little handheld machine, a lux meter, out of my pocket. It looks a bit like a Geiger counter, except it's for measuring light instead of radiation. It's the best way to check a mirror's reflectivity without actually looking at it. "Should we test it?" I ask Elliott, my voice savagely glib. "Just so you can make sure you're getting a quality product." I rip the masking tape off the mirror's surface before he can answer.

Something unravels in my gut. I steel myself against the too-familiar feeling: like there's a string tied to the mirror and the other end is wrapped around one of my ribs, a small, vulnerable, free-floating one. The sensation is weird and queasy-making, and it's been happening every time a mirror is uncovered nearby lately. Which is extra inconvenient for someone who makes a living the way I do. I haven't been sure what to make of it—some sort of physiological reaction to the danger, probably—so I mostly just try to ignore it.

The mirror's reflective surface is aimed at the wall, hidden from sight, but Elliott gets at least two shades paler. I'm shaking a little too. I've done hundreds of deals like this, but every time is still terrifying. I'm usually better at hiding it, though.

I stride over to the darkest corner in the room and put the lux meter atop a dusty whack-a-mole game. While I set the test up, I'm careful to keep the mirror turned away from me and Elliott. Any Beings and fog that are generated on the island only last a minute or two—unlike the permanent ones on the mainland—but if one of those monsters accidentally gets spawned here and now, it'd only take it a matter of seconds to finish us both off.

I turn the meter on, then step back and reach into my pocket again. There's some other stuff in there, the precautions I took just in case this meeting went bad, and I maneuver around those shapes carefully until I find the penlight I'm looking for. I pull it out and flick it on. Its tiny beam of light spears through the growing shadows.

I hold the mirror out. With my other hand, I turn the pen-light back toward me until its beam falls on the mirror's surface.

A weaker ray of light bounces off the mirror and hits the wall, and I adjust my aim until the reflected light hits the lux meter. The little machine chirps, and red numbers flash on its screen.

I turn off the penlight, lower the mirror, and carefully reapply the masking tape before holding it out to Elliott.

"There," I tell him, a dare in my voice. "I've proven it's reflective. That's my end of the deal finished. Your turn."

He's still staring at the mirror, solemn and still. I wonder if I've gone too far, if I've scared him into calling off the deal. I need to remind him of why he needs to go through with it. I don't have to ask to know his reasons for being here; there's only ever one reason for anyone to buy a mirror.

"What are you hoping to power with this?" I ask, forcing my tone into something resembling curiosity even though I'm desperate to be done with this meeting and on my way to Ty. "A desalinator? Medical equipment?"

Whenever a mirror generates a Being, the event also creates a massive electrical field that can, with a little ingenuity, be harnessed to power just about anything. Everyone who deals with me is willing to risk the Beings to harvest its energy. All of them always believe they've thought through every extremity, taken every precaution. About a third end up dead anyway. Some of them take bystanders with them too, people in the wrong place at the wrong time. It sucks for those folks, but dealing mirrors is the quickest way for me to get where I need to go, and I'm willing to do whatever it takes to make that happen.

Elliott doesn't answer, but my words snap him out of whatever trance he was in. He lifts his eyes to mine. For the first time, I see real emotion there, though in the shadows I can't quite make out what it is.

He lifts his hand and takes the mirror from me. He drops it into his pocket. Then he turns his head and glances at the front door like he's planning to bolt.

I go on high alert. No way is he going to short me, leave without giving me the info he promised. I dip my hand into my pocket and curl my fingers around the precaution I put there. Another mirror. I tug the tape off its cover and hold it in my pocket, the silvered glass cool against my palm.

Then I go still. There's a noise coming from the boardwalk, a scuff of wood, something quiet but familiar. Footsteps. Elliott must've heard it too, that was why he turned to look. I make out a shape ducking behind a booth across the way. It's a person clad in a blue uniform. The muted light of sunset glints off the gun in his hands.

Cops. The cops are outside. The cops have found me during the middle of a deal.

Panic screams through me. I spit out a curse. I take a step toward Elliott—should've trusted my instincts, should've *known* he was a damn snitch, have to get the upper hand on him now before he can officially inform on me—but he's too quick.

He lifts up the back of his shirt, pulls his own gun out of his waistband, and points it at my chest.

"Marty Callahan," he says, "you're coming with me."

CHAPTER THREE

DESPERATION RISES AT THE BACK OF MY THROAT. I can taste it.

Elliott jerks his head at the door to the boardwalk. "Move," he orders, his voice dead calm.

I cough out a harsh laugh. "Make me, asshole." I take a step toward him. Maybe I can force him to shoot me here and now, I think wildly. Take out the middleman. Sam was right: It would be better.

But Elliott is ready for me. His left hand stays on the gun while his right snakes out, grabs my shoulder, pinches some nerve there. The flash of pain makes me flinch, just long enough for Elliott to get behind me and shove me toward the door. Another blue-clad cop strides across the boardwalk in front of us, talking into a walkie. They're breaking out their walkies for me, using up precious batteries for this op. It's the worst possible sign of how important my capture is to them.

My pulse kicks up to somewhere around heart-attack level as I stumble forward. I'm going to die. This is it. I'm a goner—and all because of my determination to find a big brother I'm not even sure is still alive. A brother I can now be absolutely positive I'll never see again, because even if he's not dead, I'm about to be. I close my eyes.

"I'm scared," eight-year-old me whispers in the dark. Lightning flashes outside and thunder rattles the plywood that's nailed over my bedroom window. The wind is screaming. It sounds like a panther I heard at the Miami zoo once—high and wild, shrieking like a dying thing.

"Of the hurricane?" Ty rubs my head with a grin. "It'll have to go through me first."

I open my eyes. Fury snarls in my veins. I won't give up on Ty. Not till I take my very last breath. I've still got the second mirror in my pocket. I would never actually use one, not when I'm close enough to be a victim myself, but Elliott and the cops might not be willing to bet their lives on that. And if I can get Elliott to come one step closer with that gun, I might be able to take it away from him—and that's a weapon I *am* willing to use.

My hand is still in my pocket. As we move toward the door

I pull it out, keeping the small mirror hidden in my fist. This one has sharp edges. They cut into my palm. I barely notice.

I reach the door. I lower one hand to push the bar, ignoring my compulsion to tap on the door frame, though it's harder this time than it was earlier. The muggy island air smacks me in the face—it's gotten more humid in the last few minutes, the cloud cover simmering over almost the entire sky now. It turns the boardwalk into a sweatbox, steaming us with the smell of rotted fish and algae.

"Get on the ground!" shouts the cop who's crouched behind the booth across the way. The red-gold light of the sunset makes it hard to pick out details, but I recognize that mop of hair immediately. One of his eyes is sporting a purple beauty of a bruise, and dried blood is still crusted beneath his nose. Ginger. He's so tense that his gun is shaking. That only makes the situation more unstable.

I sweep my gaze left and right, counting. Three. Four. Five. More than enough cops to take me in. Probably more of them under the boardwalk, too, waiting to cut off any escape attempt I might make.

I swallow and raise my hand, opening my mouth to shout that I've got a mirror. But before I can speak, a blur of movement flashes in the corner of my eye, and something knocks my legs out from under me. I fall hard onto my stomach. The mirror bounces out of my grip. Everything else forgotten, I squeeze my eyes shut and whip my head away from it, my heart hammering. I can't look at the mirror. Please, God, I pray, let no one else look at it either.

No one screams.

I dare to crack an eye open. No mirror in sight. We're only a few yards from the edge of the boardwalk—it must've sailed over the edge, unseen.

I blow out a breath. No Being. But no leverage now, either.

Elliott's got one knee on my back, pinning me facedown to the boardwalk. He's the one who swept my feet out from under me a moment ago. "Cuffs," he demands now, still ice-cold calm, not even looking at Ginger as he tosses out the order.

My racing heartbeat pauses as I take in his tone. My eyes narrow. That doesn't sound like a snitch trying to make a deal with a cop. That sounds like he's . . . what, one of them? But he's too young to be a cop. He's eighteen at most, and the mayor set the age limit to join at twenty-one.

"Get on the ground," Ginger repeats at a shout.

"He's *on* the ground," Elliott snaps.

"Not him," Ginger replies, raising up out of his crouch and advancing on us, gun still held out in front of him. "You."

Elliott goes still, finally looks up. "You can't be serious."

His disbelieving tone doesn't make sense. He punched a cop earlier today, and now he's surprised that cop wants to arrest him? And even if he means to rat me out, he's got to know that the mayor tosses snitches onto the bridge just as frequently as the dealers they help catch. *Anyone* who breaks the law against participating in a mirror deal is liable to exile.

"He is serious," calls another cop from farther down the boardwalk as she advances on us, her own gun held out even though her tone sounds oddly apologetic. The name tag above her badge reads DIAZ. "Do as you've been ordered."

A note of impatience threads through Elliott's prior calm. "I'm Elliott Ackermann," he says to Diaz. Something about his name tries to catch at my attention, but the adrenaline is too strong, the panic too loud. Elliott is still talking but I barely hear him. "I'm the one who tipped you off. This is my op—"

"We know who you are," Ginger says, cutting him off.

Elliott tenses up, his knee digging a little harder into my spine. "Then how about you put the guns down? We're on the same side here. Cops," he says, gesturing at them with his free hand—and then, gesturing to himself: "Shadowseeker."

Shadowseeker. The name arcs through me like electricity. Not a snitch. Not a cop. He's much worse than that.

The bastard. The *bastard.* He knew the crowd was going to the bridge this morning, because he was the one who'd helped put Sam up there. He must've *planned* to attack Ginger to win my trust. He dangled information he knew I wouldn't be able to resist, used my own brother against me. Then he closed the trap.

"Don't make this harder than it has to be," Ginger warns Elliott—the same thing he said to me earlier. I bare my teeth, appreciating the irony.

Elliott goes still for half a heartbeat as he takes the situation in. Then, in one quick motion, he takes his knee off my spine, grabs me by the back of the collar, and yanks me to my feet so I'm standing in front of him. He puts my body between him and the cops. The cool metal of his gun brushes against my left shoulder blade.

There. He's taken that one step closer that I was needing. Maybe I can get myself out of this without a mirror after all.

Someone shouts below us, one of the cops lurking on the beach beneath the boardwalk. It's the best distraction I'm gonna get.

I step inside Elliott's reach. I duck under the gun. I ram the heel of one hand into his wrist, lock my other hand around the gun, and wrench it sideways. I'm at a weird angle because I'm used to practicing this for right-handed people and he's a lefty, but I manage to get the gun almost away from him before he reacts. He curses, his eyes widening. I have milliseconds before he gets over his surprise and fights back, and he's brawny enough for me to know he'll win if that happens. I twist inward, lift my right foot, and kick hard at the inside of his knee. He crumples to the deck. I have the gun . . . for exactly one second before Ginger knocks it out of my grip.

The gun clatters and skids a few feet away. I start to dive after it, but Ginger grabs my arm, uses my own momentum to twist me around and knock me to the ground right next to Elliott. Something cold snaps around my wrist. My heart takes a nosedive. Handcuffs. I've been cuffed. Which means I've been captured, which means I'm dead, dead, dead.

Bodies. Gnawed to pieces, shredded like they ran through an acre of barbed wire, nothing but scraps left to wash up on the beach. It'll be me soon. Will I die on the bridge, or will I get to the mainland first? Maybe there's a way I can make it to the airport there. But the nearest one is dozens of miles inland, through the fog, and I won't have a pilot, won't have anything but the clothes on my back.

Elliott is on the ground too now, shouting something. "—telling you, check with the mayor!" he yells. "I've apprehended the last mirror dealer on the island! She'll make an exception for me—"

Ginger stands back up. "You know she doesn't make exceptions," he says tightly. "She's already scheduled your exile." He aims his gun at Elliott, who goes silent, frozen in shock.

It's then that I realize only one of my hands is cuffed. I roll to my side, glance down at the matte black metal ring around my wrist, and follow the chain to the other cuff—which is locked around Elliott's wrist.

We've both been arrested. He'll be exiled along with me. I

laugh, a little wildly. Elliott turns his gaze to me. His cuffed hand curls into a fist. He reaches toward me with his other hand, his gaze burning with a cold fury that looks a hundred times more real than the cool, satisfied mask he wore earlier. I snap my mouth shut, recognizing the sudden hatred in his eyes, and try to roll away. Which is difficult when you're handcuffed to the person attempting to murder you. Elliott yanks his cuffed hand back, pulling me off-balance, and some bit of debris on the ground digs painfully into my ribs. I catch myself with both hands splayed on the boards.

Smoke seeps through my fingers.

I stop struggling and frown at the ground. "The boardwalk is on fire," I say slowly, but a sense of wrongness tickles the back of my mind.

Ginger keeps his gun trained on us as he presses a button on the walkie that's crackling at his shoulder. "Gamma team, report, is there a fire? Does Callahan have accomplices—do you need backup?" He waits a second, but no one answers. Ginger backs up a few feet toward the edge of the boardwalk. His gun is shaking again. "Report!" he shouts toward the beach below, without taking his eyes off us. "Is there—"

He stops talking suddenly, jerking. He blinks once, twice. A bloom of red opens in the middle of his chest.

Jutting out from its center is a ray of darkness.

The lines of it are crisp, unreal, an impossible razor's edge of night. Smoke—no . . . no, *fog*—bleeds out from it. From either side of Ginger, wings wrap around him softly, gently, cocooning him. The feathers are each defined, beautifully wrought, tines of void and shadow.

Ginger's gaze meets mine. Those eyes—bright green, painfully so. I called them expressive earlier. Now, they're screaming.

Ginger vanishes, encircled entirely by the wings of whatever creature is hidden behind him. There's a muffled noise, something that's almost a cry, cut off by sudden silence.

The wings unwrap. The black ray retracts. The creature sweeps gracefully back down to the beach, and Ginger's body sags, lifeless, to the ground in front of us.

Elliott and I are both silent for the space of a single breath. My hands are still on the boardwalk. The fog curls through my fingers. Warm. Smoky. Sliding across my palm, tickling my wrist. In an instant it's burgeoning all around us, cutting off the russet sunset clouds, the crashing ocean below, until everything is muted by a film of gray death.

People are screaming beneath us now, a chorus of voices. They won't stop. They'll never stop.

Because the thing that dug into my ribs when Elliott pulled me down, it wasn't debris. It was the feeling I get when a mirror is uncovered nearby. The mirror that tumbled over the side of the boardwalk must've landed near one of the officers down there. They looked at it. They loosed a Being on themselves— and on everyone else in the vicinity.

Including me.

My heart isn't racing anymore. It isn't beating at all. I'm not breathing. Not looking. Not thinking.

I have a lot of experience with fear. Sometimes it slips over you bit by bit, slow and insidious. And sometimes it closes you up so tightly in its fist that you forget you ever knew how to feel anything else.

I'm on my feet. I'm running across the boardwalk. The handcuff bites hard at my wrist, making me stagger. Elliott stumbles behind me, panting and gasping, his expression blank like he's afraid to think too. All I see is Ginger wrapped up in those wings. All I can hear is the screaming below us.

Being. That was a Being, no more than ten feet away from me.

I've heard the stories. The shadowy monsters come in all shapes and sizes. Bearlike. Tiny, crawling spiders with fangs that drip darkness. Once, when someone looked into a mirror while on a boat just offshore, it brought a vast black whale with teeth like saws and an unhinged jaw that swallowed up the sailing vessel whole. But I've never seen one myself. Not till now.

Shouting ahead of us. More cops. Thoughtlessly, I reverse directions. I can't get caught, can't get exiled to a mainland full of those things. Elliott shouts and tries to wrench me away, but it's too late—I don't see Ginger until I'm tripping over his body. I land hard on my left side, taking Elliott down with me. He scrambles to get up but slips, twisting me further toward the corpse.

Ginger's eyes are still open. Still screaming, somehow, even though they're empty. Red soaks into the boards beneath him, puddles in the divots, funnels through the cracks. I'm close enough to register the smell: coppery-bright blood mixed with the tang of fresh dryer sheets.

I roll to my side and clutch my head in my hands, trying not to throw up. I've seen dead bodies before. Some of them, the ones they plaster on posters around town as warnings, were way worse than this. Ginger died quickly. It wasn't that bad. I don't care anyway. Why should I care? He was my enemy. And now he's dead. It's good news. It's *good*.

The smell is too strong. It's clogging my brain, thicker than the fog, slowing my response times. Someone is shouting at me to get up. Elliott's fingers dig into my wrist as he hauls me around Ginger's body. "Move," he orders. I open my eyes. His voice is cold and steady but the hatred is brighter than ever in his eyes. He's holding something in his other hand. His gun. He must've retrieved it just now. It's red, sticky with Ginger's blood.

I look around wildly. Escape. That's what I should be focusing on. The fog will start to thin any minute, and when it's gone, the surviving cops will be able to find us easily. We can't go out the main entry—that's where I heard more cops shouting earlier.

We can go down to the beach. The Being will be gone when

the fog dissipates, but it's probably already killed any cops who were down there, making that our best escape route. Decision made, I start to sprint back toward the edge of the boardwalk.

Something bites hard into my left wrist, jerking me to a standstill. The handcuff. Elliott has grown roots.

"What the hell? Come on! They're going to exile you too!" I shout wildly, pulling at him, but I might as well try to move a brick wall.

He's transfixed by something behind me. I spin around. Human-shaped figures—cops—are moving toward us through the gray. There are five, six, a dozen, fanning out across the boardwalk, ducking behind booths, finding cover from us or the Being or both.

A woman's voice cuts through the fog, clear and calm. "Put the gun down."

As if he's been nailed with an electric shock, Elliott's hand opens. *Thunk.* The gun hits the ground.

The woman steps out of the fog. Violet-blue eyes, crisp white blouse, blond hair tightly pulled back. It's frizzed a little from the humidity since I saw her at Sam's exile.

Mayor Ackermann.

She came to personally oversee this operation. She put herself in danger, in the middle of a mirror deal, to make sure I was captured.

There's no escape. I'm surrounded.

My brain won't stop circling, my thoughts like panicked birds trapped in a too-small cage.

Then above us, something screeches, grating and inhuman. Everyone dives for cover. Three cops jump to protect the mayor, pushing her behind a T-shirt booth, covering her with their bodies. A winged shadow curves overhead, dives down through the fog. When it comes up again, something writhing and human is in its talons. Gunfire echoes, as if bullets will do any good.

I'm frozen in place, staring upward, and suddenly realize I should be ducking for cover too. I jerk my gaze to the boardwalk to search for somewhere to hide—and spot Elliott's dropped gun.

I glance sideways. Elliott is still next to me but his eyes are on the gradually thinning fog above, tracking the Being and the screaming thing in its talons. His face is lined with horror, his shoulders tense under the weight of his own failure. He's a shadowseeker, after all—trained to hunt down mirrors and mirror peddlers, to stop these wraiths before they're born.

I glance up at the cops, at the mayor. Their gazes are glued on the fog too, searching frantically for the Being. No one is watching me.

No one sees me pick up the gun.

The fog vanishes all at once, dissipating like steam. Overhead, the Being shreds itself into shadows that sparkle and fizz and fall, and then it's gone too. The person in its claws drops, screaming, to the beach far below. All eyes follow the man's fall—except mine.

I have maybe five seconds before everyone remembers I'm here. That's five seconds to figure out what to do with the blood-sticky gun in my hands. I hesitate—and then pivot in toward Elliott, lift the gun, and aim it at him.

The barrel touches his chest, angled toward his heart. He freezes. He swallows, the muscles in his jaw twitching with the motion. His eyes move away from the twisted body on the beach, but he doesn't dare turn his head to look at me.

"You've never killed anyone before," he says softly.

He's right. I haven't. But I'm not a good guy either. I've done plenty of stuff I should regret over the last year. And I don't regret any of it, because it was necessary. Because I will do *whatever* it takes, no matter how difficult or wrong it is, to get my brother back. Even now, even this.

About half the cops are running toward the newly dead body, but one of the others glances our way and spots us. She shouts to the others and suddenly half a dozen guns are pointed at me. No one fires yet, though.

I raise my voice. "I know he's a shadowseeker," I call. That's how Elliott knows I haven't killed anyone before. Because he's researched me, read my file, used the information to put together this operation to entrap me. "He's one of you. Let me go, or I'll kill him right here in front of you."

My voice is shaking. All of me is shaking. I don't know if I can actually kill a person, but I might have to find out.

Elliott closes his eyes, opens them again. The hatred is burning, burning. "Don't," he says to me quietly, and his voice is still calm and steady, but now there's a thread of fear beneath it. I can't afford to hear the emotion, can't afford to humanize him. He's my *enemy*. Just like Ginger.

Sickness churns in my stomach. I tighten my grip on the gun. "You have to the count of three!" I shout at the cops.

"No need," calls a woman's voice. It slices through the air like a scythe, and the cops who were protecting the mayor from the Being move aside so she can walk toward us. "Go ahead," she says to me. "Shoot him now."

Elliott's eyes go blank. He doesn't look at the mayor, instead focusing on a spot over her head. He swallows once, twice. "Mom," he says at last, and the word is mangled by its own layers, thick with a meaning that it takes me a full five seconds to register.

I stare at him. I remember the way he wielded his name like a badge earlier, when he was talking to that cop Diaz. I remember how something snagged in my mind at his introduction: Elliott Ackermann. My mind superimposes the image of the mayor over him. Same blond hair, same blue eyes, same calm, cold voice—though Elliott's isn't calm anymore.

He has to be bluffing. This is another trick. "You're lying,"

I accuse him. "You can't be the mayor's son. The mayor's son is dead."

Everyone knows that. It was the thing that solidified her iron grip on the island in the months following the Fracture. Nothing proves you're a stone-cold bitch like exiling your own son for possession of reflective material. No one talked about anything else for weeks.

Elliott keeps his empty gaze on that spot above the mayor's head. "That was my brother," he says, and I know that tone. I *use* that tone. *Don't talk about him like he's dead*, I'd told Elliott earlier, in the same voice he's using right now.

My grip on the gun loosens.

The mayor takes another step toward us. "Elliott just participated in a mirror deal," she says. Her eyes are on me as she nods at her son. "He was willing to break the law to get the proof necessary to exile you. Apparently he forgot that I put that law—and my zero-tolerance policy for *anyone* who breaks it—in place for a reason. All these deaths"—she sweeps her hand at Ginger, then toward the bodies I can now see littering the sand below us—"would have been prevented, had he caught you by legal means. But now he's facing exile the same as you. Go ahead and shoot him now, if you want. It won't help you at all."

She's got to be faking it. No way would she be okay with me murdering her own son right in front of her, even if he did mess up . . . but then again, she did exile her other kid. Would this really be that much more of a stretch?

"You're bluffing," I try. "You wouldn't just let him die."

Her gaze tightens. When she speaks, her words spark and crackle with tightly controlled emotion. "I will do whatever it takes to keep this island safe. Including, when necessary, protecting it from my own family."

Desperate, I try to figure out my next move. I can't actually kill Elliott. That would lose me all my leverage, plus with every second that passes, I get more certain I can't do it anyway. But I can't let her know that. I have to call her bluff—because surely, no matter what she says, it *has* to be a bluff—and let her know I'm serious without actually murdering anyone.

And suddenly, I know how to do that. I take half a step back, swing the gun down to Elliott's knee and, before I can think about it, pull the trigger.

Click. The gun jams. I try again. Nothing.

Elliott doesn't flinch, but his hands are clenched and his breath hitches at the sound of the gun trying to fire. He finally turns his head and his gaze meets mine.

"Arrest them," Mayor Ackermann calls, and her voice is as empty as his eyes. "They'll be exiled at midnight."

CHAPTER FOUR

THEY WALK US TO CITY HALL. IT'S DARK. THE WIND picks up, spraying pebbles and dust across us. I don't blink, because every time I blink I see Ginger's face.

I can still smell him. Blood and dryer sheets. It's crusted to my clothes, filling my mind.

The older cop, Ginger's partner, is at City Hall. He's the one who pats me down when they separate me from Elliott and process me. He doesn't call my name like we're friends this time. He doesn't even look at me.

I'm escorted to my ten-minute "trial." No one but the judge and a sleep-rumpled lawyer bothers to attend. I don't have any family to protest my exile. My aunt died last August, my parents bailed long before that, and Ty is further out of reach than ever.

No one protests Elliott's exile either, apparently. His trial takes almost exactly as long as mine. And then it's midnight, and they're shoving us back outside.

The helicopter is in the parking lot. Its blades are whirring, waiting. I stare at it until I figure out why we're being pushed toward it and then I laugh and laugh until I can barely breathe. I'll be on the chopper tonight after all—not as a stowaway hijacker, but as a prisoner on his way to an inescapable exile. There'll be no walk across Valkyrie Bridge for me. No chance to jump into the ocean and try to swim back, no chance to take a run at my escort and get shot rather than face the Beings. It's a suitably horrifying end for the island's last mirror dealer and a warning to any who might think of following in my footsteps.

Or maybe the mayor just doesn't want to hear her son screaming as he's torn apart, and that's why she's putting us on the chopper instead of the bridge.

Someone shoves me. I stop laughing. I'm jostled sideways, pulled to a stop, sandwiched between four officers. So many. I'd be honored if I wasn't too terrified to even think straight.

The red blink of the radio transmitter. The impossibly bright blur of the helicopter's lights. The mayor's face is all cold, hard angles: a woman carved from steel and bone.

She faces the gathering crowd. She praises the bravery of

those who have volunteered for tonight's mission. She speaks of her faith that the crew will find food and fresh water to resupply the island before the looming storm season. Then, as if it's an afterthought, she passes sentence on the mirror dealer who will be dropped off on the mainland on the way.

The crowd cheers at the news of my capture. The mayor quiets them. I plaster a smirk on my face and try to act like I'm not ready to throw myself at her feet and beg for mercy at the first sign she has a soul.

She keeps talking. The words dip in and out of my consciousness. *Shadowseeker. Zero tolerance. Tragedy*, she says, with no emotion at all in her voice.

The crowd shifts. Something about their quietness snags my attention, and I struggle back to myself for long enough to squint at them. The mayor has just announced Elliott as the second of tonight's exiles—and, if I heard right, outed him as a shadowseeker—but they're not cheering for his capture the way they did for mine. Instead, they mutter and frown, an uneasy energy snaking through them as they glance between the mayor and her son.

I twist to look to the side. Elliott's got his head bowed, and that pretty-boy blond hair covers most of his expression, but not enough. He's carved from steel and bone too.

The muttering in the crowd gets louder. Their restlessness grows. I realize, with a distant sort of surprise, that they're upset. *All* of them. They don't want Elliott exiled. If he's a shadowseeker, then he's a hero—one of the special-ops legends they've all admired for months.

Something like hope stirs painfully in my gut. I will Elliott to resist. To yell, to stir them up, to start a riot. Anything.

Elliott finally registers the shift in the crowd's energy. He looks up, scans them. Then he glances at the guard next to him. There's only one. It would be so easy for him to fight back. To at least try to escape his fate. And maybe I could escape too, in the commotion.

But Elliott just bows his head again and does nothing.

A sour taste floods my mouth. I realize now why he only has one guard: because they already knew he wouldn't fight. They knew it the second he dropped the gun because his mom told him to.

My handcuffs are replaced with zip ties. I'm shoved toward the helicopter. There's a brief argument about who's going to pilot, punctuated by nervous glances at me and Elliott. I try to bolt, but one of the guards kicks my legs out from under me and hauls me on board. I get in a good shot with an elbow, break his nose. After that they tie my hands to one of the loops that hang down from the helicopter's ceiling just inside the door. I can sit, barely, but my arms are numb and bloodless in minutes.

By the time we take off, rain has cracked the clouds open.

We cross the sound. We're over the mainland in minutes.

We keep going. Lightning flashes, illuminating the side of our guard's glaring, still-bloody face, casting millisecond-long shadows across the cabin.

Wind batters the helicopter. Rain lashes angrily across the windows. We dip and weave through the onset of what's probably a hurricane—a weak one, but still no joke to fly through. Our guard gets up and walks to the front to talk to the pilot. They debate whether they should dump us and turn back, search for supplies another day when there's no storm.

The helicopter's noise is deafening. I wish it were louder. Maybe then it would fill up my brain, dissolve the memories, drown out the fear of what's next. Maybe it could make me forget that it was *my* mirror the cops looked into beneath the boardwalk, *my* ambition that ended with the blood that's still on my clothes.

I know the mirrors I've sold have gotten people killed before. But I've never been a part of it—not like tonight. I didn't think it would matter. I don't want it to matter.

Anything for Ty. I meant it. I still do. I have to, or it'll have all been for nothing.

I glance at the window. We're below the storm, but above the fog that blankets the city. Here and there, the top of a building pokes up beneath us, glittering a cold, wet blue in the flashes of lightning. Directly below is a radio antenna scored and dented with enormous teeth marks. The thick metal poles are frayed and jagged, snapped off at the top like matchsticks.

I close my eyes. A memory from last year seeps in.

Ty's sideways smile. My arm hanging out the window of his ancient Camaro. Sunlight pouring over the day like a jar of upended honey, "Stand by Me" coming from the stereo.

We pass a radio antenna. I point at it. "We should totally climb that." The urge tingles in my bones: to push myself, to conquer something just because I know I shouldn't. To accept the universe's dare.

Ty raises an eyebrow. "Isn't that illegal?"

I shrug. "Gotta fulfill my daily troublemaking quota somehow."

He snorts, then shakes his head. "Sorry, your quota will have to go unfulfilled today. I told Aunt Irene we'd be there by five."

I turn my head, pretending to watch out the window as we pass the antenna, but actually working hard to hide the unease that's slithering through my stomach. Neither of us has met Aunt Irene in person yet, but she could be the coolest pseudo-guardian in the world, and I would still hate leaving my old home behind to move to some speck of an island surrounded by strangers.

But I could find a way to be okay with it if Ty were coming too.

He glances over, sees my expression. His smile fades and his brow goes all crinkled, the way it always does when he worries. "Look," he says softly. "Let's just try this, okay? I'll stay with you a few weeks to get you settled in, and if you haven't adjusted by then, I'll call it off."

And he would. He'd turn down his scholarship to study abroad, turn down a free year of living in London, to make sure I was all right. Ty is always making sacrifices for me that way. Like when he took a second side job delivering takeout so I could afford to see Dr. Washburne, my therapist, every week. If my OCD hadn't improved enough for me to move to occasional phone check-ins instead of regular office visits, Ty wouldn't even be considering this move. And even now, after his scholarship has been accepted and all the arrangements have been made, he would still stay behind if I asked him to.

Because that's what Ty does. He tears himself into pieces and then gives them up, one by one, for me. He's been doing it since even before Mom ran out on us, and he's not about to stop.

Not unless I make him.

I formulate the words he needs to hear and then force them out. If I do a good enough job I can even convince myself they're true. "Nah, I'll be fine," I say lightly. "Just do me a favor."

"What?"

"When you come back from your precious fancy-ass London next year," I say, pointing out the window at the antenna in the rearview mirror, "we climb that. Together."

He laughs. "Deal."

One month later, the day after Ty leaves for London, the Fracture happens.

I open my eyes. The helicopter banks violently, pushing me against the window. The antenna fades into the distance.

I don't know how far inland we're going. But sooner or later, they're going to drop me into the city below and I'll be alone in a vast sea of fog and Beings. If I want to survive longer than thirty seconds, if I want to have even the slightest chance at finding Ty again, there's only one option.

I swallow. I glance at the guard; he's got his back to us, both hands on his rifle, as he talks to the pilot. He turns around to check on me every few sentences, I guess in case I manage to slip my zip ties and try to hijack the helicopter with my bare hands. Or do something similarly stupid—like team up with the ex-shadowseeker I just attempted to shoot.

I glance at Elliott. "Ackermann," I say, barely loud enough to be heard over the noise of the rotors, "listen. We're going to need to work together."

"Shut up," he says tonelessly, not even looking at me. I practically have to read his lips to decipher the quiet response. The fight that drained out of him earlier is still gone.

The helicopter shudders, and my stomach twists in a way that tells me we're descending. Panic slices through my scattered thoughts. I need Elliott. Two people together have a better chance at survival, plus he'll have training and skills that might actually give us a shot. If he's already given up before they even dump us down there, though, we'll be eaten before we have a chance to run.

I need to find a way to jar him into action. A thought leaps into my mind, something I learned back at the dartboard booth: Anger is better than fear.

And I know only one way I could make Elliott Ackermann angry.

"Your brother," I say.

He looks up.

I twist my hands in their binding, try to get some blood flowing to my fingers again in preparation for landing, but I keep my gaze on Elliott. "His name was Braedan, right? He was into astronomy. Stargazing. He kept his telescope after it was added to the Reflectivity Index. That's why your mom exiled him." Everyone knows this information. Part of it was public knowledge, part of it was gossip that's been confirmed by enough sources to be taken as truth.

"I said shut up," Elliott says again, but he's still looking at me, and his response is loud enough to be heard this time.

I call up the ghost of my own brother—that golden day, the way the memory hurts and the way that hurt feels right. The way he's filled up every part of my life with his absence. It was painful to hear anyone even mention his name afterward. It still is. I bet it's the same for Elliott. I bet if nothing else hurts him, if nothing else makes him fight, his brother will.

"He didn't keep the telescope," I say.

The guard steps back toward us, toting the rifle with one hand, bracing himself against the wall with the other. He flicks a wicked-looking pocketknife out and slices through the rope that connects my zip-tied hands to the loop in the wall.

My bound arms drop into my lap, dead weight. I dare to look out the window again. In a flash of lightning, I make out a black shape rising toward us. I panic for a moment, remembering the teeth marks on that antenna, but the black shape isn't a massive Being. It's the roof of a building. The helicopter is about to drop us off.

I turn back to Elliott. He's watching me carefully, but his eyes are still dull, still void of anger.

I talk fast. I've got maybe thirty seconds before they shove us out the door to our deaths. "Your mom confiscated his telescope the day it became illegal. I intercepted it when she put it into storage, and the next week, I sold it back to him at a five-hundred-percent profit. Two days later, she caught him with it. *That's* why she exiled him."

The guard unlatches the door and hauls it open. I blink and duck my head as rain bullets inside the cabin, which is why I don't see Elliott coming until he barrels into me, knocking us both out of the helicopter and into the empty air.

I don't have time to yell. There's a blur of gray fog, black sky, silver-blue lightning, and then I crash hard on my back. All the air in my lungs is gone and I can't inhale. Rain instantly soaks me, slicing cold across my skin. Thunder cracks through the sky. I curl onto my side, trying to inhale. Water sluices into my mouth. I can't spit it out. I'm suffocating, drowning.

Another flare of lightning. The helicopter bobbles above us. The guard is half hanging out of the cabin, scrambling to pull himself back in. On the ground a yard or two away from me,

Elliott is already rolling to his feet, his back to me. He raises his bound hands high above his head and then brings them down hard across his stomach. The zip tie snaps, falls to the ground.

Elliott turns. He scans the roof, spots me. In three steps he's standing over me, then he bends down, grabs a fistful of my shirt, and drags me toward . . .

Toward the edge of the roof.

I finally manage to suck in a breath, spit out the rain, try to choke my way through a garbled sentence that even I can barely hear over the storm. My brain spins its wheels. Elliott is one of the good guys. He wouldn't even defend himself against the cops earlier, for God's sake. Surely he won't kill me in cold blood.

I twist, grabbing at him, but my hands are still bound. We reach the edge of the roof. He thrusts me out until I'm tipped over the edge, way overbalanced. If he lets go of my shirt I'm a dead man.

I turn my head. The fog is a quilt below us, pocked and marbled by the storm, so thick it looks impenetrable. The ground is hundreds of feet down. The fog is much closer. I remember the flying Being, the one that killed Ginger. How many more like it are just a few yards beneath me?

I hold very still.

So does Elliott.

I've got my hands clamped over his. I can feel the ridges of his knuckles, the tendons taut in his wrist. I'm holding on tight, trying to keep him from opening his hand, but he and I both know that effort is about as useful as trying to hold a grenade together.

Above us, the helicopter starts to lift. The guard has managed to pull himself back in. The sound of the rotors fades, overtaken by distance and thunder.

And then we're alone on the mainland.

Wind screams across the roof. We're both soaked. It's too dark to see Elliott's face, too dark to guess his expression. I don't need to, though. I'm the one who told him what I did to his brother. I know exactly what his expression is.

Finally, he speaks. "I wish I were like you. You would have let go already." Something ugly twists, fleeting, beneath the surface of the words.

I lick my lips. I raise my voice to be heard over the storm. "That's not true," I say, even though I'm not sure if it is or not.

"You pointed a *gun* at me, Callahan. And you pulled the trigger."

Wind buffets me. "I wouldn't have killed you, though. I swear."

His hand tightens, twisting my shirt a little more. "But you did kill my brother."

"I sold him a telescope." I also sold him back his own glasses, though I'm not about to tell Elliott that. "Your mom is the one who killed him."

He's silent. Wind whistles across us, pushing me sideways.

I squeeze my eyes shut. A curse, shakier than I would like, slips out before I can stop it.

But apparently the sign of vulnerability sways Elliott. He takes a half step back, just enough for my shoes to get a tiny bit of purchase on the concrete ledge but not enough to take me completely out of harm's way.

"She had to do it," Elliott says, his voice flat. The words are rote, practiced. He's said this a lot. Probably to himself.

Sensing weakness, I push harder. "After what she did to him—to both of you—you're still going to defend her? She didn't know the gun would jam, man. She told me to shoot you, let me *actually* shoot you, and she didn't know the gun would jam."

"Neither did you," he snarls.

Lightning shatters the sky, illuminating us for a moment. Below, the fog has swirled into new patterns. Fear thickens my throat.

I look back to Elliott. "We can work together," I repeat. "We have to, if we want to survive. We need each other."

He barks a short, scoffing laugh. "Why would I need *you?*"

I grimace. My plan to jar him into action worked—a little too well—but now I've got to follow through, convince him I can contribute to his survival. I talk faster. "I know how to hotwire a car. We could get to street level, find something that's still got some fuel—"

"And drive through the fog, constantly on the lookout for Beings, to try to get where? There's nothing *left*. Better to just die quickly."

I clamp my hands a little tighter over his wrist. "No, *not* better, that is *not better*. There is something left. There's London, there's Singapore. Maybe there are other places too, cities we just haven't been able to get a signal from yet."

Another surge of lightning splits the clouds. I turn my head to check the fog below again. It may be a trick of the shadows, but for a moment it looks like the fog is moving, shifting.

Or something in it is.

I squeeze my eyes shut, unable to keep my breathing even any longer. I'm gasping, hyperventilating. "Please. Ackermann, please," I beg, not even hating myself for it. If it's groveling he wants, I'll give him as much as it takes to save my skin.

Elliott pauses. Then, a sharp inhale. He's spotted the shapes in the fog too. He yanks me back onto the roof and releases me. "Go," he orders coldly.

I open my eyes, wobbling as I regain my balance. "Together or we're dead," I maintain, though everything in me is shouting to run and not look back.

He sets his jaw and then nods curtly.

Below us, something scrapes. It sounds like claws against glass.

I back quickly away from the edge. We have to get somewhere inside, as far from the fog as possible. Lightning flashes again. In the burst of light, I scan the roof and spot a door at the same moment Elliott does. I get there first, grab the doorknob. The metal is rain-slick and my hand slips off. I try again and realize it's locked.

"Move," Elliott says tersely. I get out of the way and he kicks the door hard. Once, twice. It rattles but doesn't give. He turns to me. "Can you pick the lock?"

I've got my back to him now, staring into the rain, waiting for a monster made of shadows to claw its way over the ledge. My heartbeat is a thrum in my ears. "No."

He curses. "Look for a key, then!"

I tear my attention away from the rooftop, drop to my knees and search the ground blindly. The concrete is smooth, the bricks to either side of the door featureless. No key. Desperate, I stretch my still-bound hands out farther, and something falls out of my pocket and clinks metallically to the ground. It's my key, the one that opens the padlock in my loft.

"There!" Elliott shouts, and snatches it up.

"No, that's just to my—" I start, but he's already turning it in the latch.

Snick. The door unlocks and swings open. I stare dumbly at it for a long moment. That shouldn't have worked. This key is to my loft, not to this random door on the roof of a building I've never seen before.

Then lightning flashes again, and I glance over my shoulder

and spot fog spilling across the roof toward us out of the corner of my eye. I stop caring how the key worked. I yank it out of the lock, step through, and slam the door behind me. I slide my hands upward. There: a dead bolt. I flick it shut. Then I turn and hurry after Elliott into the inky stairwell.

CHAPTER FIVE

THE DARKNESS IS OPPRESSIVE. I SCUFF MY feet to break the quiet as I feel my way down the seventh—or eighth? . . . It's easy to lose count in these conditions—flight of stairs. This stairwell is narrow and completely windowless, the air stagnant and tinted with mildew. Better mildew than the metallic smell of fog, though. We've gone far enough down that I've started to feel relatively safe; if the fog or Beings were going to follow us in here, they would have overtaken us by now.

There's a scratching noise up ahead. I freeze, until a tiny flame bursts into light a few steps ahead of me. "I have some matches," Elliott explains. The flickering fire sends shadows chasing each other over his flat expression.

I'm so relieved that my knees are about to buckle—the cops confiscated my penlight, and I thought they would've taken all his stuff too—but I scoff. "Of course you do. You're a regular freaking Boy Scout."

For a moment I don't think he'll answer, but then: "Regular freaking Eagle Scout, actually."

"Overachiever," I mutter. Good thing he doesn't know how to hot-wire a car, or he wouldn't even need me for that much.

"Underachiever," Elliott shoots back at me, his tone more cutting now. "What good is a criminal who doesn't even know how to jimmy a lock?"

I clench my hands. The key, which I didn't realize I was still clutching, digs into my palm. "What good is a shadowseeker who can't keep his own brother from getting exiled?" I retort. It's an unnecessary escalation for a conversation that had almost been borderline civil, but it's a knee-jerk reaction. If I can distract him, he won't have any chance at guessing that I never taught myself to pick a lock because I didn't want to know just how easily a person could get past all my own dead bolts and padlocks and chain slides. Knowing all the exact ways my safe places might be invaded would just add fuel to my mental loop of obsessive fears, and there's no need to make my OCD combat any harder than it has to be.

Elliott doesn't take the bait. The match burns out to a watery blue flame and then vanishes. The sharp smell of smoke tickles my nose. The acridness reminds me of the fog, and I hold my breath until it dissipates.

Another match scratches in the dark and a new tiny light flares. Elliott steps onto the next landing with a metallic rattle. "I wasn't the shadowseeker then," he says, his tone so even that I can barely detect the anger he's got under tight control beneath it. I stop on the stairs and narrow my eyes. Did he say *the* shadowseeker, not *a* shadowseeker?

Cautiously, I prod him. "What were you, then?"

"A kid." He pauses. "A failure," he corrects.

He's already a full landing ahead of me, too distant to light my steps. I jar myself into motion and follow him. The key is still in my hand. I unthinkingly put it in my left pocket—left, for locked doors—and then pause, recognizing the compulsion.

I clench my jaw. I want to laugh, and I want to hit something. I'm on the Being-haunted mainland with no allies except a guy who'd be just as happy to see me dead, and all I can think about now is this damned key and how badly I want to keep it in the correct pocket so I'll be sure to remember that my loft is definitely locked. As if that matters. As if *that's* the most urgent thing I could possibly be facing right now.

I pull my empty hand out of my pocket and do my best to shove the thoughts out of my head. I've got to focus. Got to remember that I'm stronger than my OCD. I can't afford any distractions pulling my focus away from survival.

Ahead of me, Elliott pauses. He lifts the match toward the door next to him. FLOOR 2, it says. We both peer over the railing; the next flight of stairs is the last one.

Elliott speaks first. "We should find somewhere to wait until morning. The storm might wane by then, and we'll be able to spot any Beings better in the daylight. In the meantime, maybe you can work on picking locks. Or on learning how not to be an asshole. Your choice."

"Did you just make a *joke?*" I ask, astonished.

He raises an eyebrow. "Learning how to pick locks it is, then."

It takes a little work with my still-bound hands, but I manage to salute him, lone middle finger touched to my eyebrow. He catches the gesture and gives me a look.

"What, isn't that the Scout salute?" I say innocently.

He drops the now-dying match to the concrete floor, then plants his hands on the railing and vaults down to the ground without answering. I don't feel the need for theatrics so I take the normal route down the stairs.

The match above flicks out, and Elliott lights another. We walk to the first-floor door. Neither of us moves to open it.

"So, I don't suppose you have some kind of Swiss Army knife that includes, like, a machine gun or a blowtorch or something, do you?" I ask at last. My words are flippant but the terror from earlier is still humming just beneath my collarbone, ready to burst back to life. This is the ground level. Beneath the fog. There could be a Being behind this door, but there's no way to know for sure until we open it.

Elliott reaches into his pockets with his free hand and holds out everything he comes up with. "I've got five more matches, a ration coupon, and a mint. You?"

I don't bother to check. I know what I've got—one key, plus one completely useless stuffed fox that's somehow managed to stay in place since the boardwalk.

I reach out and grab the mint from his hand, popping it into my mouth. "I've got a mint," I say, and then I push through the door before my courage fails me entirely.

The first floor is as dark as the stairwell, but it's a different sort of dark—one that drips over everything and leaves behind a film, so that whatever it touches becomes a part of it. I can almost feel it sliding over my skin, can almost taste it: thick and sticky, like blood.

I glance back at Elliott. The match is burning out, and the door is swinging slowly shut, but he's standing still, staring down at the ration coupon in his hand. CISCO ISLAND is emblazoned in bold letters across its front, with the city's official seal stamped over it.

Carefully, he folds it and tucks it back into his pocket. Then he lights another match and steps out next to me. We both stand very still, the flickering flame barely illuminating the tiles beneath our feet.

Elliott takes a breath. "You owe me a dollar for that mint, jackass," he says, and finally dares to lift the match so we can see where we've landed and if any Beings are waiting to devour us.

He turns in a circle. The light highlights tiny bits of our surroundings, puzzle pieces that we have to put together one at a time. A pillow. A white blanket, tightly tucked in over a thin mattress. The flame glints off dull metal crisscrossing beneath the bed, and then, at the bottom, wheels.

A gurney.

Elliott lifts the match farther away from him and finds another empty gurney pushed against a wall, and then a dead monitor and an empty IV stand. We've landed in a hospital.

I clear my throat. "A dollar, for a mint? That's highway robbery."

Elliott lights a new match—just three left now—and steps farther away from the door. There's open space to either side of us. We're in a hallway. There's a plaque next to the door we just came out of. CHILDREN'S WING, I make out, with an arrow pointing to the left. The arrow pointing to the right says EMERGENCY ROOM and INFORMATION DESK and PARKING GARAGE.

Elliott turns to the right, maneuvering past the gurney. "I guess you would know all about highway robbery," he deadpans.

Ahead is a row of doors, these large and wooden with room numbers next to the knobs. Room number 189 is open. Elliott moves toward it. I cross the threshold behind him. Another compulsion roars to life in my mind, and this time I don't have the strength to battle it. I lift my zip-tied hands, tap the door frame three times on the left and five on the right, hoping Elliott doesn't notice. Relief saturates me; now I'll be safe from the Beings, safe from the fog. Three and five are good numbers. They'll protect me.

But barely a second later, a tidal wave of shame rips through me, drowning the relief. I curl my hands into fists, furious with myself. I've just broken a yearlong streak of not performing any of my compulsions. How hard is it to simply walk through a damn doorway? All I had to do was *not* tap it, but somehow I couldn't even manage that much. I know tapping won't protect me. I know the relief never lasts long. I know all about the lies OCD is telling me—and I still gave in to them anyway.

I force my hands to unclench. I can't deal with this right now. I need to focus. If I can just focus on what's happening around me, maybe I can manage to forget what's happening inside my own head.

Elliott is standing ahead of me, taking stock of the room. The flame casts dancing shadows over another empty gurney and monitor, a computer built to swivel out from the corner, a dead TV overhead.

And a window.

Beyond the glass is a sea of murky gray. At first it's only slightly lighter than the complete darkness in the hallway, but then lightning flashes and the fog captures it, diffusing it into a dim, sparkling blue glow that illuminates our little room for a second. My brain instantly blinks back to middle school science class to provide me with the name of this phenomenon. Refraction: the way light bends and breaks and scatters when it's caught by a prism or by a lens. Or in this case, by the tiny droplets of liquid that make up the fog that's drowned the world.

Without a word, Elliott and I use the light of the second-to-last match to strip one of the gurneys, pull the mattress off, and push it up lengthwise against the window. Then we shove the gurney in front of it to hold it in place.

The match burns down to a speck of flickering blue. Darkness seeps from the hallway into the room, fills up the corners and cracks. My eyes are burning but I don't blink. I don't want the darkness to creep beneath my eyelids.

As Elliott lights the final match, I move away from him and close the door. It doesn't have a lock. I want to laugh, because this is bad news—a lock would be an extra measure of security against potential Beings, who after all can't go through solid objects—but instead of being scared, I'm relieved. I don't want to spend the rest of the night fighting the compulsion to get up and double-check that the door really is locked. This way I'll still be terrified, but at least I don't have to do anything about it, because there's nothing to do.

I grit my teeth. It must be the stress of the situation causing my OCD to flare up so badly. But it doesn't matter; I can still fight it. I've already beat it once, after all. Tapping on the doorway earlier, worrying about the lock and which pocket my key is in, these are just small slipups. They don't have to mean anything. They definitely don't mean my OCD is coming back full force.

I try to make myself believe it.

"Might as well try to get some sleep," Elliott says. He's sitting down in the spot where the gurney was.

I turn and eye the now-dying match at his feet. "Maybe we ought to start a fire?" I ask, though the Boy Scout has to have already thought of that.

Sure enough, he shakes his head. "No ventilation in here," he explains. "Too much of a risk."

I nod, resigned, and then hesitate as I try to decide where to sit. Instinct tells me the far side of the room—Elliott is still my enemy, after all—but he's also the only other living person within fifty miles. And, I tell myself, I need to stay close in case he tries to sneak off without me in the middle of the night.

I move to a spot a few feet away from him and slide to the floor, the zip ties on my wrists digging in at the motion. The last match burns out. And together, in the silence and the darkness, we wait for daylight.

Dawn creeps around the edges of the mattress with the gray pallor of a long-dead corpse. I'm sitting with my arms around my knees—the only position that's even semi-comfortable, as my hands are still zip-tied together—when I realize I can make out Elliott's form farther down the wall. He's sprawled out on his stomach looking like one of those chalk crime-scene outlines, snoring as if he's at a sleepover instead of waiting for death to pounce.

There's an empty IV bag next to my foot. I throw it at him.

He comes awake instantly, brushing the bag off and glaring at me. He stretches, glances at the mattress-covered window, and then stands. "Time to move," he says without preamble and opens the door.

I tense, leaping to my feet. My muscles are stiff and tired from the long night, but I ignore the ache. "What the hell? You have to *check for Beings first!*" I hiss, eyes wide.

He glances back at me. "If there's a Being in the hall, it's going to kill us whether or not I check for it."

Which is true, but unhelpful.

I follow him cautiously. Several nearby doors are open, spilling enough muted gray light for us to see in the hallway. Elliott steps around an empty gurney that's pushed up against the wall and then disappears through another door. It's a bathroom.

After a moment, I hear the squeak of a faucet turning on and then the sound of running water. Apparently the plumbing still works here, at least.

I start after him. My still-damp shoes squelch with each step. I sigh, wishing we could stumble upon some fresh clothing or a miraculously working dryer. Or a coffeemaker, while I'm wishing for impossible things; my eyes are grainy with fatigue, and my brain feels disconnected and floaty from lack of sleep.

"Keep your eyes down," Elliott calls to me, his voice tense. "I'm pretty sure there's a mirror above the sink."

I hesitate—but then look down at myself. Spots of Ginger's blood are still flecked all over my arms. Some of it stains my shirt and pants, too, and there's not much I can do about that, but I'm suddenly desperate to wash off as much of it as possible. I edge inside the bathroom, careful to keep my gaze on the white tiles beneath my feet.

Ten minutes later, we've both freshened up as best we can and, despite me making it blindingly obvious how difficult it is for me to maneuver with bound hands, Elliott hasn't offered to help me get out of the zip ties.

He's going to make me ask. "Fine," I snap as we exit the bathroom. "Are you going to show me how to do that move you did to get out of these, or what?"

He strides ahead, ducking into another patient room. There's a shuffling noise and then he comes out with a blanket over one shoulder and a long extension cord looped around the other. "No," he answers, nodding at my hands. "I like this better."

I watch as he moves farther down the hall, choosing another room and disappearing inside again. Frustrated, I twist my wrists, trying to shift the ties to a spot that isn't already chafed and sore. "You won't like it better when a Being attacks," I call after him as loudly as I dare. "You'll be getting eaten and I won't be able to help at all, because my hands are *literally* tied."

He emerges from the doorway with a handful of rattling pill bottles and first-aid supplies, tucking them into his pockets. "You wouldn't help if I was getting eaten anyway," he says. "You'd leave me behind the second you thought it was in your best interest."

I pause. It occurs to me that this is the way I've been thinking of *him*; that he's waiting for the opportunity to abandon me, that I have to stick close, or he'll leave me to my fate without a second thought. I wonder when I started assuming everyone was like me.

"Do you really think so little of me?" I ask, genuinely curious. If he truly thinks I'm such a liability, why would he bother to keep me around even this long?

He pauses and finally looks at me, his expression closed off. After a moment he shuffles through the supplies in his hands and tosses me something small and gleaming. I catch it: a little pair of surgical scissors. It's sheer luck that I caught them by the handle and not by one of the blades, which could have sliced a finger open. I look back up.

"Give me a reason not to," Elliott says, and then he turns his back and walks away.

By the time I've managed to contort my hands enough to cut through the ties and free myself, Elliott has already found the information desk. I hurry straight to the big map that's plastered to the wall above it, vaulting over the desk to read it more closely.

I squint. "It looks like the parking garage entrance is . . ."

"That way." Elliott cuts me off, pointing to the left. His expression is strange—wary, unsettled. I follow his line of sight to find two sets of glass double doors. Muted gray sunlight spills through them, which, I realize now, is why it was bright enough for me to read the map a moment ago. Beyond the doors I can make out the dim interior of a multistory parking garage. There's fog out there, but it's thin—blown into submission by the storm I can still hear at the edges of the garage—and easily allows me to see rows upon rows of cars and trucks and SUVs. We'll be able to spot any nearby Beings while we're out there, too, as the garage is small enough that it's not very dark even in the shadowed center.

"Yes!" I exult quietly, pumping a fist. Finally, a win.

"Callahan," Elliott says from behind me, his voice slow and strange, "do you notice anything weird about those cars?"

I crack my knuckles, mentally going through the list of tools I'll need to scavenge. "That there's a lot of 'em," I answer. It's good news. I've actually only ever hot-wired one car success-fully—Ty's '92 Camaro—so the wider selection means a better chance at finding one that I'll know how to steal.

"Yeah," Elliott says. "About a hundred of them on this level alone. A hundred cars—and no bodies."

I go still as the words sink in. Then, slowly, I turn. I look around. The front desk area is wide open and clean. There's a bank of dead elevators to my left, a dark glassed-in gift shop and a waiting area to my right, and antiseptic white tile beneath my feet. It was the same in all the hallways and patient rooms we've passed through: empty gurneys, vacant nurses' stations. And not a single corpse.

"It's only been a year since the Fracture," Elliott says. "There should be bodies *everywhere*. We shouldn't be able to breathe for the smell, shouldn't be able to take a step without running into a body. All those cars out there. Where are their owners?"

Unease crawls over my skin. I try to shake it off. "The Beings ate them, probably," I reason. It's the supposition that's been in the back of my mind ever since we first stepped onto the empty ground floor, but now it doesn't quite feel right. Beings have never eaten people—or at least, not completely—on the island. But maybe that's just because they dissipate too fast. The Beings and fog on the mainland are permanent.

"Then where's the blood?" Elliott persists. "The signs of struggle?"

I look around again. He's right. There should be bones and blood all over this foyer, personal belongings scattered across the floor, claw marks on the walls. Even if everyone had enough of a warning to evacuate safely, there should be signs of distress, of people leaving in a rush. But there's nothing. No half-finished paperwork on the desk. No toys left behind in the waiting area. The floor is sparkling, as if it were mopped yesterday.

Elliott points at the sign above the desk. MADRIGAL SOUTH HOSPITAL, it reads at the top. "I've been here before," he says, his voice dark and far away. "With Mom. She was the city treasurer here when I was fourteen. This hospital had just been built; she attended the opening ceremony. It's been in use for three years since then, but it still looks exactly like it did the day she cut the ribbon. Except," he says, sweeping a hand at the parking garage, "for all those cars."

I swallow. I look from him to the cars: my salvation, my escape. My first step toward maybe, somehow, getting to Ty. "Are you saying this is some sort of . . . what, a trap?"

The Beings have never shown any sign of intelligence before. But then, as far as we can tell, they're just the weapons of whatever aliens attacked us last year. So if this *is* a trap . . . I don't want to meet whoever set it.

"I don't know what it is," Elliott admits.

I brood for a moment. "We have to take the chance," I say

at last, and start toward the doors.

Elliott's mouth is set in grim lines, but he nods. "Just a sec," he says. He walks over to the desk, reaches beneath it, and fiddles with it for a second before he manages to unscrew one of its legs. He turns, hefting the solid-looking length of wood. It's ornately carved and about three feet long.

"That'll do exactly zero good against a Being," I observe.

He strides toward the doors. "It might buy us a minute or two if it comes to a fight, at least."

I move out after him, through the first set of doors and into the little foyer. My mind, which has been feeling fuzzy from lack of sleep, sharpens at the danger we're about to walk into. "Be careful of the side mirrors on the cars, and the rearview mirrors, too," I warn. "Keep your eyes up. You're my lookout."

"How far I've fallen," he mutters, and paces out into the parking garage without a backwards look. He hops onto the hood of a nearby Jag and scans the area, keeping the desk leg out and ready. He's still got the blanket over one shoulder and the cord looped over the other. He should look ridiculous. I'm kind of annoyed that he looks a little bit badass instead.

I pause at the second set of doors, holding one open but not stepping out of the foyer yet. The wind howls in the distance. It doesn't sound quite as strong as last night. We must have just caught one of the outside bands of the hurricane, or maybe it's losing strength.

I look out across the cars. The fog is light out here but I can still see it, can sense it thickening against my skin until it's almost a liquid, something clear and viscous and capable of drowning me. I can smell it, too: unnaturally metallic, ever-so-faintly burnt. The smoldering ash of a lightning strike.

I catch myself tapping on the door frame and snatch my hand down, disgusted with myself. Anxiety crashes through me, overwhelming. I *need* to finish tapping the door frame. Otherwise I won't be safe in the garage. And I know it won't actually make a difference, that tapping a door can't make me safe, but that doesn't stop the all-consuming urgency of the compulsion or the desperate need for even the few seconds of relief that the tapping will bring.

"You coming or what?" Elliott calls in a low voice, still scanning for Beings.

"Hold on," I say, setting my jaw. I will *not* give in to my OCD. I've worked too hard to backslide like this. I need to put it in its place right now, once and for all, in order to stop the anxiety. I will turn around and go back through both these sets of double doors again—three times apiece, five times apiece, just to make sure—until the urges and the anxiety are gone.

I turn around. I take one step. I glance up, and see the mirror.

It's high on the wall above the waiting area, one of those mirrored half-domes that help people see around corners. It takes me a second to register what it is. In that second, something ripples across the surface of the mirror: a rainbow sheen, like an oil slick on water. A low buzz of electricity crackles across my skin. And then comes the weird sensation in my ribs—as if there's a string connecting my smallest rib to something inside the mirror, and it wants to reel me in.

My body understands what's happening before my brain does. Horror washes through me like a storm surge. I freeze.

The oil slick on the mirror's surface darkens to a gray curl of fog. Something carved from night reaches up through it. A paw—its joints too long, too close to being fingers—curls through the mirror. Scythe-like claws scrape trenches in the wall below.

Another paw joins it on the other side. A terrible face rises up: pointed ears made of darkness, a foxlike muzzle that spreads into a panting smile. In one push it's out of the mirror and on the ground, shadows rising from its back like tendrils of mist.

It unfolds itself.

It stands up on two legs, its joints crooked and horrible.

It turns—and looks at me.

CHAPTER SIX

Y MUSCLES UNLOCK. I STUMBLE BACKWARDS.
Terror is an egg in my chest, cracking itself open,
beating its wings like a second heartbeat.

I turn and run.

Elliott is still atop the car. He's looking in the other direction,
blind to the threat. "ACKERMANN," I scream, and he whirls
around. He spots the Being. It's throwing itself against the first
set of glass doors—which, thank God, closed behind me. Elliott's
whole body goes taut and he leaps off the car with a curse. The
blanket slides off his shoulder and drops to the pavement at the
sudden movement.

"Find us some transportation, *now*," he orders, wielding the desk leg as he strides toward the creature. The Being doesn't make any sound, but its silence is even more terrible than snarling would have been. It's like a nightmare come to life. Unthinkable, unstoppable.

Elliott's words penetrate my terror. I stare at his retreating back. "What? Wait, no, we have to run! You can't *fight* it!"

"Not for long," he agrees over his shoulder, his voice tight. "Get moving!"

Everything in me is propelling me away: to run blindly, as far and as fast as I can. But Elliott is right. You can't outrun a Being. Not on foot. Our only chance is me hot-wiring something right the hell now and hoping Elliott can hold the Being off until then.

I sprint, frantically scanning the rows of cars. Glass breaks behind me. I curse as quietly and creatively as I can manage, keeping my eyes on the vehicles. *There!* Relief pours over me, an antidote to the drowning film of fog that's clinging to my skin. Just one row away is a '92 Camaro exactly like Ty's, even down to the fire-engine red color. My luck has finally turned.

I skid to a stop next to it. Behind me, glass shatters. There's an awful scraping of claws against concrete and then the thud of the desk leg striking whatever passes for the Being's flesh. The bastards are solid, but they don't bleed, and you can never actually harm them. The best outcome you can hope for when fighting a Being is to slightly delay your own death.

I put my hands on the Camaro, grounding myself to it, forcing myself not to look over my shoulder. Okay, okay, car theft. First check if the door's unlocked. People are stupid, it's not impossible. And . . . yes! The handle lifts in my hand and the door flies open. That cuts down on a little bit of time.

In my peripheral vision I spot the side mirror. I jolt backwards, turn and kick at it blindly with all my strength until it breaks off and skids under the neighboring car. Then I quickly do the same to the other side.

I throw myself into the driver's seat. The interior is all stained gray fabric that's worn through in spots, that's just like Ty's Camaro too. I remember the rearview mirror, wrench it off, toss it out. A few car lengths away, more glass breaks, and the groan and screech of metal tells me the Being has climbed atop a car. Elliott must be trying to lose it by hiding in the rows of vehicles. I hunker down sideways in my seat, both to get myself out of the Being's view and to access the steering column. Tools, I need tools. A screwdriver and wire strippers at a minimum. By force of habit, my hand snakes beneath the passenger's seat, where Ty used to keep his tool bag in his car. I'm already cursing myself for wasting time checking in this stranger's car when my fingers brush something leather. When I pull my hand out, Ty's tool bag is in it.

I stare at the leather bag in confusion, then pull my gaze up to scan the dashboard and seats. This can't be my brother's car. Ty's Camaro died last year, right after he moved me to Cisco Island.

It got scrapped. We even went to the junkyard, had a little service in its honor before watching it get smashed. But then how are Ty's tools here, in exactly the spot I'd expected them to be?

"Callahan!" comes a muffled shout. Something crashes a few rows down. "Move it!" There's genuine fear in Elliott's voice now, which tells me he must be about to reach his limit. At which point the Being will kill him and come for me.

I jolt into motion. Yank a screwdriver out of the bag, shakily remove the steering column's plastic cover. Three bundles of multicolored wires fall out.

A high, reedy voice echoes eerily through the garage, lilting up and down and then up again, like a song or maybe a wolf's howl. Goose bumps rise all over me. I'm muttering a prayer beneath my breath—I used to believe in God, and it appears I still do—but I'm not even processing what I'm saying. I was wrong before when I thought the monster's silence was worse than any noise it could make.

I search for the battery wire. *Red, it's red. There!* My hands are shaking so badly, I can barely use the wire strippers, but somehow I manage. Then I do the same to the ignition wire. Using my shirt as insulation, I twist them together.

The lights inside the car all come on. The radio starts playing "Stand by Me."

"No, damn it, shut up," I hiss, frantically jabbing at the off button. The sound dies. I hold my breath and slowly, heart in my throat, lift my head until I can just barely see over the dashboard.

Nothing. I exhale. The Being didn't hear.

Then I turn my head and see the creature standing a car's length behind the Camaro, its head cocked, its shoulders hunched, its jaw lolling open. It makes a noise, something between a cough and an eerie, foxlike chortle, and starts toward me.

But before I have time to throw myself out of the car and flee, something wooden flies end over end from farther down the aisle and smacks the Being in the side of the face. The desk leg. "Hey!" bellows Elliott. He's standing in the middle of the aisle maybe thirty feet away, exposed and now weaponless. He's trying to draw the thing away from me.

It works. The Being turns. It crouches low and then springs an inhuman distance, its freakishly long limbs carrying it ten feet in a single leap. Elliott takes off running with a curse, weaving through the cars.

I jerk my attention back down to the wires. *The starter, where's the starter . . . there!* I yank it upward, strip it—the wire is live, and I'm shaking so much it's a miracle I don't electrocute myself—and touch it to the connected battery and ignition wires.

The car roars to life. I shove myself upright in the seat and mash my foot on the gas to rev it before it has a chance to stall. The engine sputters, then levels out.

I slam the car into reverse and crank hard on the steering wheel, breaking the steering lock. The car screeches and peels out of its space. Its rear bumper bangs against the neighboring truck and then I'm free. I hit the brakes and shift into gear, twisting around to find the Being, to find the best exit route.

A muffled shout of pain. Elliott. I glance out the back. He's huddled beneath a car door that the creature must have torn off earlier, using it like a shield—but he's pinned down. The Being is lashing out with its claws, tearing through the metal of the door to get to Elliott. Sparks and metal shrapnel fly in every direction. The door will only provide maybe a few more seconds of protection.

And then the Being will come for me. I flash back to the bodies I've seen on the posters: torn apart, mutilated, half-eaten. Terror beats its wings inside my chest.

I swivel in my seat, stare through the windshield. The exit ramp is straight this way. All I have to do is put my foot down hard on the gas again and I stand a chance at escaping.

Elliott is my enemy. I can't risk death to save him. He said earlier that I'd abandon him as soon as it was convenient, and he was right. It's who I am. And this isn't even about convenience—it's life or death. Heroism is stupid, I've always known that. Plus, I can't find Ty if I'm dead.

But in the back of my mind, a little voice whispers: *Give me a reason not to.*

I curse out loud and shift the car into reverse. I'm not a hero, but I can't just abandon the stupid Boy Scout without trying to save him. He's still my best chance at long-term survival, after all. This is nothing but self-preservation—my specialty.

I hit the gas and then crack my door open and stick my head out. "ROLL!" I shout over the screech of the tires and the roar of the engine. Elliott must hear, because he shoves the car door upward and releases it, rolling sideways into an empty parking spot. The Being stays where it is, not realizing yet that Elliott is gone, too busy tearing off a chunk of the door with its jaw.

It looks up a second before I hit it. It crouches, ready to leap again, but the Camaro is moving just fast enough and slams into it before it can move, throwing it backwards a good twenty feet.

I lean over and shove the passenger door open. Elliott is staring at me from the asphalt. "Get in, idiot!" I shout. He scrambles up just as the Being shakes itself and stands, not even affected by the crash. The second Elliott's inside the car I shift gears and take off, the tires squealing and smoking. The momentum of it slams the door shut almost on his fingers.

The Being gallops after us. Its gaping, foxlike muzzle opens wide in anticipation. Shadows curl off its legs, off the things that are almost arms.

We hit the exit ramp. The fender skids against the guardrail, throwing off sparks. Then we're into the street. Rain streams across the windshield and I flick the wipers on as fast as they'll go. The fog is thick and soupy in spots but wispy in others, allowing me to make out a clear road to the left.

I don't bother wondering why it's clear when it should be littered with dead vehicles and corpses. I just crank on the steering wheel and bear the gas pedal all the way to the floor. The creature howls a threat, loping after us. It's fast, but when the Camaro hits seventy miles per hour, the Being falls behind and finally, eventually, disappears into the fog behind us.

I speed up to about ninety—beyond dangerous, when I can barely see through the rain and fog—and don't ease up for a solid ten minutes.

Elliott looks out the rear windshield one last time and then exhales, sagging in his seat. Then, after a long moment, he reaches up and buckles his seat belt.

I burst out laughing.

He stares at me for a second, then, ruefully, grins. "Safety first."

"Sure," I say. I feel giddy, my joints loose and slippery with relief.

We're heading out of the city now and into a forested area. The road is lined by towering longleaf pines, their trunks pencil-straight and crowded close together, their sparse green tops hidden far above us in the thickening gray. I slow to fifty as heavier fog patches start drifting across the road, then, thinking better of it, I let the speedometer creep back up to fifty-five.

This'll be tricky; I need to go slow enough to compensate for the fog, but fast enough to outrun the Beings that are surely roaming through it.

That's not our only worry, either. Judging by the fuel gauge we've only got a few gallons in the tank. We're going to have to find some gas pretty quick if we want to keep our getaway car running. But for now at least, we're safe.

Elliott is looking at me. His earlier smile is gone, a speculative look in its place. "For a second back there I thought you would leave me."

My hands tighten reflexively on the steering wheel. I don't need him thinking I'm going to "turn good" or be redeemed or whatever. Being good only means tying yourself to someone else's set of rules, and following rules is as likely to kill me as anything else out here. "I'll leave you next time," I promise.

He raises his eyebrows but says nothing, instead pulling off the length of cord that's still looped around his shoulder and chest. He starts working to untangle it. "So what do we do now?"

I'm silent for a moment. The giddiness starts to fade and my earlier fatigue filters back in. I'm going to need to sleep soon— but not yet. Not until I've got some sort of plan.

Ahead, a radio antenna looms out of the fog, its base overgrown by brown wire grass. The grass is about waist-high, spindly with tufted tops, and it almost manages to hide the claw marks gouged deep into the metal. This must be the antenna we saw from the helicopter, its snapped-off top sticking out above the fog. I'm almost positive it's also the same antenna my brother promised we would climb together when he got back. This has to be the road we drove last year, when he moved me to Cisco Island.

I keep my eyes on the antenna until it recedes into the fog. Then I clear my throat. "I remember there being a small regional airport a few hours' drive from here."

Elliott finishes detangling the cord and tosses it in the backseat, then roots around in his pockets. "Let's take inventory. We have an extension cord that we could use as rope, a pair of surgical scissors, and some general first-aid supplies. Aspirin, gauze, bandages." He raises his eyes to me. "None of those things will help you fly a plane."

I set my jaw. "I know that."

"And you want to go anyway? What's the point?"

"We've got to go *somewhere*."

He hesitates. "We could try to sneak back to the island."

I roll my eyes. Of course that's his first thought. "And what happens when we get caught again?"

"You've got someplace you're stashing all those mirrors and illegal telescopes, right?" His voice is sharper now. "Why don't we just hide out there?"

The phosphate mines offer plenty of hiding spots, it's true. We could lie low there for a while, *if* we made it all the way back to the island, but before long we'd need to buy food. With rations being carefully policed, there's no way we could go long without being spotted. And that's assuming Elliott wouldn't just give me up to his mom the second we set foot in her city again.

In any case, Cisco Island isn't where I want to be. "No," I tell Elliott. "We're going to the airport. We'll figure out the next step when we get there."

"The next step toward getting to London, you mean?"

Silence falls over us. "Yes," I say through gritted teeth.

He doesn't respond. Then, finally, he sighs. "I'll fly us." His tone is tired, stretched, and he's looking out his window instead of at me.

I blink. "What?"

"I said I'll fly us."

"You're . . . a *pilot*?"

He turns, faces forward, looks out the windshield into the fog. "Remember the guards arguing over who would pilot the helicopter and how bumpy the ride was? That was because *I'm* the most qualified pilot on the island—those guys can barely fly straight. I've got a license for single-engine fixed-wing planes, too."

I spit out a few curses. When my mind is clear enough to answer rationally, I glare at him, incredulous. "You're a pilot and you're only telling me *now*? Are you freaking serious? You could've hijacked the helicopter yourself when they were dropping us off! They barely even had you tied up!"

"You should be glad I didn't," he answers coldly. "The first thing I'd have done afterward is push you overboard."

I remember him holding me over the edge of the roof, my hands clutching his fist, the look in his eyes when he said he wished he was like me.

"No. You wouldn't have," I say, a little calmer now.

He glances at me sideways, his mouth a flat line.

I inhale, wrapping my mind around the new information he's given me. Outside, the rain has lightened to a sprinkle, though from what I can tell, the sky is still dark and ominous, promising that another band of the hurricane is on its way. "Okay. So . . . we'll go to the airport, find something you can fly. Can single-engine planes cross the Atlantic?"

"Depends."

"We'll figure it out when we get there." A smile creeps onto my face as my anger at Elliott fades. For the first time since we've been exiled, I have a plan that actually stands a chance at getting me to Ty. Although . . . if I'd have known Elliott was a pilot before today, I wouldn't have been around long enough to get exiled in the first place. I would have done whatever it took, including kidnapping him, to get in the air.

Lucky for him, I had no clue he'd even existed until yesterday. Which on an island the size of ours is a near miracle. I glance at him. "How can you be a pilot and the mayor's son and, apparently, a shadowseeker, without anyone knowing about you?"

He's silent for a moment, and I don't think he'll answer.

Then he sighs. "Remember when I told you I used to be a failure? I was being literal. I got expelled my sophomore year and never finished high school."

I blink, taken aback by his confession. "*You* got expelled? What'd you do, lecture someone to death?"

"No. I put my principal in the hospital."

I take my eyes off the road to look at him. He's staring straight ahead, jaw set. "Seriously?" I ask, trying not to sound impressed.

He hesitates again, then shrugs. "Yeah. My mom was city treasurer in Madrigal at the time, running for mayor there. The guy running against her—who also happened to be the principal of my school—kept airing these awful, really personal attack ads, telling all sorts of lies about her. It was working, making her drop behind in the polls. Mom was devastated. I was so *angry* that he could do shit like that to her and just get away with it. So I dug up his home address and confronted him. Things . . . escalated. We got in a fight. He ended up in the hospital. Afterward, unsurprisingly I guess, he expelled me."

I raise my eyebrows. "You beat up a dirty politician, huh? On behalf of every American, I thank you." Unwilling to break our semi-truce, I don't mention that his mom was probably just as terrible as the other guy.

I squint into the fog ahead. There should be road signs around here at some point, and I don't want to miss them. I'm pretty sure we're going the right way—the regional airport I remember is near a town called Pidgeton, I think—but it would be nice to know exactly how far we are from it. Plus, we still need to find gas somewhere. The fuel gauge is hovering on E now.

At my reaction, Elliott relaxes a bit. "My mother didn't see it that way. 'Woman sics violent son on opposition' was the headline of every newspaper, talk show, and political blog in a hundred-mile radius afterward. That asshole blamed her for my 'attack' and ended up winning their race anyway." His words are easy, but his tone is hard, brittle. "Mom was furious; she blamed me. She said if I'd left things alone she could've at least gotten some sympathy votes, but after what I did everyone hated her. When we picked up and moved to Cisco Island to start fresh, she made sure no one would use me against her again. She kept me home, had me study to get my GED instead of putting me in another school. She asked me to 'stay out of the public eye.'"

"So you did," I say, mentally slotting in another piece of the puzzle that is Elliott. Not only did he take the blame for what had happened, he tried to make up for it by letting his own mother pretend he didn't exist.

"So I did," he agrees, one corner of his mouth tilted up in a humorless smile. "While she thrust Braedan into the spotlight, I stayed home, stayed anonymous, and tried my best to make her proud of me again."

"Flying lessons," I realize. "Eagle Scout."

"Yeah."

"Did it work?"

"She exiled me. What do you think?"

The air between us thickens. I ignore the warning in it. "I think you should've guessed she'd exile you," I tell him frankly. "Did you really think she'd make an exception, after you broke the law, after what she did to Braedan when *he* broke the law?"

Up ahead, a shape rises out of the fog. I tense until I register that it's a green road sign—not a Being—but it recedes into the fog behind us before I get the chance to read it.

Elliott's lips turn up in an expression that's too sharp to be called a smile. "I was willing to take that risk if it meant ridding the island of every last mirror dealer. That's why I became the shadowseeker, after all."

Ah, here we are again, at this conversation. "*The* shadow-seeker?" Another sign flashes past, but I don't even look at it, too focused on the topic at hand now.

"Yeah. 'The.' After Braedan got exiled for possessing reflective material, I made it my personal mission to hunt down every black market dealer on the island. I went undercover, again and again, to locate the proof my mom needed to arrest them."

"And exile them," I say, anger quickening in my gut. "Sam Garcia, did you arrest him too? He was underage. Seventeen. And your mom made him walk Valkyrie Bridge." I remember the way I felt when the officers started dragging him toward the fog, when I saw the panic in his eyes. Not that I'd liked the guy, or even known him—but no one deserved what he'd had to face. Or what we're facing now.

Elliott's arm is resting next to the window. His hand curls into a fist. "His business put the whole island in danger."

"You didn't hunt him down, hunt any of us down, because we put the *island* in danger," I accuse, my fingernails digging into the steering wheel's leather. The speedometer starts creeping up again, and I have to force myself to slow back down to fifty. "You did it because you wanted revenge for your brother. Because you wanted to make your mom proud of you, wanted to protect her from us just like you 'protected' her from that politician—even though *she*, not the mirror dealers, was the one who fed Braedan to the Beings. Do you still want to make her proud, now that she's exiled you, too?"

"Shut up," he warns, his voice low, his eyes on the road.

"No," I say more loudly, the anger sparking and brightening. "You helped her put dozens of people on that bridge. Your blind loyalty to her makes you just as bad as any dealer—"

"No," Elliott snaps, and stabs a finger at the window. "Shut *up*, and look."

There's another green road sign just ahead. I glance at it— and slam my foot on the brakes.

The car fishtails. The smell of burning tires filters into the

Camaro. We come to a stop a few yards past the sign.

My hands are clamped like a vise on the wheel. My foot is still on the brake pedal, bearing it all the way to the floor. I turn my head and look outside: towering pencil-thin pines, clumps of tufted wire grass, two-lane asphalt highway, fog. Nothing unusual.

Except for that sign. I only had a second to read it, but it was enough.

Elliott and I look at each other silently. After a long moment, I shift gently into reverse, take my foot off the brake, and ease the car backwards. The back of the sign approaches. I keep going until we can see the lettering on the front. I read it.

YOU DID IT BECAUSE YOU WANTED REVENGE FOR YOUR BROTHER, the sign reads, in reflective white lettering on the green background.

CHAPTER SEVEN

GOOSE BUMPS RAISE ON MY ARMS. I SWIVEL IN MY seat, stare blindly into the fog for whoever could've . . . what, put the sign here? They would've had to have known in advance what we'd be talking about, our exact wording, exactly where we'd be when we said it.

"How?" is all I can manage.

Elliott's gaze is still glued to the white lettering. "The other signs," he says.

I hit the gas again. We reverse back down the road at an unsafe speed, swerving crazily. Confusion and foreboding tangle in the pit of my stomach.

The prior sign comes back into view. I slow enough to read it. THAT'S WHY I BECAME THE SHADOWSEEKER, AFTER ALL.

"What," Elliott says quietly, "the hell."

I hit the gas again, doing forty in reverse now. It's reckless. I don't care. My confusion strengthens, the foreboding mushrooming into fear.

The third sign rises out of the mist. Before the car comes to a complete stop, Elliott has the door open and he's climbing out, striding through the waist-high wire grass to read it. It's incredibly dangerous in this fog, with the mainland full of who knows how many Beings lurking who knows where, but I clamber out too. Fuzzy tufts of grass shed onto my jeans as I come around the car and join Elliott in front of the sign.

THERE SHOULD BE ROAD SIGNS AROUND HERE AT SOME POINT, AND I DON'T WANT TO MISS THEM.

"I never said that." My voice is too loud. It rings in my ears.

Elliott frowns. "It doesn't match the others, then. So, what? It's . . . a pattern? A puzzle? A message? This one is important for some reason?"

"No," I correct his assumption, unable to tear my eyes away from the reflective white letters. "I never said that *out loud.*"

Elliott looks at me. He looks back at the sign.

"I thought it," I tell him. Something—my heartbeat?—is roaring in my ears. "I thought it, in *this exact wording*, and then it appeared on a road sign ahead of us."

Elliott stares at me for a long moment. Then: "Get back in the car." The words crack through the fog like gunshots.

I bolt. The doors slam. He buckles his seat belt. I do mine too, but it doesn't make me feel safer. I shift back into drive and put my foot on the pedal, shoving it to the floor.

Forty miles per hour. Fifty. Seventy. The engine sputters and then catches again, running on fumes now.

"The road signs know our thoughts," Elliott says at last.

"I don't—I don't know." I keep my eyes glued on the road, afraid to look at anything other than the asphalt.

"Is this the aliens messing with us? Are they mind readers or something?" His voice is too calm. He shouldn't be calm. He should be raging, panicked, petrified.

Mind readers. I don't want anyone in my mind. It's bad enough *I* have to be in there. If the aliens can read my thoughts, root out my compulsions, spy on my fears . . . I don't stand a chance.

The engine sputters again. I press the pedal all the way to the floor, as if I can keep it going by sheer force of will. "We need to find some fuel *right the hell now*," I say, my voice tight. I glance around, desperate for a gas station or another vehicle we can siphon fuel from. Anything that would keep me from getting stuck in the middle of this road, forced to walk unprotected through fog and Beings and maybe-telepathic aliens.

The engine dies.

Silence. It crackles all around us, static in the air, ringing in my ears.

I keep one hand on the steering wheel as the car coasts. With the other I reach down and snatch the starter wire, sparking it against the ignition and battery wires. The engine coughs for a few seconds. The radio turns on automatically again, and the chorus of "Stand by Me" plays at full volume.

The engine sputters back out. The music keeps going, fraying my nerves. I reach out a hand to smack the off button.

"Wait," Elliott says suddenly before I can touch it. "That happened earlier, too, didn't it? The music. It came on in the garage, when you first started the car."

I nod, not seeing how music matters at all right now, white-knuckling the steering wheel as the car slows to sixty and then fifty.

Elliott is frowning at the dashboard. "This car doesn't have a CD player or a tape deck, though," he says. "Just the radio. But somehow . . ."

He turns the music off. Silence fills the car, louder than before, until Elliott presses the button again. "Stand by Me" continues.

No. Not "continues." It starts up again—in exactly the same spot it did a moment ago, at the beginning of the chorus.

Elliott slides the little lever to switch through the FM stations. The chorus starts over and over again on each and every one.

I'm frozen at the wheel. "That's . . . how are you doing that?"

Elliott shakes his head, still looking at the dial under his hand. "Callahan. The entire mainland is dead, empty. Covered in fog. There shouldn't be *anything* on the radio."

The second he says it, the song cuts out to static.

I turn my head slowly. I stare at him. The static is so loud, it's making it hard to breathe.

"A song that plays on every station," he says, still too calm, too logical. How can he be so logical right now? "Road signs that can hear what we're saying *and* our thoughts. And there were no bodies in the hospital, and too many cars in the garage. What else has happened that shouldn't be able to happen? What else might give us a better idea of what we're dealing with out here?"

The answer strikes me. I stare at the steering wheel under my hands. "The car," I say numbly.

Elliott's gaze snaps to me. "What?"

"This is my *brother's* car." I swallow. "It's the same—color, model, year, everything. Even his tool bag, it was exactly where he kept it. But it can't be the same car. We watched that car get junked a year ago. And . . . and, 'Stand by Me,' that was his favorite song. He was always listening to stupid old music. Campy stuff."

The static is filling up the car like a third presence. I risk taking a hand off the wheel to slap the off button. The silence that takes its place seeps in the same way the darkness did back at the hospital last night, filling up all the cracks, suffocating me.

"And the key, too," I remember, trying to force myself to think straight, clinging to lucidity like a drowning man grabbing for a raft. "The key that opened the door on the hospital roof, it shouldn't have worked. It was my key, to *my* loft. It had fallen out of my pocket right before you saw it."

Elliott's eyes narrow in thought. A strange expression steals over him. He stares at the dashboard again for a long moment, like he's trying to concentrate on a difficult riddle, and then, suddenly, he squeezes his eyes shut. "I've never been on this road before," he announces. "I have no idea where it goes or what's on it."

My brow crinkles. "Is that supposed to be some kind of metaphor?"

He shakes his head. "No, just—look, tell me what you see on the side of the road."

"What? Why?"

"Just do it. Outside, the things we're passing. Tell me."

I hesitate—but there's an odd note in his voice, something that sounds almost excited. It makes me think he might've figured something out. I decide to humor him just in case he really has, and squint through the windshield. We're coasting at about thirty miles per hour now. After a moment, a bulky, mechanical shape looms through the fog on the side of the road. "It's—"

"A broken-down dump truck," Elliott interrupts.

I cut a glance at him—his eyes are still tightly shut—then look back at the rusty green and brown truck as it disappears behind us. "Yeah. I thought you said you've never been down this road before."

"I haven't. A playground, a mile marker. A little farmers market stand with a yellow sign." His eyes are still closed. As he names each thing, they rise up in front of us and pass by. The playground has a bright blue slide and three red swings. The mile marker says 221. The roadside stand has a sign that reads A LITTLE FARMERS MARKET STAND WITH A YELLOW SIGN in bold white lettering.

"What the f—" I start, hitting the brakes so violently that the seat belt cuts off the rest of my words. The farmers market sign is already gone, vanished into the fog behind us. I twist around, straining my eyes, trying to see it.

"A gas can," Elliott finishes, and then opens his eyes. He glances at me—and then his gaze goes past me, over my shoulder. Expecting a Being or an alien or, shit, I don't even know what at this point, I whip around and follow his gaze.

But it's not an alien. It's . . .

A gas can.

For a second I just stare at it. It's old, dull red and smudged with dirt. It's sitting next to the caved-in ruin of what used to be a gas station. The nearby pumps are overgrown with vines, useless without electricity to power them—but that doesn't matter, because I can see from the way the light hits the gas can that it's full.

"It's a trap," I say finally. My voice sounds tight and foreign. "It has to be. The aliens are planting this stuff, everything you said just now, to lure us out of the car."

But Elliott is shaking his head. "They don't need to trap us. We're sitting ducks already—and anyway, we were out of the car just a few minutes ago, at the road sign. They could've ambushed us then if they wanted to."

"Then they're messing with us. They want to watch us run."

If that's their plan, they've devised a good strategy. I *want* to run. I know there's nowhere to go, that we're outmatched and possibly surrounded, but it doesn't matter. I need to get out of here. I need to at least *try* to escape. *Unbuckle*, I think, but I can't pry my fingers off the steering wheel.

A door slams. I jerk upright, but it's just Elliott. He's striding around the car, grabbing up the gas can. Judging by the way his muscles strain when he carries it, my guess about it being full was right. He stops at the back of the car and shouts, "Open the fuel door!"

"What are you doing?" I call, struggling to keep my voice down. "Get back in the car, idiot!" He's going to get eaten. All that work to save him back at the garage, wasted. I laugh, then immediately snap my mouth shut, hearing the edge of hysteria.

He doesn't answer for a moment. Then, slowly, his voice

muffled through the window, he says: "I have an idea."

"Is your idea that *you're about to get us both eaten?*"

"Open the fuel door and I'll tell you," he says stubbornly. With a muttered curse, I do as he asks.

He pours the gas. He drops the can when he's done and opens the passenger door, remaining miraculously uneaten, at least for now. I wait for him to get back in but he just leans down to look at me, his eyes bright and gleaming. "My idea is that I know what's happening."

"Which is what?" I demand, too loudly, my hands still clamped on the steering wheel.

He waves a hand at the playground and the mile marker and the roadside stand that are somewhere behind us, swallowed by the fog. "I thought about things I might expect to see on the side of a road. Pictured how they might look as I said them. And then they *existed*. Exactly the way I imagined them."

I finally catch his meaning. Fear slithers down my spine, and a leaden sort of shock seeps into my veins. My hands fall from the wheel and drop, dead weight, to my lap.

Elliott looks back at me. "It's not the aliens that are changing this stuff," he confirms. "It's *us*."

CHAPTER EIGHT

I YANK MY SEAT BELT OFF. IT'S TOO CONSTRICTING, cutting off my breathing, but when I thrust myself out of the car I can't get any more air than before. "How?" I demand. "How is that possible?"

"I have no idea," Elliott answers, straightening up. He's animated, excited. He turns and starts toward the woods, leaving the passenger's side door hanging open, talking over his shoulder as he goes. "But it has to be true. That key on the roof worked because I expected it to work. There were no bodies because that's the way I remembered the hospital, from when I was there last time. You found a car just like your brother's—

with his tools, his favorite songs—because . . ."

"Because that's the only car I know how to hot-wire," I finish, my lips numb. "Because I was looking specifically for something like it."

"And earlier, that first road sign, you said you'd thought that, right? That there should be road signs and you didn't want to miss them?"

"Yeah," I manage.

Elliott disappears into the fog between the pine trunks. His voice weaves out toward me. "So up pop road signs, right when you were thinking about them. But you had no idea what they should say, plus I bet you were concentrating more on our conversation than the road—so the things you were thinking about the hardest, that's what went on the signs. *We're* controlling our surroundings, or at least small elements of them—with our thoughts, our memories, our expectations."

I turn in a circle. I stare out into the fog. Patches of it blow across the street and the forest, thickening in spots, wisp-thin in others. The things Elliott willed into existence are less than a block away. If I go inside the little ramshackle stand, will its shelves be stocked? Are our imaginations powerful enough to create a hundred minuscule details with a single sweeping thought?

Dread clutches a tight fist around my chest. My thoughts are not about gas cans and mile markers. They are not helpful, not easy to control.

Especially when I'm worried they could actually come true.

"Yes!" Elliott exults, striding back toward me, his form fuzzy through the fog. "Callahan, come check this out!"

My legs move. I follow him, trying to keep my mind blank. Empty. A white slate, a clean landscape. But fear and exhaustion are fizzing at the backs of my eyes, making it even harder than normal to keep my thoughts straight.

It was bad enough when I thought the aliens could read my mind. But *me* . . . I trust me even less than I trust aliens. I've had my own brain turn against me before, and it was the worst experience of my life. And that was when my thoughts *couldn't* accidentally come true.

Elliott is standing in front of a cement slab the size of a small house, inlaid in the grass. At its edge is a reinforced metal door that opens upward. He pulls on the handle and disappears down some stairs.

A light turns on. A *light*. Electricity, where there should be none.

A white slate. A clean landscape. *Don't think.* I tap the frame, follow him down and close the door behind me. There are two dead bolts. I slide them shut. Drop my hand. Then reach up and double-check that I really did lock them. That they'll *stay* locked when all I can think about is them accidentally sliding back open.

"Come on," Elliott calls. I have to finish my fifth round of double-checking before I can tear myself away from the dead bolts, turn around, and walk down the stairs.

It's a basement. Bunk beds in one corner, with thin green military-esque blankets and pillows. A bathroom with a tiny shower. A dresser, with fresh clothing folded on top of it. A big, humming matte-black contraption in the far corner that I'm guessing is the emergency generator responsible for the electricity. And taking up half the room: rows and rows of metal shelves, all loaded with prepackaged food.

Elliott grins. "It's a decommissioned prepper hideout. I visited it once on a Scout outing somewhere outside Madrigal, but it was years ago and I couldn't remember exactly where it was except that it was across the street from a gas station. So I just walked into the woods hoping to find it somewhere nearby, and—here it is. Just like I remembered."

I stare at him, aghast. "You did what?"

He takes in my expression. His smile fades. "What's wrong? I brought us a *prepper hideout* just by thinking about it, for God's sake. This is the best news we've had all day!"

I try to gather myself. "This is nice. Very helpful. Food, gas, electricity, locks on the doors to keep out the Beings. But have you even bothered to think about what else we can do with our thoughts? What I could do with *my* thoughts?" The words get louder until I'm shouting, my voice wavering under the strain. I feel like I'm going to break—the anxiety, the horror, it's so strong it's finally just going to snap me in half.

Elliott's eyes narrow. "Are you threatening me?"

"No!" I'll have to tell him. He needs to understand. I start pacing. "Look. I have OCD. Obsessive fears and compulsions that I do to try to stop my fears from coming true. I used to have to keep my keys in different pockets so I'd always know which doors were locked. Had to check doors after I locked them, to make sure they were *really* locked, over and over again. Three times. Five times. When things got really bad, sometimes it was all night long." I wave at the door above us. "I tap door frames to make sure I'll be safe in each room."

He frowns. "I noticed you tapping the doors, but I didn't know it was OCD. What does that have to do with anything though?"

"OBSESSIVE FEARS," I repeat at a yell. "Didn't you hear me? Obsessive. Meaning I can't stop *thinking* about the things I'm *afraid of*. Like unlocked doors that will let a Being in. Or a hundred hidden mirrors that we don't see until it's too late. Or this whole place caving in on us, leaving us buried and suffocating. I'm very imaginative, I promise you."

The danger finally registers for him. "Oh," he says at last.

"Yeah. *Oh*." I ball up my hand and punch the railing as I pass it during my pacing. I have to *do* something, have to find a way to negate the danger. But how can I negate the danger when the danger is coming from my own thoughts?

Oh, God. This is my worst nightmare.

"I went to therapy for months before I got better," I tell Elliott, my voice raw with agony. "I had to learn to accept my fears. To be okay with uncertainty instead of turning myself inside out trying to be certain I was safe. I had to figure out how to let my intrusive thoughts exist without trying to force them away."

"Well, can't you do all that now?"

"No!" I shout, wheeling on him. "Because now my obsessive fears might *actually come true*." I turn back to pacing. Maybe if I can wear myself out I'll calm down, be able to control my thoughts better.

Elliott steps forward and grabs me by the shoulders, forcing me to stop. "But they could come true before too."

"What? No! *No*, I've never been able to make gas cans and farmers market stands and prepper hideouts appear by— imagining them into existence, or whatever!"

"That's not what I mean. You just said you had to learn how to be okay with uncertainty, right? So your obsessive fears faded not because you were ever able to make sure they could never happen, but because you accepted the possibility that, however small the chances, they might."

I stare at him. Slowly, my therapy reasserts itself. "Yeah," I say finally.

"And what you're doing now, trying *not* to think about dangerous things. Is it working?"

"Not at all," I say bitterly. "The harder I try not to think about something, the more I think about it."

He turns me around, hands still on my shoulders, and propels me toward the bunk beds. "Then stop trying. You can think about all the terrifying things you want. They might happen, they might not, but trying to avoid thinking about them apparently only makes it worse. In the meantime, I'll concentrate on keeping everything locked and safe and hiding us from the Beings. So between you thinking of scary things and me thinking of safe things, we'll probably have about the same odds of getting eaten by a Being that we would've had if we weren't able to control anything with our thoughts."

His words startle me enough that I don't fight him when he pushes me across the room. Instead, I mentally go back over what he's said and prod his plan for holes. It might be because I'm so exhausted I can't think straight, but his idea actually sounds reasonable. Some of the terrible pressure, the responsibility of trying to keep my thoughts from acting on my world, eases. Not all the way—but enough to let me relax, just a little.

He pushes me onto the bottom bunk. "Go to sleep," he orders, almost gently. "I know you didn't get any rest last night, which can't be helping this situation. I slept plenty, so I'll stay up and focus on keeping things locked down until we can get back on the road."

I look at the bed. I *am* exhausted. And his plan sounds like it might work. I can't be sure I'll be safe—but then, I never can be, can I?

Elliott settles down into a chair next to the bed and puts his hands behind his head, leaning back. He's telling the truth. He'll stay here, awake and watching, keeping us safe while I'm asleep. A surprised sort of security steals over me. I remember huddling with Ty in my room while a hurricane raged outside. I can still feel the way he ruffled my hair: *It'll have to go through me first.*

"Thanks," I say to Elliott, the word laced with something I can't quite name.

"Go to sleep," he repeats firmly.

I close my eyes and obey.

When I wake up, it's storming again—a fact I'm able to deduce from the four inches of steadily rising water that's flooded the floor.

I sit up in bed. "Great. My shoes *just* dried," I say aloud, looking balefully at the sloshing brown water. Then the sleep clears, and I remember where we are and how we got here, and the conversation I had with Elliott earlier. Anxiety slams into my brain like a car crash. But this time, it comes with anger.

This is a ridiculous situation. It should be impossible. It

seems designed especially to torture me, and I have no way to fight back. I'm forced to rely on *Elliott* to keep me safe, which is beyond humiliating. I should be able to fend for myself.

I rub my hands through my hair, trying to force myself to focus on the techniques I learned from my therapy sessions with Dr. Washburne. Anger is useful, I remember. I just have to channel it in a productive direction: at the OCD that's disrupting my life, not at myself for being vulnerable. That's what helped me recover in the first place—getting angrier at my OCD than I was afraid of it and using that energy to push myself through the hardest parts of exposure and response prevention therapy. I don't know how much good it'll do me in this situation, though.

Elliott breaks into my thoughts. "I can't do anything about the shoes, but there's fresh clothes over there."

I glance up. He's draped in an oversized black poncho, standing next to the metal shelves, rifling through boxes and stuffing supplies into a big green duffel bag. He motions at the dresser, where a fresh set of clothes waits.

I narrow my eyes at the dresser. "Are those clothes imaginary?" I ask. "If I put them on, will they disappear later?"

He shrugs, grabbing a few packets of what look like dried banana chips and tossing them in the bag. "Warm and dry and imaginary is better than wet and cold and real, in my book."

I swing my feet out of the bed and onto the floor. My stomach grumbles and I slosh through the water toward the shelves in search of breakfast. Or—dinner? I have no way of telling time in this bunker.

"We're going to have to head out pretty quick," Elliott informs me. "We need to reach the airport before the hurricane strengthens."

"Why can't we just wait it out here?"

He nods at the ankle-high water. "Apparently there's a reason this place was decommissioned. It just started raining again ten minutes ago. At this rate, we're going to be swimming in about an hour. Plus if the eye wall is headed this direction, it might damage the planes—which means we'll need to try to take off as soon as we get there, before it hits. Luckily I have at least a little experience flying in storms."

I raise my brows. He seems suddenly much more eager than before to fly us to London. I'm glad he's come to his senses, but I'm positive that taking off in the fog, in the middle of a hurricane—even a small one—isn't going to be nearly as easy as he makes it out to be.

At least we have provisions now, though. I reach the shelves and tear open a box. It's prepackaged freeze-dried meals. I make a face; at least back on the island, we had fresh-caught fish included in our rations. I pull another box over to check it and then stop. If I think hard enough about a steaming plate of lasagna, will it appear in here?

Unease mingles with my anxiety. The mixture slowly eats

through my veins, like rust through an old fence. I shake my head. "You know what I hate most about all this?"

Elliott's on the other side of the shelf. He glances at me from between the boxes. "Besides the evil monsters made of darkness that want to devour us?"

I ignore him. "I hate not knowing what's real. If I eat this food, will it actually nourish me? And the bodies, back at the hospital—if they were only missing because you remembered the hospital without them, then where did the actual bodies go? Were they there the whole time and we just couldn't see them? Did they stop existing? Can you *do* that?" It's terrifying, to think my mind, or anyone's, might have that much power.

I look back down at the box between my hands. Here's one way I could find out just how powerful my thoughts are. Biting back my trepidation, I concentrate on Mom's lasagna, the kind she used to make after she'd left us alone all night to go clubbing or had to work a double shift at one of her jobs. *Guilt lasagna*, my brother and I called it. It was my favorite meal because the only time I ever felt like we were a real family was when we were all sitting together eating it.

When the image is so strong in my mind that I can almost smell the meat sauce, I open the box. It's full of freeze-dried peaches. I push it to Elliott, trying to hide my relief. "You need to imagine us some better food, because apparently I'm no good at it."

"Sorry, you're up a creek. Both literally and metaphorically," he adds, wading through the now shin-high water to grab two flashlights and a handful of batteries from the next shelf over. "I did some experimenting while you were asleep. I figured instead of driving to the airport, why not try to just conjure up a plane right here? But it didn't work. Apparently we can only change things—and only relatively small things, as far as I can tell—when our subconscious can reasonably expect those things to appear in that particular way. So I can find a prepper hideout across from a gas station just the way it was during my Scouting trip in this area, but I can't summon a three-layer cake from thin air or, unfortunately, imagine up a cellar door that doesn't leak."

"So there are limits." I cling to the thought with all my might, and try to ignore what a weak reassurance it is. Accidentally imagining the door unlocked is well within the realm of *reasonable*, and it can get us killed just as easily as anything else out here.

Elliott pauses in the act of zipping the duffel bag closed, apparently hearing the tension in my voice. "You okay?"

I grab the clothing. He's right about warm and imaginary being better than real and soaked, I suppose. "No," I answer, "but let's go anyway." I turn and start toward the door before I can lose whatever scraps of courage are left to me.

Behind me, he sighs long-sufferingly. "It's fine, don't worry, *I'll* carry the enormous bag full of supplies for both of us, which I painstakingly packed all by myself."

"I'm just looking out for you," I reply over my shoulder. "You've got all that muscle . . . wouldn't want it to atrophy from disuse or anything."

A folded poncho hits me in the back of the head. I catch it before it slides into the water and pull it on, smothering a smirk. I tuck the clean clothes into the poncho's large internal pockets.

Then I'm standing beneath the door. Streams of rain waterfall down from its seams, splattering my poncho. I wrap my fingers gently around the handle. It's still locked, both dead bolts drawn closed. Thanks to Elliott's concentration.

I glance back at him. He's shrugging the bag's strap over his shoulder, wading toward the stairs behind me, not saying a word about how my presence is a liability or how maybe he'd be better off on his own. I was asleep on the bed for who knows how many hours and he didn't abandon me.

Yesterday, he was my enemy. I was a mirror dealer and he was the shadowseeker. But now . . . I don't know what I'm supposed to make of him. I've told him about the most vulnerable parts of myself, and he accepted them without a quibble. We'd both likely go back to trying to kill each other in a hot second if we weren't dependent on each other for survival—after all, he did get me arrested, and I did sell his brother a telescope—but still, at this moment and in this place, something feels different between us.

I flip the dead bolts and push the door open.

The wind catches it immediately, ripping it out of my grip and nearly yanking my arm out of its socket in the process. I stagger and throw my hands up to shield my eyes from the driving rain. The wind is screaming like a wildcat, tearing at my poncho. It's pitch-black out; I must've slept through the whole day and into the night.

Something scuttles across my shoe. I jolt and shake it off: a little brown scorpion, probably looking for somewhere dry to shelter. It skitters down the stairs and onto a floating pile of debris. "Good luck," I mutter.

Elliott glances up at my words and spots the floating scorpion. His eyes go wide and he leaps sideways away from it, splashing loudly and nearly knocking the dresser over when he runs into it. The waves he makes topple the debris, dunking the scorpion into the water where we can no longer see it. At this development, Elliott launches himself toward the stairs, vaulting over the railing to land on a dry step behind me. He shudders, shaking the folds of his poncho as if the scorpion might have teleported into his pocket.

He spots me watching. "Shut up," he mutters, flushing, and pushes past me into the night.

I raise my hands in surrender as I follow him. I have a thousand snarky observations I could make about his fear of a relatively harmless creepy-crawly, but he didn't make fun of my issues, so I won't make fun of his.

We stagger through the storm. It's a good thing Boy Scout seems to have an internal compass, because there's no way I'd be able to find the car again in these conditions. The poncho whips around my knees and arms as I lurch from tree trunk to tree trunk, using the pines to steady myself against the wind. Bits of bark flake off on my hands and the rain quickly washes them away.

I squint through the fog. It's patchy here, thinner than earlier today, but I still can't make out anything farther than a few yards ahead of me. If a Being attacked right now we'd be completely and utterly screwed. We haven't seen any on our drive yet, though, just the one in the garage this morning. And that kind of freaks me out—it's like they're toying with us, waiting for the right time to strike.

"Up here!" Elliott shouts, his voice wavering through the wind. Headlights flick on and I follow the beams to the Camaro. The passenger's side is closest, so I throw myself into it and slam the door. The noise of the storm cuts to about half as loud as it was before. I start to take off my poncho, then think better of it and quickly use it as a tent to change under. The dry clothing feels soft and cottony, but my skin still crawls where the imaginary fabric touches it.

Part of me wishes I could be excited about the possibilities of thinking things into existence, the way Elliott is. The way almost anyone else would be. The people back on the island, they'd all be thrilled to have soft clothes, extra food, running vehicles. As far as I'm concerned, though, it's just a massive relief that this mind-control magic or whatever it is never worked there. It would've made the whole last year a living hell.

I pause at the thought, frozen in the act of stuffing my poncho in the backseat. A theory spins itself out in my mind.

Elliott interrupts my thoughts from the driver's seat. "I went ahead and started the engine," he explains with a nod at the twisted-together wires that are dangling from the exposed steering column. "Guess I did it right, since nothing exploded. I tried to make another gas can appear too, just to top us off, but apparently that's only reasonable enough to work once. We should be okay for fuel anyway though."

I'm still in my own head, but at his words I glance at the gas gauge. We have just enough to reach the airport, which is about a two-hour drive from here, if I'm guessing correctly. We'll be backtracking, retracing most of the path the helicopter flew to dump us out here. Once we take off we might even be able to see Cisco Island.

Elliott eases the car onto the road and accelerates. The wipers work frantically to combat the rain, but it's a losing battle. We creep along at about twenty miles per hour, which makes me itchy with nerves—the Being we fought earlier could run much faster than this—but the weak headlights and heavy rain make it hard to see and we can't risk wrapping the Camaro around a tree. At least we don't have to worry about traffic. Other than the dump truck, there's not a single other vehicle on the road.

After about ten minutes of silence, I finally speak my earlier theory aloud. "I think it's the fog," I tell Elliott, raising my voice to be heard above the storm outside.

He glances at me. His features are just barely outlined by the dim light of the glowing gauges. "What about the fog?"

"It has to be what's enabling this . . ." I wave my hands in the general direction of his head, "mental voodoo. Think about it. There's fog on the mainland but no fog on the island, and we can control stuff with our thoughts here but not there."

Elliott frowns, considering.

I go on. "Mirrors produce Beings *and* fog. We've always assumed the fog was just there to, like, provide the appropriate murdery ambiance, but what if it's supposed to be a tool in itself? I say the fog is what's creating all these telepathic abilities."

Elliott is quiet for a moment. "The Beings are the aliens' weapons, or at least that's what we've always assumed," he says slowly. "Does that mean the fog is supposed to be a weapon too?"

"A torture device, more like," I mutter.

He hesitates. "You still worried about your . . . what, intrusive thoughts? That's what you said earlier, right?"

My first instinct is to get defensive. To say something

flippant and snarky, or maybe turn the conversation back on him, bring up the scorpion he was terrified of or something. But the instinct fades after a second, and I decide to risk honesty.

"Yeah," I answer. "They're these weird, out-of-the-blue thoughts that don't feel like something you'd normally think. Like you're standing at the edge of a road, minding your own business, and out of nowhere you picture yourself pushing the lady next to you in front of a semi truck and then you panic, wondering why you'd think that. Or in my case, you're shopping at the corner store when you stop dead in the middle of reaching for a Twix because you suddenly get this awful, graphic mental image of your brother being murdered during a home invasion."

I'd dropped everything and run all the way home, panicked to the point of incoherence because the image had felt so *real*, and even though I knew it was just a thought, I also knew that if he did get murdered it would be *my fault* for not locking the door. That was the first time I started to realize something weird was going on in my head.

"So intrusive thoughts are caused by OCD?" Elliott asks. He sounds intrigued, not judgy, which is encouraging.

"Yeah," I reply, then think better of it. "Well, actually, no. Almost everyone gets them, but non-OCD people tend to just shrug them off and forget about them. People with OCD freak out about them, try to figure out if they could really come

true, whether they're a bad person for having them, et cetera."
I shrug, but the gesture feels tight and uncomfortable. "I actually
don't get the intrusive-thought part of OCD nearly as bad as
some people, though."

I remember one girl from my support group who had harm
OCD—she was terrified she was "secretly evil" because of the
violent intrusive thoughts she had. She refused to touch knives
or anything that looked even vaguely like a weapon, and would
tie herself in knots to avoid being left alone with her little sisters
for fear she'd "go crazy" and hurt them.

She wasn't secretly evil, of course. Her OCD just focused
her fears on what was most important to her: being a good person and the safety of her family. OCD is a bastard like that.

"So what part of OCD *do* you get, then?" Elliott asks.

My discomfort level rises a few more notches. But as hard as
this is to talk about, in a strange way, it's also kind of cathartic.
There are so few people who understand me. For some reason, I
want him to be one of them.

"My obsessions are mostly about safety. Like, I think something along the lines of *what if I left the door unlocked*, then I
think about all the catastrophic things that could happen if I
did. Then I can't focus on anything else until I do my compulsions to make sure I'll be safe. And the more I give in to my
compulsions, the stronger they get."

I notice that I'm talking about my OCD in present tense and

grit my teeth. I *used* to give in to my compulsions, and they *used* to get stronger as a result. But I broke that cycle. Things aren't that bad anymore.

Except they are. How many doorways have I tapped in the last twenty-four hours? How many times did I check the dead bolt in the hideout?

I shake my head. I'm better. I'm *better*. I refuse to backslide. This is just a hiccup, just a momentary fumble.

"You know what the funny thing is?" I say to Elliott, my voice bitter with irony. "I think I'm as scared of my OCD getting bad again as I am of this damn fog making my fears actually come true. How messed up is that?"

The car fills with silence. Outside, the wind howls. The road dips into a low spot, and the car forges a path through the small stream that's formed there.

Elliott doesn't answer. He doesn't give me some inane response like *It's all in your head*—as if that should be calming rather than frustrating and terrifying—or *It's okay, everyone's a little bit* OCD, like the diagnosis is a personality quirk instead of a sometimes-debilitating mental disorder. Instead, he just stays quiet and gives me the chance to talk more, if I want to.

I don't. I'm done talking. I just want to be out of this goddamned place and safe with Ty already.

After a while, Elliott speaks again. "About the fog. If you're right about it being what enables the mind control, then I think it's supposed to be a tool for the aliens, not a weapon to hurt us."

I glance at him. "What do you mean?"

He's staring into the storm, keeping his eyes on the road as he navigates. "The aliens probably mean to use it to make changes to the planet, wouldn't you think? Build whatever passes for their homes, even create the right kind of atmosphere they need to breathe or whatever. You and me, we can only make small changes using our thoughts, but if the aliens invented the fog, I'm betting they know how to use it for much bigger stuff." There's a downed branch covering half the road ahead, and Elliott carefully slows down and steers around it. "You have to admit it would make for a pretty efficient takeover. Beings to kill the humans; fog to make the planet habitable for the aliens."

"So the fog is . . . terraforming Earth," I conclude, dread lying like an iron weight in my gut.

The car speeds back up—if you can apply the word "speed" to the turtle-crawl Elliott is keeping the Camaro at—after we pass the downed branch. "Right. And maybe we haven't seen any actual aliens because they aren't here yet," he adds. "They could've sent the Shatter Ring ahead, let it do all the work, then when we're all dead and the planet is covered in fog, they move in."

I stare out the window. A crack of lightning spears through the sky overhead. The fog refracts its light, making it sparkle like it's magic instead of death. "So the only thing holding the aliens back are the cities that have somehow managed to resist the fog and the Beings," I guess.

Elliott cuts a glance at me. "The cities that have managed to resist the *permanent* fog and Beings," he corrects, his tone sharp, reminding me that my wares have brought plenty of the temporary variety to Cisco Island.

My shoulders tense up, but I ignore him. "You know, we could probably get a prime price for this information once we get to London," I speculate instead. "The fog could be used to resupply the city, don't you think? People could walk a little ways into it and think up an abandoned truck of canned food, or something."

It's my favorite kind of plan, the type that uses one of my problems—the mind-control fog—to solve another. If I can sell intel this valuable to whoever's running London I'll be set for life. I won't have to bother with black-market mirrors anymore. Not that Ty would approve of my present vocation anyway. Once we're together again, he'll likely go right back to looking out for me the way he always has, and his definition of looking out for me tends to include keeping me on the straight and narrow by force when necessary.

I smile at the thought, just a little. It's been a long time since I let myself fantasize about what it would be like to have my family back. That's what Ty and I have always been: our own family. Dad died when I was little, and Mom was barely present even before she left for good, but my brother and I always had each other.

"I guess I shouldn't be surprised that your first thought is extortion," Elliot says, jarring me out of my fantasy.

"What?" I say, frowning at him. His hands are tight on the steering wheel, and the speedometer's needle is ticking upwards of forty now. I can barely see out the rain-slicked windshield.

"If the fog can be used to resupply cities, we can't hold that information hostage for *money*. That wouldn't be ethical." His voice is flinty.

I go stiff. "What did you think we were gonna do with it? Just hand it over without asking for anything in return?"

I can practically hear him grinding his teeth. "We should give this information to the cities, and then *after* they have it, trust them to express their gratitude."

I laugh in disbelief. "Trust? Really, Ackermann? This could be our golden ticket! Look—when we land in London, there's no way it's not going to be a huge deal. We'll be the first people to travel through the fog and actually make it anywhere. Sooner or later the folks in London are going to mention us in one of the transmissions they manage to get through to Singapore and to *your mom*, and then the London officials will find out we're exiles. What do you think they'll do then? Throw us a parade to 'express their gratitude'?"

"We could ask for asylum in exchange for the information," Elliott says, his wording oddly careful. "Making a plea for refuge wouldn't be unethical."

I ball up my fist. "I don't want asylum. I want to be safe, and rich, and with my brother. *That's* why I've spent the last thirteen months selling mirrors. Not so I can get locked up in a jail, trying to be grateful that at least they didn't toss me back out into the fog!"

"Look," Elliott snaps, his voice suddenly loud, "London is—"

Something gray in the road ahead catches the corner of my eye. I slam my hands on the dash and shout, "Look out!"

Elliott hits the brakes. The car squeals and jitters sideways, hydroplaning, throwing me into the door. The rear of the Camaro swings around past the front until we're moving backwards, then one of the tires catches on the water again and we complete the violent spin. There's a horrible wailing of metal giving way and Elliott and I are both thrown forward. Our seat belts—thank God I actually wore mine this time—catch us. The jolt gives me instant whiplash.

The Camaro stops. The engine sputters and cuts to silence. The headlights flicker. One dies, but the other stabilizes after a moment.

I peel myself off the back of my seat with a muttered curse. I glance at Elliott—he's fine—then peer through the now-spiderwebbed windshield to squint at the thing we've crashed into.

Lying in the road is a massive tree.

And in front of the tree, splayed unmoving on the asphalt, is a body.

CHAPTER NINE

RAIN SPLATTERS THROUGH MY BROKEN WINDOW, spraying over my shirt in spurts of wind. I unbuckle, grab my poncho from the backseat, pull it on. I glance again at the body: it's a huddle of rotted flesh, white bone, and torn clothing, curled in on itself beneath the tree. Whoever it was, they've been dead a long time.

Praying desperately, I reach over Elliott—he's frozen, staring at the body, hands stiff on the wheel—and pull the starter wire out from the spot where I'd tucked it away. I touch it to the battery and ignition wires. Nothing. The engine doesn't even turn over. We're dead in the water. Literally.

A blinding, biting, helpless sort of fury rises up in me. I punch the dash. We're *hours* away from the airport, stranded in a hurricane that's likely to get worse. We can't go back to the hideout. It's at least half an hour away by car, which means it's just as unreachable as the airport by foot. But that's not even the worst of it. I have no idea how strong the eye wall is or if it's headed this way, but Elliott was right before about it potentially destroying the planes. Even if it doesn't, a spin-off tornado could easily do the same damage. And I'm stuck here, unable to do anything. Unable, yet again, to get to the one person I've been trying to find for a year.

I punch the dash again. What else could possibly go wrong? My brain obligingly spits out a highlight reel of the worst options: we get struck by lightning, get crushed by debris, stumble on a mirror that releases another Being. It's a good thing Elliott is concentrating on keeping us safe, or my thoughts right now would get us killed in seconds.

I glance over at him. He's still in the same position as a moment ago: paralyzed, staring at the body in the road. I frown. Surely he's seen a dead person before. He saw all those murdered cops at the boardwalk, at the very least. I can't blame him for being a little shaken up—I remember how it felt to have my hands sticky with Ginger's blood, after all—but right now we've got to focus on getting out of here.

I give him a shove, try to shake him out of his paralysis.

"Wake up, and imagine us . . ." I try to think of something that would be both reasonable and helpful, "a non-broken-down dump truck, maybe, or another hideout? Or better yet, just get the car to start again. Imagine the damage isn't as bad as it looks from this angle."

He doesn't respond. His face has gone white in the dim interior lights.

My nerves fraying, I strive for patience. "Look," I say, glancing from him to the road. "It's just a body. Right? We knew we'd run across some eventually. All the mainlanders are dead."

Without responding, he unbuckles his seat belt. He pulls the latch to open the door, but the crash has stuck it shut. He kicks it open. Rain pours inside as he exits the car.

"Ackermann!" I shout after him. No response. I curse and heave open my own door. The fog is soupy here, so thick I feel like I'm swimming when I walk toward the fallen tree. I hunch into myself, staying on my guard, but it's hard to keep an eye out for lurking Beings with the storm buffeting me. "What are you doing? Get back in the car and *do something* to get us out of—"

I stop. The hair on my arms and legs is suddenly standing straight up, clinging to the inside of my poncho. I barely have time to throw myself to the ground before—CRACK. Lightning erupts, turning the world white. Splinters of wood fly over me. The crash of thunder is so loud it rattles the inside of my head. An acrid, chemical sort of smell washes over me. Ozone.

I army-crawl away; splinters of wood mean the lightning hit one of the pine trees lining the road, which means I'm probably about to get crushed by falling debris.

I freeze. A horrific understanding washes over me. Struck by lightning; crushed by debris. My fears from a few minutes ago. They're coming true. Because Elliott is no longer concentrating on our safety.

Something cracks and groans above me. The lightning-struck tree, falling. I shove myself sideways just in time. Its long, thin trunk crashes against the back of the car, smashing its rear half.

The dust settles. Elliott and I are trapped between the two downed trees, which shelter the spot where we're standing so the wind isn't quite so strong. The totaled car forms the third leg of the triangle. I stare at the freshly felled pine, its branches on one end and upended roots on the other disappearing into the fog.

My first two fears came true. Lightning. Debris.

The third fear was a mirror.

I squeeze my eyes shut and clamp my hands over my head. My breathing is loud, uneven. Elliott's safety measures aren't working anymore. My thoughts are acting on the world, unfettered. I can't look at anything. If I don't look at anything, I won't see the mirror, I won't bring a Being. The only way I can stay safe is to keep my eyes closed.

I laugh out loud. It sounds more like a rattling gasp. The familiarity of this response—huddling into myself, trying desperately to stay safe, not daring to look up for fear of what I might see—is achingly familiar. This is how I used to deal with my OCD. Keep your head down, try not to think about what terrifies you. Try not to think about how the fear that it *might* come true is worse than actually having a Being right here in front of me. Because if I were facing a monster, I could run, I could hide.

But I can never get away from myself.

"Ackermann!" I shout over the wind and rain. "You've got to focus!" *You've got to help me*, I want to say, but I bite down hard on the words and they stay thrashing and unspoken in the back of my throat.

There's no answer. I stumble forward blindly. Fingers clamp around my arm. I go still. The hand is warm, but the grip is painfully tight.

It could be Elliott. Or it could be something else.

I keep my eyes shut. "Help me," I say finally, the words trembling on the air, twisting like a fish caught on a line.

The storm howls. The wind savages my poncho, the rain pelts my face.

"He wasn't a mainlander," Elliott says at last, in a voice I can barely hear above the storm.

The relief that it *is* Elliott who has ahold of me is so staggeringly great that it takes me a moment to register his tone. It's flat and cold, and it makes me remember his expression when his mother exiled him: empty eyes, a face carved from steel and bone.

I shake off the image, my eyes still squeezed tightly shut. "What are you talking about? I don't—it doesn't matter! You have to focus on—"

"Open your eyes," he says, still in that dead tone.

I breathe. The air shudders into my lungs, flees back out. "I can't."

"Open your eyes," he repeats, "and *look at what you've done*."

His hand is still locked around my arm. It pulls me off-balance, drags me to my knees. I slip on the wet asphalt and catch myself on something that gives with a sick, wet *crunch* beneath my hand. I freeze.

The body. We're kneeling in front of the body. Elliott wants me to open my eyes and look at—

What I've done.

And suddenly, I know whose body is beneath my hand. I don't want to look at it, but I can't keep my eyes closed now either, so I open them and look at Elliott instead.

He's crying. No. That's not the right word. No word is quite right, not for this.

Except maybe *broken*. Maybe *anguish*. Maybe *hate*.

I tear my gaze from his. But I still can't look at the body, so I look at the massive tree behind it. This one was felled a long time ago: bare limbs, a few clumps of shriveled brown leaves, twisted roots that have long since been washed clean. Its trunk is scored with gouges. I don't want to think about what put them there, what felled this tree, what killed the person lying in front of me.

I can't delay any longer. I lower my eyes to the body.

Rotted skin, white bone. It's gouged too. If the storm wasn't so violent, if the air wasn't filled with wind and rain and ozone, the smell would be terrible.

I raise my eyes a little higher. The single remaining headlight casts sharp shadows over the body, but I can still make out clumps of hair on the corpse's scalp. He was a blond. Just like Elliott. He's wearing a gray T-shirt, the same one he was wearing when he walked across Valkyrie Bridge last autumn. His glasses—the glasses I sold him—are crooked, and one lens is broken.

Braedan Ackermann. The first son the mayor exiled.

"We can't stay here. We've got to move," I say, but I don't stand up. I can't look away from the body.

He was my enemy, I tell myself. Just like Ginger. Just like Elliott. It doesn't matter that his body is in front of me now— I've known for a long time that he was dead and that it was because of the things I'd sold him, and I didn't care.

But I do now. Because he wasn't ever actually my enemy, was he? He wasn't the shadowseeker, wasn't even some random cop. He was just a guy. The same age as my own brother. The brother that I want back so badly, the brother I've been determined to do anything to find.

And now the cost of my determination is rotting beneath my hands.

I jolt to my feet, take a step back. Distance myself.

I still need to find Ty. I'm still willing to do whatever I need to do, for his sake. This doesn't change anything.

"You've got to focus on keeping us safe," I say to Elliott. I make my voice strong, clear, certain. The opposite of how I feel. "A mirror is going to appear somewhere, so you have to counter my—"

"The stars were wrong," Elliott says in that awful, empty voice, looking at his brother instead of me.

I stare at him. Thunder booms, shredding the air between us. "What?" I dare to say when it stops.

"That's why he needed the telescope. He noticed it a week after the Fracture. Stars disappearing, whole constellations moving independently through the sky. No one else noticed. No one else ever looked up. But he did."

I lift my hand. It hovers in the air. I'm not sure what to do with it . . . put it on his shoulder? Shake him out of his trance?

"He made it so *far*," Elliott says. His voice doesn't sound empty anymore. Now it sounds like it's being wrenched out of him by some external force. "He must have walked for days. How many Beings did he have to face before one killed him? How much did he suffer, how many nightmares did he live through while I was safe on the island?" His hands twist into fists in the fabric of his brother's shirt. "While you were safe on the island."

I drop my hand. I say nothing.

Elliott bows his head. I can't make out his expression, but once again, I don't need to. "You're not even going to admit this is your fault," he says. It's not a question.

I take another step back. My defenses snap into place. "I didn't do this to him! Your mother—"

Elliott comes to his feet, his words a roar. "—did what she had to do!"

My own hands curl into fists. This is ludicrous, arguing about someone who's been dead for months when the fog is roiling all around us, when a horde of Beings could be waiting on the other side of a mirror that'll appear at any moment—but my mind is bubbling with panic and horror and something like guilt that I refuse to feel, and lashing out at Elliott gives all that energy a focus.

"That's just what you want to believe!" I shout back.

His eyes are alight, and the hatred from earlier has overtaken the anguish and brokenness. All his energy has found a focus too. "What?" he demands, his voice a low warning.

I ignore it. "You're so blindly loyal to your mother, so desperate to think she's somehow a good person, that you've managed to excuse her exiling *your own brother*. Exiling you, even! And do you know why you're so desperate to believe she's good?"

"Enlighten me," he bites out, daring me to answer.

I never turn down a dare. "Because if she's a good person," I say, "then she might actually love you back."

I don't see the punch coming. Elliott is too fast, lashing out with that brutal left hook of his. It sends me staggering sideways, agony shooting through my cheekbone.

"You really think you have any right to lecture me about family?" he seethes, not even shaking out his hand. "Your business gets people killed. Do you seriously think *your* brother would've been okay with that?"

Something warm and wet mingles with the rain that trickles down my face. I swipe a hand across it; it comes back watery red. "Shut the hell up," I order, my voice groggy with the pain and shock. I should've known he'd lash out. I would've been prepared for it yesterday. But tonight, after the way he talked me down in the hideout, after he protected me from a Being while I hot-wired the car—it put me off my guard. It let me forget that neither of us can change what we are.

But Elliott isn't done. He's shaking, glowering at me, his brother's body shadowed at his feet. He wants to hurt me the way I've hurt him. "Do you seriously think Ty would still love you after what you've done?" he demands. "That he'd even *want* you back, if he was still alive?"

Anger flickers in my veins, sparks through a live wire. I straighten up. "Don't talk about him like he's dead."

Something in Elliott's expression shifts subtly, hardens, goes cold. "He is dead," he says.

I don't move. Lightning cracks again nearby, flashing the world a brilliant white, making the fog gleam and shimmer.

"What?" I say at last.

"He is dead," Elliott repeats. His words are a scalpel's cut: measured, cleanly vicious. "There is no London. No Singapore. They're a lie, a way for my mom to keep everyone calm and hopeful and under control. There've never been any ham radio signals. No signals of any kind. The whole world is dead; Cisco Island is the only thing left."

The smell of ozone is almost gone now. Traces of it linger in the air like ghosts. After a moment, even they are driven away by the wind.

I swallow. I'm shaking now too. "You're lying."

"No."

"You're LYING!" The scream is swallowed by the rain, by the dead trees, by the body at Elliott's feet.

Elliott shakes his head. His expression is wild, fierce with anger and hatred and vindication. "Your brother," he says savagely, "is as dead as mine."

CHAPTER TEN

WHITE NOISE DROWNS OUT ALL MY THOUGHTS. Adrenaline takes over.

I scoop up a piece of broken brake light from the ground and pitch it at Elliott. He throws his arm up to shield his eyes, and before he can lower it, I'm on him. I bring my foot down hard on the side of his knee. He curses and staggers sideways, grabs ahold of my arm and wrenches it up behind my back. It hurts like hell, but I follow the momentum, twist around, throw my free elbow at his face. The blow lands on his cheekbone, the same spot where he punched me. He flinches but the pressure on my arm intensifies. He's going to break it unless

I stop him. I've got plenty of dirty street fighting tricks but he's all battering-ram power, sharply focused violence, crisp punches that'll break bone if I let him get ahold of me.

I go limp. He shoves me forward, up against the huge trunk of the long-dead tree, to avoid being dragged to the ground by my weight. With my free hand I snap off a dead branch next to my face. I stab it blindly backwards. Elliott yells and releases me, dodging. I whirl, shove him hard. I've caught him off-balance, and he reels backwards, stumbling into the car. I dart toward him to press my advantage.

There is no London. The words loop in my head, warping, scattering apart and gluing themselves back together as I try to force them to make sense. *Your brother is as dead as mine. There is no London.*

It can't be true. It can't. My brain throws information at me, a shield of evidence against Elliott's words: He was so eager to get to the airport. He drove through a hurricane to try to reach the planes. Why would he do that if he truly believed there was nowhere to go?

I stop in my advance toward Elliott as a sick realization washes over me. "You were going to take us back to the island. Back to your *mother*."

He pushes himself off the car and wipes blood from the corner of his mouth. He doesn't say anything but only watches me warily, that wildness still bright in his eyes, waiting for his chance to rush me again.

I remember more. "That shit about asking for asylum." My muscles are so tight they ache with the pressure of holding me in, holding out the awfulness of what Elliott's said and done. "You meant asylum *there*. You were going to just hand her the information about the fog and hope she'd spare your life in return. You always meant to go back!"

"It's the only place we *can* go!" he shouts.

I don't wait for him to come at me again. I throw myself at him before he can move, blinded by the urgency of shutting him up, of stopping him before he can say any more awful things. He's ready for me, of course. He ducks sideways, snakes one arm under mine, yanks me around and punches me hard in the side of the head.

My skull rings. I stagger sideways, trip over something soft, hit the ground. When my vision clears, I'm on the asphalt staring into Braedan's empty eye sockets. His glasses are still hanging over what's left of his nose. One lens is intact, the other shattered. Lightning flashes again. The fog catches its light, and the intact lens glimmers with its reflection.

I freeze. Its *reflection*.

I sold Braedan these glasses. His own glasses, which had been confiscated, because they'd been added to the Reflectivity Index.

The lightning's blue hue has faded from the fog around me. But it hasn't faded from the glasses. There, the reflection is swirling, intensifying, thickening. A rainbow sheen washes over the mirror—and then a black mass begins to coalesce behind it.

Something twinges inside my abdomen. The feeling intensifies and spreads until it feels like a rope wrapped around my waist, tugging me forward. An invisible electric field buzzes over my skin.

I put my hands on the ground. I push myself backwards until I hit the dead tree. "Ackermann," I croak.

A shadow crawls out of the lens. It's a few inches long, a thing with gleaming pincers, too many eyes, too many legs. A fat stinger curls above its back and darkness drips from its tip like acid. Its features are distinct, impossibly vivid, each of its tiny scales rendered in hues of charcoal and ebony. The monster looks like a twisted version of the scorpion I brushed off my shoe earlier, but this one is far from harmless—and it's not alone. In the lens behind it, the onyx shadows are still writhing. Another scorpion Being crawls out. Then another, and another. A dozen. Two dozen.

I scramble sideways. I trip over Braedan's leg, kick hard to propel myself across the concrete. The scorpions scuttle after me. Where their stingers drip on Braedan's body, his flesh sizzles and turns black. One of the Beings reaches my shoe. I shake my foot violently, but the creature's pincers clamp tight on my shoelaces and now two more are skittering toward me, the clatter of their claws against the asphalt audible even over the rain. I remember hearing about the spiderlike Beings that came out of a mirror back on the island, remember the way their victim—a girl my age—had screamed when they'd bitten her. The way she'd writhed and wailed for hours after being "rescued," her arm slowly turning black and falling off before she finally died.

Frantic, I shove my shoe off with my free foot, leaving the scorpion on my shoelaces behind. I scramble up. The scorpions are a tide now, a crawling mass, a flood. I turn to run from it— but they're spreading out in every direction, and I'm trapped between the dead trees.

The car. Its hood is crumpled against the massive, long-dead tree, its trunk crushed by the recently felled one. If I can get on top of it, I can run along the bigger trunk and get to the woods, get away.

I reach the car, plant my hands on the hood, vault up. The windshield cracks further under my weight. I clamber to the roof.

It's only then I think to look for Elliott.

He hasn't moved from where he was a moment ago: hands fisted, standing a few feet away from Braedan's body, a deep purple-red bruise already spreading over his cheekbone like an inkblot. The rest of his face is as gray as the fog that surrounds us. He's staring at the Beings. I remember his reaction to the normal scorpion earlier. If he was that terrified of a regular, harmless one, these must look like death itself.

I consider leaving him. After all, this is *his* fault. If he had kept concentrating on our safety, or if he hadn't *lied* to me, I might never have seen the glasses and we wouldn't be getting attacked now. And after what he's said, what he's done . . . I want to see him hurting. I wouldn't care if he died. But I still need him in order to survive out here, so I take off my remaining shoe and throw it at him.

It hits him square in the side of the neck. His head snaps around, his gaze finding me, his eyes going from frozen back to furious. "Get up here if you want to live, douchebag!" I yell, and he finally jolts into motion just a few inches ahead of the scorpions.

The flood of Beings turns, spreads out across our slice of the road. They swarm the car. Elliott springs onto the hood and then follows me onto the roof. He pushes past—none too gently—and leaps onto the massive tree.

I eye the distance. The top of the trunk is several feet higher than the roof of the car, and I need to jump from this height to have any chance at sticking the landing, but the distance looks just a little farther than I'm comfortable with. Elliott is much more athletic than me—to no one's surprise—and he's hauled himself onto the top of the trunk already. He runs the length of the tree, disappearing into the soupy fog.

Something explodes with a bang beneath me. A tire. The car jolts, and I nearly lose my footing. Two more tires follow in quick succession, falling victim to the scorpions' acid. I glance down; the first few scorpions are crawling up onto the hood now.

I spit out a curse, back up a step, and take a running leap for the tree.

I don't make it. My shoeless feet can't get any purchase and I slide toward the ground, helplessly clawing for a branch, loose bark, anything I can latch on to. Splinters dig in beneath my fingernails. Below me, the scorpions have covered the hood in a tide of shadows. A few of them start to jump toward me. I snatch my legs up and they miss, falling back into the writhing mass on the ground, but all I've got to do is slide a few more inches and I'm toast.

I squeeze my eyes shut. My breath is a high, reedy trembling in my ears. Maybe I should just let go. Stop drawing it out and let them kill me quickly. I don't want to scream for hours, don't want to watch myself fall apart before I finally die. And there's nowhere left to go anyway, nowhere that I'd be able to ever get away from the world full of monsters—either the ones made of shadows or the ones made of flesh and bone like the mayor. But my body overrules my brain and my fingers hook into the tree, scrabbling at it, trying to gain enough purchase to support my weight.

I drop a few inches lower. I open my eyes; another Being is leaping off the hood. One of its pincers latches on to the hem of my jeans. I kick wildly, feeling the solid *thunk* when my foot connects with it, but I can't manage to dislodge it. Panic wells up, drowns me, pulls me under.

A hand grasps mine. Elliott. He came back. He hauls me upward, and I push at the tree with my feet, gaining purchase now that I have help. I scramble onto the top, bark scraping at my stomach and arms. The Being on my jeans flails wildly in the air, its stinger plunging downward, missing. Drops of acid hiss and eat into the tree bark.

Elliott spots the Being. There's a split second, a held breath, the space between one heartbeat and the next when he's frozen. And in that second, the scorpion leaps from my pants to his leg.

In my head, I hear the screams of the spider-bit girl. I see Braedan's rotted flesh turning black. I see it happening to Elliott.

A moment ago, I thought I wouldn't care if he died. It isn't true.

My hand moves. It jerks forward. It wraps around the scorpion. The Being is cold and smooth, like volcanic glass, an impossibility writhing in my fingers. I wrench it off before it can sting Elliott and lob it back into the thrashing mass below.

Elliott's head snaps up. He stares at me.

I curl my left hand—the one that was just holding a Being—into a fist. There's no time to think about what I've done or why. "MOVE," I shout, and then I'm following my own advice, running pell-mell down the length of the massive trunk, dodging broken-off branches and slipping on bits of loose bark. The wind whips at me and rain pelts my poncho, but I don't slow down. Elliott's footfalls shake the trunk behind me. The scorpions have started climbing the tree after us but we've finally got a lead on them.

We run blindly into the fog. Within seconds, the dim light from the car's single remaining headlight is gone and the thick darkness has swallowed us whole.

I slow down, feel my way forward. The scorpions' chittering has been swallowed by the noise of the storm. We might actually make it.

"Get down here," Elliott shouts. His voice comes from below me, on the ground.

I sit on the trunk and let myself slide blindly downward. I land wrong and something in my ankle twists too hard in the wrong direction. I yelp and hiss through my teeth, but force myself up and hobble off the road and into the grass. The storm lessens a touch, the forest blunting some of its force.

A light flicks on—one of the flashlights Elliott put in his pockets earlier. He tosses me another and I catch it with my right hand because my left is tingling and cold, like it's still clutching the ghost of the writhing Being. I don't want to think about the eerie sensation. I flick on my light. It casts a dim yellow glow around me, enough to let us flee at a slow jog without running face-first into a tree. I hold an arm up to shield my eyes from the driving rain.

"Don't think about anything dangerous," Elliott shouts from ahead.

"What?" I pant. I can hardly put any weight on my ankle, but I'm hobbling after him as fast as I can manage.

"I can't focus on keeping us safe right now. Don't think about anything."

Ice slicks through my veins. "*What?* You know that doesn't work! I can't—I keep thinking about—" More Beings. Faster ones. More mirrors, everywhere.

A crackling noise ripples out through the forest around us. It could be the wind but it might be something worse. I speed up, grab Elliott's shoulder, shove him around. "You have to FOCUS," I yell in his face.

"I can't, okay?" he shouts back. His hair is plastered to his forehead and he shoves it off like he doesn't know what to do with his hands. "Those scorpions—I can't—" He shakes his head and his voice drops. "It's like someone reached into my head and pulled out all my fears and let them loose in the world."

I laugh, a little wildly, because I know just what he means. But our fears are exactly the problem. If we can't pull it together—if *he* can't pull it together—we're dead.

My hands are still on his shoulders. I shake him. His gaze drops, and he looks at my left hand like he has no idea how it got there. "You've got to try—" I start, but he cuts me off.

"Marty," he says. The word sounds strange, like a foreign language, like it means more than itself. I realize it's the first time he's called me anything other than *Callahan*.

He's still looking at my hand. I follow his gaze.

On the back of my left hand—the hand I used to wrench the scorpion off him—my knuckles are crisscrossed with jagged black streaks like veins of lightning. Slowly, I take my hand off his shoulder. I turn it over. In the middle of my palm is a perfect, dime-sized circle of dead white flesh. Angry red skin encircles it, making an ugly bull's-eye, and black veins creep from its edge toward my wrist and fingers and over the back of my hand.

The strange coldness, the eerie feeling of something still writhing in my palm. It wasn't a memory.

It was venom.

CHAPTER ELEVEN

RAISE MY EYES AND STARE AT ELLIOTT. THE YELLOW glow of the flashlight turns his face to a skull, all sharp shadows. "Marty," he says again, and then the pain hits me.

It's an inferno. The whole world is a burning building and I'm trapped inside. The agony intensifies, going from an unbearable burning to an ice-cold acid. My body bows in on itself and I drop to my knees. The flashlight clatters to the ground. I curl around my injured hand, my breathing jagged like I'm going to scream.

I do.

Elliott is on his knees in front of me. He grabs me by my

good arm. He shakes me, and the scream cuts off, but the silence is almost as bad. The night seems to twist around me.

He searches his pockets frantically, pulls everything out. Aspirin, bandages, gauze. None of which will help a Being sting. He searches through my pockets next. There's nothing except my key and that stupid stuffed fox, which only reminds me of that first Being back in the garage, the one with the foxlike muzzle. The one that felt like *my* fears brought to life.

Elliott looks down at me. He knows what neither of us are saying: that I'm as dead as the spider-bit girl, whether I die right here or hours from now.

The pain ebbs, retreating until it's a throbbing coldness in my left hand. It'll be hours, then. There's a part of me that wants it over now, but my well-honed survival instinct rears up and overshadows it. It pulls me, staggering, to my feet. It orders me to move. *Move.* Don't think about what other fears could come true. Don't think about—

That crackling noise from a moment ago ripples out around us again, loud even in the storm. The sound reminds me of a chandelier: a thousand pieces of glass clinking against each other.

Gingerly, slow with the echoes of pain, I pick up my flashlight and hold it out. I turn in a circle. I take a step—and yank my foot back with a hiss. Something sharp is sticking up from the ground. I aim the flashlight downward. The fog is thicker than ever, and I have to bend low to make out what's stabbed me.

I blink. It's a blade of wire grass. This plant isn't too tall, maybe three inches, but each thin blade that arcs up and out from it looks as hard and sharp as a knife. And it's difficult to tell through the fog and the night, but the grass is a strange color—a sort of yellow-white, and almost metallic. I reach out to touch it with a fingertip. Something like static electricity crackles off it, buzzing beneath my skin, and I pull my hand back before touching it.

Lightning flashes. The fog catches its light more brightly than ever, sparkling like blue magic, and the blades of grass sparkle blue too. Almost like they're . . .

Reflective.

My inhale freezes somewhere in my throat. Veins of frost reach into my lungs, wrap in icy bands around my chest. This time it's not an effect of the venom. It's terror.

The grass isn't grass. It's *mirrors*. Every blade, every tuft, is an impossibly detailed silvered-glass sculpture. Numbly, I lift the flashlight. More grass. More bladed mirrors. A nearby pine tree: every knobby flake of bark reflects the flashlight's yellow-white beam back at me. I point my light at the ground. I take a step. My foot skids on the flat, glassy dirt. It's slippery with the rain that now beads on its surface, streaming across it in rivulets.

Mirrors everywhere, I thought a moment ago. And now my fears have come to life.

But something flickers behind my breastbone—a protest,

a thought, a single ragged heartbeat. We aren't supposed to be able to change anything big. Elliott said it himself. Only small things, he claimed. Only reasonable things.

I spin in a slow circle. My light catches on everything and reflects back at me. This is not small. Not reasonable.

Above the din of the storm, a tinkling clatter reaches me: tiny claws on glass. Elliott and I look at each other. The scorpions are still coming for us. And I've got a twisted ankle, and a poisoned hand, and we're surrounded, *surrounded*, by mirrors.

Something moves in the mirrored tree trunk next to me. A rainbow oil-slick ripple. Then comes the shadow, swallowing up the beam from my flashlight. It flickers, swells across the ground, the grass. It flares and stretches like some great dragon unfurling its wings.

An invisible rope twists around my ribs. It tugs me out toward the tree. Reels me down toward the grass. I'm a fly caught in a spiderweb; there's nowhere to go.

But insistent as the tugging is, it also feels oddly gentle. And with another wave of agony building up in my hand, a tide of scorpions at my back, and a forest of mirrors all around, some fatalistic part of me almost wants to obey the tugging. To walk toward the mirrors—toward my fears. To fall into my own reflection. To face the coming Beings in whatever twisted alien world they come from, rather than ending my life hunted and tortured here on what's left of the mainland, drowned in fog, without even a last glimpse of the stars.

The *stars*. "The stars!" I say out loud. And then I laugh and laugh. The sound reminds me of when I was clawing at the tree's bark earlier, the ragged scrabbling of it, the way splinters burrowed beneath my fingernails.

Elliott looks at me. His face is pale but set; he's done running. Which is good, because there's nowhere left to run. Nowhere we can get away from ourselves. "What exactly is so funny?" he says sharply.

I turn around, point through the darkness toward the road we've just left, toward the body of Elliott's brother. "The stars. You said there was something wrong with the stars. That's why Braedan wanted the telescope. The stars, the constellations, they kept disappearing and moving in ways the laws of physics shouldn't have allowed. Well, I don't think the laws of physics *did* allow it. I think the stars themselves are still out there, completely normal. It's just our view of them that's changed."

The skittering of claws on glass intensifies. Tiny mirrored pebbles vibrate on the ground in resonance.

"Does that really *matter* right now?" Elliott says, and in his voice I hear the same fatalism that singed me a moment ago. No brother, no plane, no escape. No point. But a new realization has caught fire in my mind, and it's burning through everything.

I sweep my light in a circle. It reflects back, a thousand

iterations of me hovering above the monstrous dark. "This forest, these mirrors—you said something like this wasn't possible. That we weren't supposed to be able to do anything big or unreasonable. But my thoughts made this happen anyway."

Elliott's brow crinkles. "Are you—do you mean, you think we could . . . conjure up a plane after all, or something?"

There's a faint stirring of hope in his voice. I squash it. "No. I'm saying, even if we could conjure up a plane, it wouldn't matter. Because there is nowhere to go. There's no safe haven here, because we changed the forest, and there's no safe haven on Cisco Island, because *someone changed the stars.*"

Elliott swallows. I see the fire start to catch in him too, but in his panic he tries to smother it. He shakes his head. "No. That can't be what happened. Thoughts can't change things on the island, there's no fog there, it's safe—"

"It's not the fog that's doing this. What happened to the stars means that things *can* be changed on the island. Which means things can be changed anywhere. Which means everything, *everything*, around us could be imaginary. These woods. The road we were traveling. The hospital—you might've just remembered the whole building into existence, the same way you did the prepper hideout. If the stars are wrong, the whole *world* could be wrong." I laugh again. The beam from my flashlight jerks wildly with the motion of it. "Nothing is real. Nowhere is safe."

Elliott lifts his light. At the edge of its yellow circle, a charcoal scorpion crawls out of the forest. Elliott takes a step backwards.

I do too, involuntarily, even though I already know there'll be no escape this time. Maybe we could get away from the scorpions. We definitely won't get away from the vast shadow stirring in the mirrors around us, though.

My left hand throbs, and beneath the skin, a cold ache gathers strength. I watch the scorpion Being skitter closer, watch the terror on Elliott's face, and my wild humor drops away. "Even them," I realize slowly.

I sweep the flashlight outward. It pans over the dozens, hundreds, of tiny Beings surging through the fog toward us. Elliott, who is scared of almost nothing, is terrified of scorpions—and then a legion of them crawl out of his brother's glasses. And the foxlike Being from the garage . . . *I'm* creeped out by foxes. It's too much to be a coincidence.

I said a second ago that everything could be imaginary. If the hospital and the Camaro were our memories and the road signs were our expectations, then . . . "The Beings are our fears," I say aloud.

I bring the beam of light up. It arcs over the monsters that are even now coalescing behind our reflections. What will be in the mirrors all around us? What else am I scared of?

So much. Everything.

Elliott doesn't ask what I mean. He looks at me, and I can see in the set of his jaw, in his squared shoulders, that he understands. Ever practical, he asks, "Then how do we fight them?"

And that's when it hits me.

If I've learned one thing from my OCD, it's that you can't run from your fears. And the more you do to stop them, the more powerful they become. We're surrounded by fears made literal, Beings made of darkness that could tear us limb from limb, and I finally know *exactly* how to fight them.

I look back at Elliott. "We don't."

He looks at me like I've suggested lying down and letting the Beings eat us, which must be what it seems like from his perspective. He doesn't have the experience with fear that I do; he doesn't understand. He shakes his head. "Do what you want," he says, and hefts his flashlight like a weapon. "I'm going down fighting."

The scorpions flood around us, cut off our escape. They make a circle. It starts to close.

My hand starts to tingle, another wave of agony rising. The darkness in the mirrors starts to solidify: a slitted golden eye the size of my torso. A vast wing covered in delicate feathers. Scales. Claws. Teeth.

The tugging in my ribs gently reels me in. It's a question. A dare. And I never turn down a dare.

I grit my teeth. I look around. There's a tree next to Elliott, a big pine-turned-mirror, that's just barely inside our quickly narrowing scorpion-free circle.

"How much do you trust me?" I ask him.

He gives a ragged smile, eyes on the Beings. "Not at all."

"That's what I thought." Only one thing for it, then.

I take a deep breath. I launch myself at him. And I push us both toward the mirror.

My shove catches Elliott off guard. He only has enough time to turn his head, to grab my arm, to widen his eyes, and then we're falling toward the silvered pine. I hit its cold, glassy surface first. There's a buzz like static electricity on my skin. It folds over me. The mirror—*liquefies*. It's mercury, ice, a silvery sort of coldness that drags me in and swallows me up. The forest is gone. The Beings are gone. The mirror has pulled us through.

The world breaks down into a kaleidoscope of sensations.

A chemical smell. Something acrid. Something burnt.

A rainbow sheen that flickers through the mercurial ice around us. It's trying to tell me something. I can *almost* understand it, as if the colors are words with half their letters scrambled. If I could just decode them—if I could just put them in the right order . . .

Elliott's grip on my arm tightens. It vanishes.

And then I wake up on a cold, hard floor—alone.

CHAPTER TWELVE

INHALE.

My ribs creak with the motion, like I haven't breathed deeply in eons. The world is dark. My thoughts are fuzzy and gray around the edges, like the fog has crept into my brain, too. I can still smell it: metallic, faintly burnt. But the world isn't made of ice anymore, and the dizzying kaleidoscope of sensations is gone—and so is the noise of the storm. There's no howling wind, no booms of thunder. The silence is vast around me.

My brain sends an order to my fingers. *Move.* But nothing twitches.

I exhale.

Some of the fog clears from my brain. I realize that the reason the world is dark is because my eyes are closed. My brain sends another order. This time, it's obeyed. My eyes open.

I'm staring at a field of stars.

I squint. My eyes feel rusted shut, like I haven't opened them in eons either. I try to move my fingers again, and this time, my right hand obeys. I rub my eyes. Open them again. The stars are above me, impossibly clear and bright, the arm of the Milky Way spangled with purples and blues overhead. A phrase snags in my mind: *The stars are wrong.* I don't have any idea which stars I'm looking at or whether the constellations above me are correct, but somehow these stars look clearer, brighter, and sharper and more painfully *real* than anything I've seen in a long time.

I sit up. The floor beneath me feels like glass but is opaque, and a gentle shimmer of rainbow light flows across it like a mirage. Chartreuse, sapphire, candy-apple red. It's hypnotizing and distracts me for a long moment—until I realize I'm wearing shoes.

I frown. Some more of the fog in my brain clears. I wasn't wearing shoes before. Was I? No. I'd kicked one off to get rid of a scorpion, and threw the other at . . . someone, I think. But now I'm somehow wearing them again, and they look nearly brand-new, the way they used to look last year when I first bought them. And—I'm wearing a different shirt, too, a nice button-down with a crisp white undershirt. None of my clothes have been white, not for months, not with the electricity on the island so carefully guarded that hardly anyone can afford to use a real washer and dryer.

I smooth down my pants—they're different too, nice khaki cargo pants instead of beat-up jeans—and freeze when I spot the jagged black veins creeping across the back of my left hand.

The scorpion. The shadows. The *pain*.

I clutch my hand. I tear off my button-down and wrap it around the wound, like that'll help. At least this way I won't have to see it. I won't have to remember that I have a Being's venom crawling slowly up my arm, that my veins are full of shadows now as well as blood.

I stand up. I stagger at first—I feel somehow lighter than normal and off-balance. But after a moment I stabilize. Warily, I scan my surroundings. The field of stars above, the soft rainbow-lit floor below, in all directions, for as far as I can see.

No Beings. But also . . . no Elliott.

Elliott. That's who I threw my shoe at. I took him with me through the mirror, I know I did. But I remember his grip vanishing—maybe a Being overtook him, or maybe he didn't make it through.

I can't see very well in these conditions. The floor's wavering light is dim and dizzying, rippling out into infinity, and the only other lighting is the gleam of stars filtering down from above.

Maybe Elliott is nearby and I just can't make him out.

I cup my hands to my mouth. "Ackermann!" I shout. My voice echoes off the rainbow floor, off what I can only assume is the translucent glass ceiling. There's no reply except my own voice fading into nothingness.

I wait. I give him time to answer. He doesn't.

I should stop making noise. This place, whatever it is, is where the Beings come from. They probably don't realize I'm here yet, but if I go around yelling at the top of my lungs they'll find me soon enough.

But: "Ackermann!" I yell again anyway, something like worry humming just below my breastbone.

A swell of burnt-orange light flicks across the floor a few yards away. It lights up a prone body—someone lying on their back, as still as death. The orange light ripens into a beeswax gold and then shatters outward, a starburst of sparks. It's enough light for me to make out that the person on the ground is a woman.

I hold stock-still for a long moment as the bright colors fade into blue. Then, cautiously, trying to look in every direction at once in case this is some kind of trap, I approach the body.

Her skin looks gray in the wash of blue light. Her hair is blond and fanned across the floor in mussed waves. Her eyes are closed. She's silent, unmoving—but I can still remember the way her violet-blue eyes spark when she speaks, and the way her voice crackles like lightning looking for something to burn.

"Wrong Ackermann," I whisper.

I stare down at the mayor. She shouldn't be here. She was on Cisco Island—what, yesterday? I watched her turn her back on the helicopter, watched her walk away while her son and I were exiled. So what is she doing *here*?

Something dark and ugly threads through me. I don't care what she's doing here. I should get rid of her. Tie her up, at the very least. She seems to be asleep, her chest rising and falling with shallow, steady breaths, but I've been around long enough to know that you don't underestimate Mayor Ackermann no matter how harmless she looks. I don't have a rope, though, or anything resembling a weapon.

I close my fists, ready for a fight, and dare to inch closer. I nudge her shoulder with a shoe.

Nothing.

I nudge her a little harder, almost but not quite a kick. My muscles are taut from holding myself in, from tamping down the adrenaline and the urge to hurt the woman who took everything from me—no matter how innocent she looks at the moment.

She doesn't wake. Doesn't even stir. I get down on my hands and knees and stick my good hand beneath her nose. She's breathing, but nonresponsive.

"What the hell?" I say out loud.

Something in my left hand twinges. I'm so distracted by the

mystery of the mayor that I don't register the feeling in time to prepare, and when the wave of agony washes up my arm, I'm caught off-guard.

My whole body jerks. There's a red-hot poker knifing through my hand, rupturing my veins, shredding my skin. The pain burrows into my arm. Claws its way through my chest. Rummages through my veins and arteries and nerves and organs until it finds the center of me, and then it clamps down and *squeezes*.

I'm screaming. I'm sure of it. But I can't hear anything above the pain.

I fold downward. Barely manage to catch myself on the floor. The shirt that's binding my stung hand is shoved off with the violence of the movement, and the bull's-eye center of the scorpion sting presses against the cool floor.

Darkness bursts out of my injured hand and spreads across the floor, like I'm bleeding shadows. All the lights, all the colors, ripple out of existence as the wave of black touches them.

The pain dissipates. I gulp down one breath, and then another, shaking. I stare down at the floor—and realize it's not dark. Not completely. There are tiny speckles of light in it, like someone's sprinkled fairy dust over obsidian tile.

I squint as I recover from the wave of pain, trying to make out what I'm seeing. This scene, it looks . . . familiar. And then, slowly, the speckles begin to move. They shift sideways.

Something massive slides into view below me. A huge circle pocked with glowing yellow veins.

My breath stutters. No. It's not a circle. It's a *planet*. One with a familiar shape: dark swaths of ocean, green-brown continents stretching wide. Earth. I'm above Earth. That continent right there, that's Asia. Right next to it is Europe. And that tiny speck of an island clinging to its edge—that's England. That's *London*—and it's free of fog. There's no fog anywhere on Earth, as far as I can tell.

I stare at the mayor's body, which is still lying asleep next to me, and then look into the vast distance beyond her. This floor, it isn't a floor. It's a window. It's translucent glass just like the ceiling. And those glowing yellow veins on Earth below—they're—

Lights, supplies a small-sounding foreign voice, its grave timbre resonating deep within my mind.

I gasp and instinctively rear back. The second my hurt hand loses contact with the floor, it washes back to the colors, and Earth disappears from sight. This time the colors move faster, though, circling and shifting, agitated.

I stare wildly around me, searching for whoever's spoken, but there's no one except the mayor. I should probably run at this point, but—that voice. It sounded . . . *young*. Its tone called up a memory I'd forgotten long ago: of myself, eight years old, sitting silently in a closet with my knees pulled up to my chin.

It had been the first time I'd gotten off the school bus and no one was home waiting for me. Ty was at a game, I knew, but Mom was just . . . gone. The house felt awful in its silence, profound in its emptiness. And somehow this voice, whatever it is, feels like someone who's been sitting in the closet for a long, long time.

Slowly, I lower my injured hand back to the floor. That seemed to be what set things off last time. And it does it again—a gray-green light swirls around me before the floor goes back to translucent.

"Hello?" I say quietly.

Hello.

My breath catches at the word. It was in my head, not spoken out loud, but it wasn't my own thought either. The hairs on the back of my neck prickle. What exactly is it I'm talking to?

As if in response, the floor slowly tilts. I go tense by instinct, expecting to slide away, but gravity keeps me right where I am as if we're not moving at all. The planet below dips to the side. A line of some sort of metallic debris—huge shards of polished silver—comes into view. The nearest pieces are massive, the most distant appearing as tiny flecks that curve around the far side of Earth, catching the light of the hidden sun as they slowly spin in their orbit.

The Shatter Ring. We're in the Shatter Ring.

Is that what you call it? asks the voice. The words are tinted with curiosity and feel somehow . . . azure, as if the feeling of curiosity has a color.

I hesitate, still uncertain of who I'm talking to and whether they're dangerous. This is the place that births Beings, after all, and it creeps me out even more that this—person?—can apparently sense my thoughts. "What do you call it?" I ask cautiously.

The voice is silent for a moment. The floor tilts again until the earth is below us and the Shatter Ring is barely visible off to the sides. *Pieces of my body*, the voice says at last, somber and small.

I gape. "Who . . . what *are* you?"

The voice seems to fumble. I sense it rummaging through itself, searching for the right words. After a moment, a collection of thoughts and pictures and memories pour into my head. Light. Dark. Colors where you don't expect them. Something shimmering in an empty place. It's too much. I clutch my head with my right hand. "Stop!" I gasp.

The thoughts and pictures cease at once, like they've been snatched back. *I'm sorry*, says the voice. Contrition shades into my mind, carrot-orange. It flickers across the floor too, radiating outward before it vanishes, and I get the sense of a person trying to rein in their emotions, trying to hold very still so that a spooked animal won't run away.

Making me the spooked animal. Which means the voice, whose emotions apparently project across the floor, and whose body is somehow also the Shatter Ring, is . . .

Holy ever-loving *shit*. I swallow dryly. "You're an alien. An . . . alien ship? The alien ship who showed up during the Fracture."

Yes, says the voice, a bit sadly. The child in the closet tucks itself a bit farther back.

I hesitate. I recall the images and phrases it tried to show me earlier, when I asked who it was. The colors, the shimmering, the light and the dark. I think it was trying to tell me its name, but it didn't quite translate. I think of a word that seems to at least mostly match the description it gave of itself—a word I thought of when I first saw the colors on the floor. "Mirage?" I supply tentatively.

Azure curiosity blinks through my mind again, then, slowly, it swells into ripples of cobalt blue. The ship likes that name. *Yes. That's close,* it says.

It. That doesn't feel right. Whatever Mirage is, the ship isn't an *it*. "Do you . . . have a pronoun?" I ask.

Mirage considers the question. *I think I like "he,"* he says after a moment. Shades of purple swirl around the words. Or—it's more like the colors *are* the words, like my mind has somehow learned a new language when I wasn't looking.

I shake my head. The sensation of someone else talking in my mind, of colors bleeding from an alien ship to me, it's impossibly weird. I want to pull my wounded hand back—the only time he seems able to communicate with me is when my injury is touching him—but I want answers, and Mirage is the only one who might actually be able to give them to me.

I am sorry about your injury, Mirage says softly. There's a vast ocean of grief resonating behind the words, a heavy, dark veil of slate gray. I remember what he said before: that the Shatter Ring was pieces of his body. He's injured too, then. Maybe even dying.

Like me.

I look down at my hand. The crooked black veins have reached across my knuckles now, and have also spread a few inches past my wrist and up my forearm. The pain has receded to a throbbing ache, but I know another wave of agony will come soon. I wonder how long it will take those veins to reach my heart. My brain.

"Do you know if—my injury, maybe it's not so—?" I can't manage more than that.

I'm sorry, Mirage says again, confirming my fears.

I bow my head. I don't want to think about my impending death, so I ask another question. "Is it what's allowing me to talk to you?"

Your injury is part of the reason I'm able to reach you, yes. The thing that stung you, it was . . . Again that sense of Mirage rummaging through himself, trying to find the right words. *Made by me.*

I freeze. My muscles go taut. "What?" I say, confusion and

anger burgeoning. I'd just begun to believe Mirage might not be my enemy.

Mirage fumbles again. *I didn't want it to harm you. I would heal the wound now, if I had enough energy.*

Hope surges through me, erasing the anger with startling alacrity. "Why don't you have enough energy?" Maybe I can help him. Maybe he can fix me. Maybe I can live. And if I'm going to survive, then I could think about those yellow veins on Earth below—and maybe I could dare to ask Mirage whether they're true. Whether Earth's power might really have been restored somehow, whether the fog is truly gone. Whether anyone managed to survive down there until now.

Whether *Ty* managed to survive.

The hope strengthens. But I learned a long time ago that hope is much more dangerous than any Being, that it can freeze like water over the cracks in your life and burst them open and leave you with even less than you had before.

Mirage is an alien. I have no idea what he wants. And, more important, the Being that stung me somehow came from *here*. I rein in the hope, seal it back underground, caulk carefully over the cracks.

Because I'm keeping them alive, Mirage tells me. A burst of muted green whirls at my side, around the mayor's body.

"Them? You mean Mayor Ackermann and—what, more people?" I lift my head, scan my surroundings. Field of stars above, Earth below, the Shatter Ring stretching out to either side—it's incredibly disorienting, and the darkness makes it impossible to see if there are any other bodies nearby. Who is Mirage keeping alive? And why does he *need* to keep them alive?

"There was a guy I came here with," I tell Mirage. "Elliott Ackermann. Where is he? Is he okay?"

I'm not sure, Mirage says. *I will begin a search for him, but it may take some time.*

I bite back the urge to curse at the ship. So Elliott could be just fine, wandering around somewhere in this vast darkness without the ability to communicate with Mirage—since he didn't get stung by the scorpion Being, thanks to my idiotic heroism, which I still can't quite wrap my head around—or he could be dead. Or stuck back in that clearing.

No, Mirage says, sensing my thoughts again. *He is not on Earth. He is somewhere inside me.*

I blow out a breath in relief. "So he did get through the mirror?"

I don't know.

I narrow my eyes. "You just said he's somewhere here."

Yes.

Something must be getting lost in translation. I try a different tack. "How did the mayor get here? This . . . woman," I finally say, though it's definitely not the first word that comes to mind, "in front of me. I saw her yesterday at the island.

How did she escape? Why won't she wake up?"

I—she's not . . . Burnt-umber frustration undulates over the floor, then flashes suddenly to gold. *I could show you, I think. May I show you?*

Immediately wary at the eagerness in Mirage's tone, I lean back. "Show me what?"

What happened last year. The fog, the mirrors. Why you're here. Everything.

I curl the fingers of my left hand, prepared to lift it from the floor. This is nuts. Just because Mirage *sounds* young and harmless doesn't mean he is. This could be a trick, a trap. Maybe he's going to send me back to the Beings. He's apparently the one who made them in the first place, after all.

But then I look through my black-streaked fingers, at the planet below. At London. At the lights that wreathe it, beautiful and impossible.

Shadows in my veins. Lights on Earth. It's a choice and not a choice at all.

Because I don't want to die. Of course I don't. But most of all, I don't want it to be the darkness that kills me. I've been terrified of it for a year and now it's inside me, corroding me, one wave of pain at a time. I don't want to watch it consume me. I don't want to belong to it. I don't want any part of it to own any part of me.

If I let Mirage show me what's happening, maybe I can find

a way to help him. A way to get him the energy he needs to heal my wound.

Maybe I can find a way to escape the shadows inside me.

"Okay," I say. "Show me everything."

Gently, Mirage reaches into my mind—and then pulls me into his.

CHAPTER THIRTEEN

'M IN THE DARK. THIS TIME, THERE ARE NO STARS.

I raise my hands and try to feel around me. Nothing. I spin—and hit a solid surface. Something digs into my arm. I know instantly it's a doorknob, because I'd know the shape of a doorknob even in my dreams.

I run my hand down the surface in front of me—a door, paint flaking off from it under my fingers—and put my hand on the knob. It feels oddly familiar. A round, cool sphere, except for a small imperfection under my index finger: a tiny scratch etched into the metal, sharp enough to cut skin along its edges. The front door back at my old house, the house Ty and I left last year when he took me to Cisco Island, it had a scratch just like this.

I hesitate, staring into the darkness all around. "Mirage," I whisper at last, because this expanse of emptiness seems at once too small and too large for anything other than a whisper. "Where exactly am I?"

Your body is exactly where it was a moment ago, he answers.

"So I *am* in your mind."

Not quite. I am building a—mental construct for your consciousness to move through.

My fingers tighten on the doorknob. The resulting numbness in my fingers is a too-familiar ache. The scratch on the knob slices shallowly into my finger. "And what sort of mental construct did you build?"

I do not know. I have no control over the form it takes. I supplied the memories I want you to see, and your mind has built a home for them.

I want to laugh, but I can't quite manage it. My mind has built a home for the memories of an alien ship that creates monsters but is somehow also both lonely and vulnerable. Where else would my brain put someone like that, except here?

I start to twist the doorknob. A compulsion twists at me and I try to shake it off. This is a mental construct, a dream, a hallucination. Whatever the room beyond is, it isn't real. The door frame isn't real. I don't have to tap it.

Except I *do*. I close my eyes and lean my head against the frame with a quiet *thunk*. Why do I have to be like this? I'm already dying. Is whatever's beyond this door really more dangerous than what's already happened to me?

It doesn't matter. I still have to tap it. So I do: three times on the left, five on the right, at shoulder height, giving up everything I spent grueling months of therapy working for. Giving up a little more ground, receding a little further into my fears. Just like the coward I used to be. The coward I still am.

I twist the doorknob.

It's locked.

I frown, then sigh. With my left hand, I dip into my pants pocket and a cool sliver of metal falls against my injured palm. My clothing may be somehow different, but my key is exactly where I left it. It feels strange—the teeth aren't quite right, this isn't the key to my loft—but it slides into the door without a hitch.

I turn the key. *Click*: the lock disengages. I pull the key out, hold it gingerly so it doesn't touch my wounded palm, and nudge the door.

It opens with a creak. Yellow light spills out, carving a bright rectangle through the shadows that stretch out behind me.

A pile of dirty plates spread out across the Formica counter. Four mismatched chairs are pulled up to the table. The centerpiece is a potted fern. Ugly gray and pink floral curtains hang limply over the window that overlooks the front yard. I hate those curtains. I hate this window. This is where I always stood when I waited for Mom to come home, my little nose pressed against the glass as I scanned the darkness for someone who often didn't show until long after Ty had pried me off and sent me, protesting, to bed.

My movements feel disjointed, dreamlike. I push the door closed. Reach up to the lock—eerily familiar in my fingers—and engage it. I leave my hand on it for a long moment, but the second I take it away and turn my back, I'm no longer sure enough that I really did lock it.

Come on. I can do this. I've done this, much more than this, before. I'm *recovered*. I'm *better*.

Even I can't believe myself anymore.

A flick of motion from behind the ugly curtains catches my eye. Something is outside the house. I check the lock again—just one more time—and then drop the key back into my left pocket. Left, for locked.

I step toward the window. The beige carpet muffles my footfalls. I pass the lumpy chocolate-brown monstrosity of a couch, the only piece of furniture that isn't stained or tattered.

"I love it," I'd said when the furniture company dropped the couch off on our porch.

Ty squinted. He walked around it, shook his head, and sat on it. "This," he pronounced, "is both the ugliest and the most comfortable piece of furniture my ass has ever had the pleasure to grace."

"I told you!" I folded my arms smugly. This was the first purchase I'd ever made with my own money, earned from my very first job as a grocery store bagger. The furniture was on clearance and I'd had to spend my whole hoard of savings—my entire first month of paychecks—to buy it and the accompanying coffee table, but the pleased surprise in Ty's eyes was worth it.

He'd been providing everything for me since Mom left the year before. And now I'd finally provided for us too—something small, yes, but permanent.

I avert my eyes from the couch. It's just a memory.

The flicker of motion behind the curtains catches my eye again. I slow as I approach it. Carefully, with one finger, I move the curtain half an inch to the side.

The window—isn't a window. It's a screen. There's a field of stars, and something silver and massive. I open the curtains wider so I can see. One of my fingers brushes the screen.

The house disappears. A memory—not mine—reaches out and clamps around my mind.

I was created for first contact, it whispers. The house around me fades away. Something brilliant—*nebula*, the memory hums—blooms around me in the open vastness of space.

I jerk my hand away from the screen with a sharp exhale. The nebula vanishes. I look around. Window, couch, table, potted plant. Nothing unusual. Nothing terrifying. But the vertigo of being suspended above a nebula in open space is still clawing at my mind, and I have to put out a hand to support myself against the wall.

The memory waits patiently for me to get my bearings.

I gulp down a deep breath. Straighten my spine. Reach out to it again, steeling myself for the mental transition this time. My palm presses against the cool not-window.

The memory wraps me up in itself. This time, I let it take me all the way in.

———

I was created for first contact.

I was birthed deep in the heart of a nebula, brought into the universe alongside newly formed stars and molecular clouds spangled with novae and dust. I was a greatship, the only one of my kind.

My creators gave me many things. The ability to communicate with a vast variety of intelligent species through unique telepathic capabilities. Sentience, so that I too would be intelligent. They even made me beautiful, an immense, mercurial oval, so that other species would be drawn to me.

But they never gave me a name.

They sent me out into the endless dark of the universe to find life. I had a directive: Make first contact, determine whether the life-forms I encountered were capable of joining the larger community of worlds, and if so, return to my makers with a delegation so that introductions could be made.

I searched. I was happy, because I had a purpose. I told myself this often.

I was capable of faster-than-light travel. I had to be, to get anywhere in the vast emptiness. But in that blurred space between dead star systems, between galaxies that gleamed with the false promise of life, sometimes I wished I could move slower. I wished I could stop. I wished I could stay—somewhere.

Years stretched to decades, and then centuries. I gave myself a name; it was in my makers' language, but translated loosely to Mirage. I told myself I chose this name for my ability to induce hallucinations, to communicate with other species through the filter of their own mental constructs. But really, it was because a mirage was what I felt like: something that was merely a dream, nothing but scattered light gleaming against a horizon I would never reach.

Then I found the humans.

I was too eager. It was my own fault. I caught the signals from afar; radio first, crackling and staticky, so faint that I almost missed it. As I drew closer, the signals grew more recent, and more technologically complex.

I had finally found what I was looking for. I dipped toward Earth's atmosphere, mirroring the signals I had caught as a greeting, as an invitation.

The humans shot me out of the sky.

I jerk back, breaking contact with the screen. I trip over the coffee table and fall across the memory of a couch. "What the hell?" I demand, eyes wide. "That was . . . that was . . ." But there's no word that can quite describe the strength of the secondhand memory that just took over my brain.

That was my birth, Mirage supplies. *How I came to be.*

I ease myself back to my feet. The memory felt so *real*. The loneliness of it had been crushing. The hopeful boredom, the painful eagerness when he found Earth—

My palm throbs, reminding me of why I'm here, and I shake off the alien feelings. I need to get all the information I can as quickly as possible. "What about the fog and the Beings? Were they . . . what, your defense mechanism, or something?"

There's more. Deeper inside this construct, Mirage answers.

I glance toward the closed doors in the hallway behind me and press my lips together. "Of course," I mutter, and march toward them.

I pass the beat-up old piano, one of the few things Ty refused to pawn off when times got tough. He loved to play. He tried to teach me, but I was worse than hopeless at it, and he eventually gave up on the endeavor. I still loved to listen to him, though. Whenever a storm hit, we'd board up the windows and huddle in the living room, and I'd listen to Ty play the soundtracks to my favorite movies. He was incredible. If he hadn't loved botany so much, he might've studied music.

There are three doors in the hallway. One goes to the bathroom, one to Mom's room. I open both doors and glance inside—if I just glance, I don't have to tap—but there's nothing unusual. The final room is mine and Ty's.

Drywall stretches down the middle of the room, separating our halves. There's nothing on my side except my bed, the ancient bookshelf I used as a dresser, and a few band posters. Ty's side is covered in greenery. Succulents on the windowsill, cacti on the desk. A few different types of violets he'd been experimenting with are shoved against the corner of the far wall.

And something is outside his window.

I tap the frame and edge closer. At first I think the window screen is frozen. It's just flat gray, with no sound or movement. But as I get closer I spot the subtle swirling.

It's the fog.

I brace myself, take a deep breath, and brush my fingers across the glass.

───

I was crashing.

Or pieces of me were, anyway. My elegant oval shape had been shattered by the missiles. When I recovered from the shock, from the awful pain—something I had never experienced before—I quickly used what was left of my nearly ruined power source to suspend the shards of myself in stable orbit. One piece slipped past, though. I calculated the shard's track. It would crash into an island. An island that was full of sentient life-forms, whom I would be responsible for killing.

I had hardly any energy left, and only moments to choose a course of action. With seconds before the shard hit, I swept up every human on the island and deposited them safely in my core.

The island was destroyed. But the people were saved.

Their physiologies weren't suited to teleportation, though, and the trip rendered them unconscious. They were asleep on a ship that was slowly dying, slowly crashing, and nothing I could do would wake them up.

Because they were dreaming.

Using my unique capabilities, their minds had created a shared mental construct. They dreamed of their island. Of being the only people to survive a cataclysmic event. They'd been awake long enough to see me explode, long enough to see my shards suspend in orbit, but had no way of knowing what had happened afterward. Their unconscious minds rendered that unknown as fog—a vast bank of it that stretched from coast to coast, with no one left alive but them.

Weeks went by. I was using more energy than I could spare to keep the humans alive, and they were siphoning off even more to maintain their construct. I sifted through their memories and built them escape pods so they could return to Earth, but they refused to wake up and use them.

I had no control over the construct. It was maintained by the humans' shared memories and expectations. And because their island was so stable, because there were so many people's thoughts contributing to making it feel lifelike, their brains believed the dream was real.

So I tried to reach them from inside the dream. I couldn't change anything within the construct, but I could attempt a moment, a single split second, of communication. I could try to show them an exit.

It manifested in the mirrors.

It made sense. People trusted mirrors to reflect reality; if the mirrors reflected something else, perhaps the people would understand that the dream they inhabited was not reality. All they had to do was accept that, and step through the exit I managed to create with what little energy I could scrape together—and they would wake up. They could go home.

But I didn't anticipate the fear.

When the humans looked at the mirrors, my attempt at communication came as a rainbow wash of colors—the language of my makers, like the colors that danced on my floor. This startled the humans, who feared the unexpected and the unknown. And in a dream where a city's worth of humans believed malicious aliens had murdered the rest of the world, the unknown was dangerous.

Their fear manifested as shadows. As monsters. As Beings that erupted out of the mirrors and devoured everything they touched without mercy. The monstrous fears faded after a few minutes, but by then the damage was done. And I learned that the combination of the humans' vivid imaginations and my own ability to render them was so strong that anything that happened to the humans in the dream also happened to their real bodies.

Dozens died.

I was helpless to stop what I had started. As months passed and my power continued to drain, I was less and less able to resist the gravitational pull of Earth below. My core was the largest and heaviest remaining piece of myself, and if I couldn't manage to keep it in orbit, then I and all the humans I had tucked away within myself would die. Many of the humans on the planet below, as well.

I kept trying to wake my passengers. As they took precautions against mirrors, I was forced to use less-reflective materials to try to show them the truth of the dream. None of them understood; none of them realized that an exit lay just beyond the monsters. But I began to realize that when a human was exposed to mirrors, to exits, over a long period of time, I could communicate with them a little bit more.

It wasn't much. Just a nudge—a sensation, a gut feeling. Like someone beyond the mirror was trying to reel them in. It was a meager invitation, but it was the most I could manage.

Outside the dream, the pull of the planet below intensified. I began to burn. To fall.

I shut down more of myself, sacrificed all the systems I could, and pulled up just enough. I bought a few more days.

And then—one of the humans finally saw through the dream. Finally recognized the monsters. Finally took the exit.

And Marty Callahan woke up on a rainbow floor above the world he'd believed dead.

CHAPTER FOURTEEN

BREAK CONTACT WITH THE WINDOW. I'M REELING backwards—away from the screen, away from the knowledge that's sent cracks shuddering through the whole of my reality. Through the whole of what I *thought* was reality.

I knock over a floor lamp. It hits the ground. The bulb pops and blue light flashes bright, a half-second supernova. I hit the coffee table, knock a book off it, course-correct and keep moving. I don't stop until I'm pressed up against the wall that divides the kitchen from the living room.

A dream. I've been living in a dream for the last year.

"Mirage," I say, the word barely more than a shaky croak.

Yes? he says immediately. There's a quality to his voice that tells me he would be hovering and wringing his hands, if he could hover, if he had hands.

"Earth. It's alive." It's a question, but also not really a question, because I can't bear to frame it as one. Can't bear to acknowledge the smallest possibility that I might've somehow misunderstood—that it might not be true.

Hope. The thing that seeps, and freezes, and floods, and drowns.

Yes, Mirage confirms. *The shard's crash did some damage to coastal areas but the fatalities were limited, from what I can tell.*

I close my eyes and let my real question slip out. "Is my brother alive?"

I'm sorry. I don't know. I barely have enough power to stay in orbit, to keep everyone alive, with my passengers draining so much of my energy for the shared dream. There's not been enough power left over to try to contact anyone on the planet below, and it's too far away for me to scan.

My eyes are burning. I open them, desperate to distract myself—to contain my emotions, to contain the terrible hope.

I look down at my arm. The black veins, they reach almost to my elbow now. My skin is marbled with them. I have no idea how long I have left before the venom finishes me off. Maybe a few hours. Maybe a day. Maybe enough time to take one of the escape pods Mirage mentioned to Earth—just in time to die, screaming in agony, a literal victim of my own fears.

Would it be enough time to find Ty?

London is dead. Elliott said that not twenty minutes ago. I'd been desperate for it to be a lie at the time. But the thing is, after that initial shock, knowing for sure that Ty was gone had also brought an awful sort of relief. It had taken so much energy to make myself believe he was okay. That I could see him again if I just worked hard enough, if I just sold enough mirrors, if I just stayed at the bottom of the mayor's shit list. I was constantly clawing at the edges of that certainty, as if it were a cliff I had to cling to with all my might. Part of that was because of my OCD—we're the worst with uncertainty—but part of it was also just me, trying to force myself to believe in something I wanted so badly to be true.

And now I'm back to that old desperation. Now I'm back to *maybe*. And I hate—I *hate*—maybe. But I have to cling to it anyway. Because if there's even the smallest chance I can see Ty again, even if it's only for a few hours before I die, I have to take it.

Some vast, unnamable feeling spins through me. It surges into my system and then centers in my injured palm, tingling like pins and needles.

I take a breath. My face is wet, but I don't move to scrub the tears away. "Mirage," I say. "Can I see him?"

A slight hesitation. *I'm sorry, I don't understand.*

"My brother. Tyler Graham Callahan. You're using my

memories to show me a dream of my house. I want to dream about him."

Another hesitation, longer this time. *I cannot build a construct of a sentient being,* he replies, a bright, apologetic orange washing through my mind along with the words. *It is against my . . . programming. The rules my creators gave me.*

"Can you break them?"

I don't understand, he says again.

My hands curl into fists. "The rules. Are you capable of breaking them? You said your creators gave you sentience. Sentience means you can weigh each situation, make choices, break rules. Please, Mirage. Please show me my brother."

I'm begging. It hurts. I usually don't mind humiliation if there's something to gain by it, but this—this feels different. This feels like I've got no barriers, no defenses, like I'm an insect pinned to a display.

Mirage doesn't respond.

I open my mouth to plead again, but I've already said everything there is to say, so I just wait.

Nothing happens. Seconds tick by. Then, slowly, something shimmers in the air just beyond the piano. Gleaming lines spill to the floor. They come together, wind and twist like threads on a weaver's loom.

And then my brother is standing in front of me.

He's wearing his favorite blue hoodie, a ratty old thing he

likes to pretend is lucky but really just wears because he hates spending money on himself. His brown hair is tousled—I used to give him a hard time about how much product he put in it. He's smiling. He was always smiling.

At first, seeing him feels like being crushed. Like the air is solid and heavier than lead, too dense to breathe, impossible to move through. But then I notice the details that are wrong. The leather cuff he wore on his left wrist, it's not there. And his hair—it's dull, just a few shades off. He's two or three inches too tall. His eyes are . . . dark. Glassy, empty.

I step away from the wall. I circle him. His shape flattens out at the side, thins to a beam of light. A hologram.

A mirage.

I'm sorry, the ship whispers. *It's the best I can do.*

I don't respond. I step back to my spot next to the piano, where I can see Ty in full, and drop my head. I press my hands into the wall and ignore the sharp pain of the Being sting, focusing on the texture of the paint beneath my fingers. I used to use this trick to ground myself. To remind myself of what was real. None of this is real, I know, but it still *feels* like it is. I could still convince myself that it is. If I just tried a little harder.

The pain in my injured palm intensifies.

Earlier, I'd let Mirage show me all this so that I could figure out a way to help him. A way to get him the power he needs to heal me. But that was before I understood the magnitude of what it would take to free up his energy.

Everyone—the whole of Cisco Island, nearly three thousand people—would have to wake up. They would have to face the monsters, face their greatest fears, and step through the mirrors. And before all that, they would have to *know* to step through the mirrors. In the last thirteen months, exactly two people have done any of that, and one of those people only did it because I pushed him.

I've found Elliott Ackermann, Mirage says into the silence, once again reading the direction of my thoughts. *He is awake as well.*

I choke on a laugh. Elliott. I'd nearly forgotten that Mirage was running a search for him. And now that he's found him, what am I supposed to tell him? That we can get to Earth—to the real world—where there's no fog, no Beings, no Valkyrie Bridge and no mother to make him walk across it? I don't want to tell him. I don't want him to leave me.

I can't *afford* for him to leave me.

Because I think . . . I think I might still need his help.

An idea blooms in the back of my mind. It's terrible. Risky. But it makes the desperation fade, just a little. Just enough.

I lick my lips. "You said you'd heal me if you could," I say to Mirage. "If you had enough energy."

Of course.

"What if everyone woke up? Would that free enough of your power to fix me?"

I—don't know. I've never had to cure anything remotely like a Being sting before. But if I was no longer having to sustain any mental constructs or keep anyone's physical bodies healthy while they sleep . . . I'm not sure. I think I might have enough energy to at least try to make you well again.

"Good enough," I reply. I step away from the wall. I don't need to ground myself anymore.

Mirage pauses, confused. *But I've been trying to wake everyone for over a year and nothing has worked. And now I only have perhaps a few hours left before I crash.*

I move toward the door. At this distance, Ty's image is distorted again, but that's okay. I'll see the real Ty soon.

Whatever it takes. Still. Always.

"Put us back in the dream," I tell Mirage.

What?

I step past the couch. I barely notice the way the familiar carpet feels under my shoes. I don't even look at the curtains. "Can you do that? Put us back on the island, in the shared dream?"

I . . . think so. If you were to fall asleep, you should automatically be reinserted into their construct. I could probably direct an electric shock that would render you unconscious. I wouldn't have any control over where you appear inside the construct once you're there, though.

"We'll deal. Knock us out, me and Ackermann both." I reach the door, put my hand on the knob. I grit my teeth and tap—trying not to feel the flash of relief it brings, trying to shove the shame of it down. I have more important things to focus on than my own failure now.

I'm going to wake everyone up. I'm going to save the whole goddamned island, whether they like it or not. And Elliott is going to help me.

I twist the doorknob. I step into the darkness, and it blinks out of existence. I'm kneeling on the rainbow floor, my left hand still pressed against the rippling colors on the ground.

I glance at the sleeping form of the mayor. I'll have to go toe-to-toe with her for the plan I've got brewing to work, and she won't be asleep and harmless once I drop back into the dream. Part of me wishes I could just get rid of her right now, but for better or worse, I already proved back at the boardwalk that I don't have murder in me.

Shouldn't you inform Elliott of what you've learned before you go back in? Pink uncertainty bleeds through Mirage's words, the color surging around my hand as well.

"No. I'll tell him what he needs to know later." Meaning I'll tell him what I want him to think, to make certain he'll do what I need him to. Guilt flits through the back of my mind and I shove that down alongside the shame. I've known for a year that I would do anything I had to in order to get to Ty. If that includes lying to the Boy Scout, so be it.

Elliott would probably want to save everyone anyway, I tell myself. It seems like the sort of thing he'd do. But if I were in his shoes—if I could safely go home to a living world, if I knew beyond a shadow of a doubt that I would never see my brother again no matter what I did—I'd leave everyone else behind in a heartbeat. Especially the guy responsible for my brother's death.

That's a chance I can't take. I can't risk the possibility that maybe, deep down, Elliott might be like me after all.

I lie on the floor. I stare up at the stars, then change my mind and roll onto my stomach. Earth glows beneath me, a sliver of its edge washed in the brilliance of dawn. I stare at it long enough for the lights to stay in place even when I close my eyes.

I'm coming, Ty, I promise silently. *Whatever it takes.*

"Okay," I tell Mirage. "Do it."

Good luck, he whispers.

An electric jolt sparks in my brain. I jerk once. And then I wake up on Cisco Island.

CHAPTER FIFTEEN

AND PROMPTLY FALL FLAT ON MY FACE.

Splat. I manage to catch myself on my hands and knees in ankle-deep standing water. It immediately soaks through my clothes—the old shirt and jeans I was wearing back in the clearing, along with my socks, as I'm once again shoeless. Cold wetness sluices over me and I shiver.

The ripples of my landing flatten out. The water is still. I spot my reflection—lank dark hair, pale skin, black veins creeping under my sleeves—and instinctively scramble backwards, my brain screaming, *Mirror!*

"What are you doing? Stop making a scene," hisses an unfamiliar voice.

I go still. I don't reply, for fear my voice will be recognized by whichever islander is addressing me.

But someone else replies for me. "The mayor is the only one allowed to make a scene," she quips, half mocking and half bitter. The first voice shushes her.

My pulse stutters. *I wouldn't have any control over where you appear,* Mirage said. Apparently he wasn't joking. Wherever I've landed, there are at least two people who don't seem to have noticed my appearing-from-thin-air trick but still might recognize me at any moment. The best I can hope for is that these two islanders are the only ones nearby. I can handle two people. But the way they were talking about the mayor kind of made it sound like . . .

I pray very hard—apparently all it takes is a life-threatening situation or two to make a convert out of me—and turn my head.

Shoes. *Lots* of shoes. Attached to lots of feet.

Mirage has dropped me in the middle of a crowd.

I swallow. My pulse climbs. I spend a beat trying to convince myself that I can just stay down here on the ground, but deep down I know that makes me even more likely to draw attention and get recognized, so I clamber to my feet. I keep my head down, hoping my hair might hide my face.

But when the mayor's voice rings out, my head snaps up.

"As one of the few remaining bastions of humanity," she says, and hate instantly floods my veins at the reminder of her lies about London and Singapore, "we can no longer tolerate those who would harm our *good* citizens, who would drain our precious resources. Especially after the tragic loss of our helicopter and any supplies it might have been able to gather."

Her voice is strong and clear and marbled with a grim sort of certainty. It draws my gaze upward against my will. I fight the urge to look as long as I can, but it takes everything I've got, and as a result I don't process her words for a moment.

Then I understand; they lost the chopper. The night it dropped us off, it never made it back. Either the pilots didn't have enough experience to make it through the storm or Beings got them. They never brought any resources back to the island.

"I've long delayed enacting true martial law," she continues. "I required clear proof to convict criminals, kept the judicial process intact. I wanted to preserve our humanity— preserve the rights our country fought for—but the cost has become too great."

I dare to allow myself a quick glimpse at my surroundings. I'm fenced in by a mob. Hundreds of islanders in ponchos and rain boots, standing in the water that's flooded the street, staring forward at . . . shit, *shit.*

Valkyrie Bridge.

This is an exile ceremony.

The sky is overcast with a strange, eerie yellow tint. Several of the coconut palms next to the bridge are downed, and leaves and felled branches litter the road around us. I can hear thunder nearby, rolling in from the sea as well as from across the sound—but it's overshadowed by birdsong. Every bird in the world has been locked in an echo chamber with us, from what I can tell. I spot two little gray and white terns trying to huddle beneath a hulking pelican atop one of the downed palms, and a whole flock of shrieking seagulls circle overhead.

As a native Floridian, I know exactly why the birds are here. We're in the eye of the hurricane. The only safe place for miles.

"That's the reason for today," the mayor is saying now. "We all mourn the necessity of the new exile policy. But we can no longer waste our precious resources on jailed criminals. We can no longer hold ourselves to a due process standard that doesn't work. We have purged the island of mirror dealers; now we must make certain that our city will no longer be an environment that allows new ones, or *any* criminals, to flourish."

My head snaps back to the mayor. A slow horror ices through me at the look on her face, that awful, familiar steel-and-bone expression. She's standing at the bridge's entrance, surrounded by the Valkyrie warrior statues as if she has any right to a place among them. At her back, a few yards in front of the fog, every cop on the island stands shoulder to shoulder, weapons drawn, eyes on—

—on the prisoners kneeling in front of them.

The pit of my stomach drops. There are *dozens*. There's one middle-aged woman I recognize from a few months back, who got caught stealing beans out of the dispensary and was jailed for it. Next to her are two college-aged guys—one with a black eye, one who's silently sobbing—who I'm acquainted with through my black-market contacts. They sell fish illegally, I remember. But they never got caught. They're way too slippery to give the cops the proof they'd need to exile them. Then again . . . I guess the cops don't need proof anymore.

Rations are getting low, and the mayor is desperate, Elliott told me at the boardwalk. Apparently that much wasn't a lie. She's going to exile all these prisoners in the middle of a hurricane no matter how trivial their crimes, because she doesn't want to waste supplies on them for even one more day.

A helpless anger burns through me, and I try to swallow it down. These people don't matter to me. I shouldn't care what the mayor does to them; two dozen fewer people on the island is two dozen fewer people for me to try to wake up. But I clench my jaw anyway, imagining the screams that'll echo over the bridge in just a few moments, the way they'll cut out one by one. There are mirrors up there, in the fog just past the Valkyrie statues. That's how the residents of Cisco Island get rid of any reflective materials that can't be ground up into powder or discarded safely in the mines. It's also how they ensure that exile results in a suitably horrible death. Like the kind I'm facing, if I fail.

I take a slow, deep breath. Focus. I have to focus. This exile ceremony could actually be good news for me, for my mission. I need a way to get a message out to as many islanders as possible, as quickly as possible, and the equipment I need to do that is usually present at exilings.

I scan the ground in front of the mayor. There: a chestlike box with blinking red lights and rows of dials and switches. The radio transmitter. I smile, the expression feeling vicious. I thought I was going to have to hunt this down, steal it right out of City Hall. Instead I can take it now, and maybe give these prisoners a chance to escape the mayor's "justice" to boot.

First, though, I need a distraction.

I turn my head, searching for something that might work to throw the mayor and the cops off for long enough to let me steal the transmitter. If I had a mirror, that would do the trick, but my thoughts alone won't work to summon one here. Mirage said that Cisco Island is stable because of everyone's expectations working together. Their minds are a grinding machine, and my will is nothing against it.

At that thought, an unexpected quicksilver relief pours over me. I can't change anything here. Can't summon up my fears, can't let my uncontrolled thoughts loose on my world. I am safe.

I hold back a manic laugh. I am the farthest thing from safe in the world. The woman who sentenced me to a horrific death is less than twenty yards away. I shouldn't feel *comforted* just because my stupid brain can't conjure up scary things.

I shake my head and force myself to focus. I'm still scanning the crowd for inspiration, for something that might work as a distraction. My gaze snags on someone a few rows ahead of me. There's something familiar about those tense shoulders, the sharp lines of that square jaw—that pretty-boy blond hair.

Elliott. He's here. Less than a hundred feet from his mother.

Go ahead, shoot him, she told me back at the boardwalk. That's what she'll say now, too, if she spots him.

He knows that. He knows what she'll do to him, what she's *already* done to him. But he isn't trying to keep his head down. He isn't trying to hide or blend in with the crowd or quietly escape. Instead, he's staring right at her, like he *wants* her to see him.

Because of course he wants her to see him.

That *idiot.* Is he still trying to rationalize her actions? Does he truly still think, deep down, she might actually care about him? Is he even thinking about what would happen if he's spotted—the pandemonium it would cause when every cop on the bridge comes after him?

I pause. I let the scene sit in my mind for a second as another probably-bad idea forms. I was just wishing for a distraction, and now Elliott's handed me one on a silver platter. And a way to get him out of here too, before he gets any bright ideas about turning himself in to his mom.

I wait until the mayor turns to glance at the opposite side of the crowd. Then, as slowly and casually as I can, I weave between the three people separating me and Elliott.

I reach him. He's looking straight ahead, laser-focused, as if his mother is the only person in the world. I remember how empty his eyes were the last time he saw her. They're not empty anymore, but the emotion in them is something too private and painful for me to have any right to name, so I lean in and speak instead.

"Thirty feet north down this road is a storm drain. The grate comes up easy," I say in a low tone.

He startles, his gaze darting to me. His eyes widen and that painful emotion washes away, replaced by alarm. "What are you doing here?" he whispers, then shakes his head, a tiny flick of a motion. "I don't know what's going on or how we got back, but you have to get out of here. She'll see you."

"No. She'll see *you*," I say. "The storm drain leads to the sewers, which eventually connect to the mines. Underneath the southernmost part of town is an old hydraulic elevator with a padlock on its back wall. Find it and wait there."

He stares at me for a second. Then his eyes drop to my arm. To the black veins that are creeping higher by the minute. Something flits across his expression, softening it. "No," he says. "*You* go. I'll cause a distraction."

I bite back a groan. He has to make everything harder,

doesn't he? Stupid hero. "Yes, that's kind of the point," I say, a little ruefully.

His eyes narrow. He knows me well enough to be suspicious, but he's also remembering how I grabbed that scorpion off him, and how I'm dying for it now.

Not for much longer, though.

I cut off his internal debate. "Good luck," I tell him, echoing Mirage's words from earlier.

His whole body goes tense. "Callahan. What are you talking about?"

I take a long step back. I put myself between him and his mother, cutting off the line of sight between them, being careful to keep my own face hidden. Then I point at Elliott and yell: "Oh my God, he's got a mirror!"

The crowd explodes.

The islanders scream and flee in every direction. Water splashes everywhere. The birds on the ground nearby take flight, a chaos of feathers and screeching. A gun fires into the air. The mayor yells and leans to the side to try to see who I'm pointing at. When she can't get a good angle she strides into the mass of panicking humanity and starts shoving people, making her way in our direction. A good two-thirds of the cops scramble to follow.

"What the hell," Elliott snarls at me, but he doesn't get any further than that, because I shove him hard.

"The *storm drain*, idiot," I hiss at him.

He hesitates. He glances around, but I'm still blocking the line of sight between him and his mom. He looks back at me. "Callahan, I have no idea what you're doing, but if we get out of this alive—"

"You're going to kill me, yeah, yeah," I say, and shove him again. I raise my voice. "Oh my God, the mirror! It's somewhere on the ground, where did it go?!"

More people scream. Several are knocked over, and their flailing bodies trip others, putting more obstacles in between us and the approaching cops. Elliott lets out a string of curses and then, finally, runs northward.

I turn toward the bridge. Several of the more industrious prisoners are leaping up and scuttling into the crowd, while others are frozen. The radio transmitter is on the ground, unguarded. I start toward it.

Someone knocks into me. I spin sideways, catching myself against another body. The man shoves me away, gets a good look at my face, then gasps and yells my name. A cop a few yards away hears and turns to look. It's an older black officer, and at the sight of his face I can almost hear his voice calling my name like we're old friends. Ginger's partner.

I freeze in place. Then an alien urge fills me up, propels me forward against my will. I want to apologize. To ask him if he can still smell the blood and dryer sheets, too—if he can still see that bright green of Ginger's eyes, still remember the way his body arced under that column of darkness.

I stop myself. The cop is shoving people aside, coming toward me, and he doesn't look like he wants an apology. He looks like he wants to kill me. And, I remind myself, that would be extremely counterproductive for all of us.

I pivot, locate the transmitter again, and charge toward it. There are no wires—it's battery-operated, remotely connected. When I go to pick it up, something small falls off the top and clatters to the ground. A remote. I grab it, find the button to stop the broadcast, press it, and then drop the remote into my pocket.

I scoop up the chest itself, and then pause. This thing is about thirty pounds. There's no way I'll fit down the storm drain with it. And I can't just quickly send out the message I need to right here and now, either. I need Elliott's help for that—and I just sent him into the sewers with every cop in the city on his tail, so I could make sure he wouldn't give himself up to his mom.

I spare a quick glance down the street. Elliott has disappeared—hopefully into the storm drain and not into police custody—and the mayor and the cops are now dispersed throughout the crowd, searching for him, grabbing escaped prisoners.

A shot rings out and I flinch. No one except the older cop has spotted me yet, and he's gotten distracted chasing down the fleeing fish-selling brothers now, but it's only a matter of time before other officers recognize me and come after me.

I won't get far in a chase lugging this transmitter. And I can't risk anyone even realizing I have it yet, or my whole plan could go up in smoke. I search for ideas. Can't go down the drain, can't flee on foot. That leaves only one option.

I curse under my breath. I take three long strides. And I step onto Valkyrie Bridge.

CHAPTER SIXTEEN

I COUNT TO FIVE AND THEN STOP WALKING. I KEEP MY gaze fixed on the gray nothingness over my head so I won't accidentally look into any of the mirrors that have been thrown on the ground farther in. I may know the truth about what they are now but that doesn't make them any less terrifying, or any less deadly. I listen carefully—for the scuff of shoes behind me, for the breathing of any Beings ahead of me. I keep my own breathing shallow and try not to think about the smells.

The heavy acridness of the fog. The cloying undertone of death that clings to it.

All I have to do is hide. Just for a few minutes. The cops will go after the fleeing prisoners, and the looming eye wall of the hurricane will drive everyone else back to their shelters. Then I'll be safe. Then I can escape without being spotted.

That smell of death. I'm trying not to think about what it is. *Who* it is. But I can't stop picturing Sam Garcia's panicked face. I wonder how far he got. Halfway across? Did he make it to the mainland before they got him? Or is it really what's left of him that's rotting right now, hanging heavy on the air?

My stomach flops over, and I half turn back toward the entrance. This was a terrible idea. I've been through some wild shit the last few days, it's true, but to *voluntarily* walk onto Valkyrie Bridge? This place has been the source of my worst nightmares for a year. I should get the hell out of here as fast as my feet can take me.

But there's nowhere else to hide. No other way I can keep the transmitter safe till I can get it to my loft. It's boiled down to a choice between stepping onto Valkyrie Bridge or failing to do what I came here to do, and apparently the bridge is the lesser evil.

I keep my breathing even, listening to the fog-muffled sounds of the chaos outside. A slow minute passes. Then another. By the time I count to five hundred, the distant din of thunder is all I can hear.

I should give it another minute or two just to be safe. There could be a cop out there, stationed to watch the entrance the way they usually do after exile ceremonies, to stop anyone trying to return. I should wait here until I'm certain they're all gone.

One more minute. I'll give it one more minute. I've been through all the fog on the mainland, faced down multiple Beings, even held one in my hand. I can manage standing still on Valkyrie Bridge for sixty more seconds. I let out a long breath that shakes only a little.

Beneath a roll of thunder, I hear the clink of glass on concrete.

I whip around, my eyes straining to see past the smothering gray. That came from the direction of the mainland. Farther down the bridge—where there's nothing alive.

Or . . . did I get turned around? When I came in here I walked straight toward the mainland and then stopped, or at least I thought I did. But I've shifted my weight a few times, and I did half turn toward the entrance a moment ago. I swivel my head back and forth, trying to recalculate, but the more I try to be sure which way is which, the more lost I feel. I understand now how exiles can get turned around in here, how their plans—to just walk past the mirrors with their eyes closed, to find the edge of the bridge and jump off it—fail so easily in this disorienting haze.

Claustrophobia clamps its jaws over me. The fog is too thick, too heavy. With every breath I take I can feel it clogging my throat. I need to *run*. Need to get away. Need to be safe.

I force myself to take a long, slow inhale. The fog isn't clogging my throat. It isn't even real, I remind myself. I need to think clearly. If that sound came from the island, that means someone is out there waiting for me, and if I accidentally run toward them I might as well serve myself up to the mayor on a platter. But if the sound came from farther down the bridge—where the Beings are permanent, where they've been known to lie in wait for new exiles—and I run *that* way . . .

Deep in the fog, the clinking echoes again. My body makes the decision for me. I turn ninety degrees and sprint in the opposite direction of the sound.

My footfalls smack against the concrete. My breath comes in gulped-down gasps. I've taken more than five steps by now. Haven't I? It's too far, farther than the entrance should be. I'm running toward the mainland. Which means I need to turn around.

But before I can, a shape looms out of the fog ahead of me.

I curse, my fingers tightening around the transmitter as I try to stop, but its weight pulls me off-balance. The best I can do is turn so that my shoulder crashes into the shape rather than the transmitter. My foot lands wrong and I slip, then hit the ground hard on my back.

I go still.

Birds sing. Thunder rolls. My right shoulder aches from the impact. Whatever I hit, it had no give to it. Not like a person would. But it didn't have that cool obsidian feel of a Being, either. I dare to lift my head.

A Valkyrie statue looms above me, blank gaze fixed

somewhere on the horizon. I'm at the bridge's entrance.

I close my eyes and drop my head back to the ground, muttering a brief but fervent *thank you*, and then clamber to my feet. My back is soaked from the standing water, but I managed to keep the transmitter dry and intact, at least.

I look around. The road is empty. There's no one in sight. The sky is still oddly yellow and cluttered with birds, and the distant rolls of thunder are getting much louder. I glance at the beach below the bridge's steep embankment. The storm surge looks high, and the waves seem bigger than they were when I went into the fog. The eye wall is approaching fast.

It's good news. The radios will have been brought into the town's designated shelters for the length of the hurricane, in case of emergency transmission from City Hall. I'll be able to reach most or even all of the islanders with a broadcast now, which means my plan might actually stand a chance at success.

If I can make it to my loft undetected. If Elliott escaped capture.

There's a discarded yellow poncho snagged on a downed tree branch a few yards away. I slosh over to it, pull it off, and wrap it carefully around the transmitter. It's not much of a disguise, but it'll have to do.

I grip the chest tightly, breathe through my anxiety, and start toward the city.

The only nearby entrance to the mines that isn't a storm drain is through a condemned building in the middle of town. The streets are deserted, but as I walk through them, the hairs on the back of my neck prickle. All the times I've been stopped and searched here, all the cops who were so eager to catch me in the act. Back then, the need for court-worthy evidence kept them at bay. Now, if just one of them recognizes me or realizes what I'm carrying, we're all done for.

My steps splash in the ankle-high water as I turn onto Banyan Lane. The intertwined trees arc overhead, their prop roots stretching toward the ground, dripping from the rain. The quiet, sheltered space beneath them feels like a cathedral. *I can see why the tourists like them so much*, my brother whispers in my ear.

The northeastern horizon is a dim gray between the branches. Ty is no longer that way, was never that way. But he still pulls at me like a lodestone anyway.

Whatever I have to do, I promise him again. My plan won't be pretty. But there's a chance it'll work, a chance it'll get me to him, and that's all that matters.

I glance at the street ahead. I've reached a fork. To the left and right are boarded-up businesses. The building in the middle is an old bank, wedge-shaped, with broken windows and doors nobody bothers to lock. When I slip inside, my palm tingles with a faint, icy pain, making me wince. I shift the transmitter's weight away from the injury as much as I can. The black veins have crawled all the way across my left shoulder now. I wish I could flip up my collar to hide them, even though nobody is nearby to see. How long has it been since the last wave of pain? With any luck, I'll manage to get to my loft before the next one hits.

I wonder whether Elliott will be there waiting for me. If he escaped, if he's okay. If my unthinking sacrifice with the scorpion was pointless anyway. I regret doing it. Probably.

I pick up my pace as I weave through the shadows inside the bank. Past the dusty tellers' desks, through the back office area. I duck behind the biggest desk, a mahogany monstrosity too heavy for anyone to steal. A sheet of rusted metal is pushed up against the wall here. Careful not to make any noise, I set the transmitter down, tap what passes as the "door frame," then nudge the metal away and duck into the gaping hole behind it. I quietly slide the metal sheet back into place once I've got the transmitter through. A few of its dials are still glowing. I pull the poncho partway off so that I can navigate the tunnels by their dim light. As I weave my way into the familiar darkness, I breathe a little easier. I made it. I'm safe now.

I come to a crossroads where the mines connect to the sewers. Storm runoff rushes through the tunnel ahead of me, a knee-high river of snarling white water. Bracing my steps carefully, I start to cross it. There's the faintest of stirrings to my right. It's my only warning before a body crashes into me at full speed.

I go sprawling. By sheer luck, I manage to twist so that I land halfway out of the river and halfway into the tunnel I'd been aiming for, managing to keep the transmitter dry once again.

"Who's that?" demands a voice. A female voice. A commanding and lightly accented female voice, which almost certainly belongs to a cop. *That's* why I didn't see any of them in the city above—they must have suspected Elliott escaped through a storm drain and went down themselves to search for him.

"No one of consequence," I reply in my most charming tone, stalling for time while I frantically search for ideas. I reach out with my left hand, looking for a rock or debris or anything that I can use as a projectile or distraction. By sheer luck, my fingers close on what feels like a broken chunk of concrete.

Splash. The woman steps closer. The dim red light glints off her badge. The name tag next to it reads DIAZ. She was at the boardwalk with Ginger, I remember, on the team that apprehended me. Which means I'm screwed.

She comes to the same conclusion. "Hands up," she snaps, lifting her gun.

My palm is starting to ache. I shift my grip on the chunk of concrete, then realize it aches not because my grip was awkward but because there's another wave of pain building up, about to incapacitate me at the worst possible moment.

It's now or never, then. I let my gaze go behind her. "No, don't!" I shout. She doesn't take the bait and look to see who I'm talking to, but she does hesitate for just a second—long enough for me to hurl the concrete chunk at her face. She jerks away, taking the impact on her forearm instead, and I scramble to my feet and flee.

I yank the poncho back down over the dials so Diaz can't track me by its glow. I hold my injured hand out, following the wall on my left. There's cursing behind me and then several loud splashes in quick succession. She's coming after me, and she's pissed.

I feel a break in the wall, a gap barely big enough for me to squeeze the transmitter through. It's a shortcut—a dangerous one—but I'll have to take it. I shove myself in, trying to be as quiet as I can. The walls here are bowed in by pressure. Too many of the supports have snapped and the earth weighs heavy on the remaining ones, ready to cave in entirely if another of them breaks.

The pain in my hand intensifies. I grit my teeth and try to breathe through it the way Dr. Washburne taught me to breathe through my anxiety. It helps, but only a little.

I count the supports as I go, feeling the rotted wood graze my fingers. Three. Four. Five. I pant with the effort of not crying out. Just a few more . . . and then I'll . . . I'll turn off into the tunnel leading to my loft—maybe she'll be far enough away that she won't hear by then—

Agony lights up every cell, fingertips to collarbone, a writhing supernova of pain. My veins feel alive. They're snakes beneath my skin. Venom drips in their wake, eating through my body like acid. I gasp in a breath and hold it, clamping down on myself, my vision blurring with the effort of staying silent. I can't stay on my feet. I fall sideways against the wall, then to the ground.

I curl around the transmitter. I scream.

Through the haze of agony, I hear footsteps. Diaz heard me. She's coming through the side tunnel after me. I'll be caught. I'm doomed—we're all doomed.

My legs spasm. One of them catches a support beam. It shudders and the earth around me creaks and groans.

Diaz's footsteps pause.

I have an idea. Something about—caving in, blocking the path . . .

The distraction costs me my concentration, and I scream again. It's a terrible sound—an awful keening, something you hear in the woods at night, prey being torn apart—and I try to muffle it, but it's like trying to stop an avalanche. I spasm again, my whole body this time. With my last ounce of lucidity, I turn a bit so that one of my feet catches the support beam again.

It snaps.

Diaz shouts. Her footsteps scramble away from me. Something is rumbling all around us, grinding and shrieking, like the earth's bones breaking.

I have to get up. Have to move. This tunnel opens into a bigger, better-supported tunnel a few yards down—but I don't think I have a few yards left in me. I roll onto my side, still curled around the transmitter, but can't manage more than that.

The earth around me groans and rumbles, growing louder. The ground beneath me trembles. Something heavy lands on my leg, pinning me: a fallen support.

I'm going to die in here. Alone. Without Ty, without even Elliott. I'll be crushed in a cave-in, unable to escape because I'm incapacitated by the sting of a creature I created with my thoughts. In the end, I'll have effectively been killed by my own fears. I would laugh if I could. How ironic. How absolutely, perfectly terrible.

Someone yells. Not Diaz.

A hand wraps around mine. It's bigger than Diaz's would be. It feels familiar. I remember this grip. But I remember it the other way around, I think—my hands over his, clamping down over taut tendons, white ridges of knuckles. Like trying to hold a grenade together. I thought he would let go. He didn't. He doesn't now, either.

He hauls me forward. My leg is trapped. Century-old dust fills the air, clogging my throat. He shifts his grip, hands under my arms, and pulls harder. I help as much as I can, trying to push with my other foot, and I finally come free. But the pain is still strengthening—too much, it's too much. I close my eyes.

I'm dragged a few yards and then dropped back to the ground. Earth's rumbling slows and stops, but the pain is still twisting, wringing, scorching. There'll be nothing left of me soon.

Someone shakes me, not gently. "Don't die, you jackass," he says sharply. "I still have to kill you, remember?"

He picks me up. I fade out, in, out.

The clattering of feet against metal. A sense of swaying, like the floor is suspended over empty space. *An old hydraulic elevator with a padlock on its back wall.* Someone said that. Me?

A familiar clatter of metal: a padlock rattling on its chain. A low, muttered curse. Whoever's carrying me shifts his grip. He reaches into my right pocket. *No,* I try to tell him. *Right is for unlocked, left is for locked.*

Except suddenly I'm not sure if I'm remembering my system correctly—which pocket is for which keys. And what if I accidentally put it in the wrong pocket? Or worse, what if I'm not even remembering right from left correctly?

Dimly, I realize that I'd forgotten this part of OCD. The way it worms into your head, plants doubt, makes you question the most basic, fundamental crap until you can't be sure of *anything* anymore, and it is exhausting and petrifying and aggravating as hell because goddammit, I am freaking *dying* and I *still* can't stop worrying that maybe, somehow, I don't actually know my left from my right.

I try to laugh again. Nothing but a choking sort of wheeze comes out.

The *click* of tiny metal teeth sliding perfectly home in the padlock: a sound I've got memorized. The person carrying me must have found my key after all. I'm taken into a room. I didn't get to tap the doorway. I need to tap the doorway. I can't manage to form the words, though.

There's a clattering, many objects hitting the floor all at once, and then I'm lain—gently this time—on a hard surface. Rough fingers yank up my sleeve, then stop. It's my left hand. Injured hand. I have no idea how it looks by this point, but it must be even worse than before, because there's a long pause full of . . . something. Then the fingers move to my other side and, more carefully, roll up that sleeve. Fingers rest on the inside of my wrist.

"Marty," he says, which is my name, I think. His voice sounds tight, helpless. "Your . . . your heart is beating too fast. Breathe. Try to breathe."

I inhale and choke on the dust that was kicked up by the cave-in. I cough and wheeze and finally manage a breath. Then another.

"There," he says, the tightness in his voice easing a little. "That's better."

The pain is fading. It slinks back across my shoulder, sulks its way down my arm, and recedes to my palm, where it curls up and waits.

I know what it's waiting for. The next time it comes back—the next time that wave crashes down on me—it'll kill me.

My eyes are still squeezed shut. Stars blink in and out behind them, twinkling, falling. I know it's just a symptom of the pain, but they make me remember the real stars, the ones I saw from Mirage's floor. And the planet in the midst of them—its glowing golden veins, its beautiful *aliveness*.

Ty is down there. I will get to him. I'm not dead yet.

I sink back into myself. I test out my senses slowly, one at a time. Touch: I'm on a rough wooden surface, pocked and dented. Sight: A dim, flickering yellow bulb illuminates an earthen ceiling crisscrossed by support beams. To the side is a row of gaping open-air windows overlooking a larger pitch-black cavern. Sound: That never really went away, but at least now I can think clearly enough to name the person who's been speaking. The one who dragged me out of the collapsing tunnel and carried me here.

"Ackermann," I cough, "I formally request a stay of execution. I'm in far too much pain for you to kill me right now."

The hands at my wrist tighten a little, then release me. "I'll take that under advisement," he says. There's something incredibly *tired* about his voice. I wonder if it's from my situation, or seeing his mother again, or both.

I ease up onto my elbows, open my eyes, and find him. He's standing at my right side. His clothing is soaked, his hair plastered to his face, his expression haunted. And that's not even taking into account the dark blue bruise spreading over his cheekbone from our fight in the clearing. "You look like shit," I note.

He summons up something akin to a glare. "You try swimming through a flooded storm drain with half a dozen cops on your ass."

I wave him off. "I got you here, didn't I?"

Here is, of course, my loft. It's hidden right beneath the city, its entrance tucked away behind an elevator shaft. The flickering light overhead is powered by a generator that I traded for in one of my deals. I'm lying atop my battered old desk. All of the things that used to be on its surface—a few sheets of precious, stolen paper, a covered hand mirror for emergency defense, and a picture of Ty and me in a haphazardly glued, homemade wooden frame—are scattered across the floor. My sleeping bag sits off by itself in a corner, rolled up to keep the spiders out.

"Yes, you did," Elliott answers, "and now you owe me an explanation."

His words cue up a flood of memory, and I jerk upright. "The transmitter," I say urgently, looking down at my empty hands. "The transmitter, holy shit, tell me you saved it from the cave-in."

Elliott gestures to the side, at the stairs that lead down into the darkness of the empty cavern below. Sitting on the landing, looking a little banged up but with its red lights still glowing steadily, is the transmitter. I sag in relief.

"You saved it, actually," Elliott says, his voice unreadable as he watches my reaction. "Kept a death grip on it until we got in the door. I'm guessing this is why you needed me to distract everyone back at the bridge? So you could steal that?" He shakes his head, a sharp, jerky motion that betrays the frustration he refuses to show in his tone. "I know you're up to something, Callahan. I know you know something about . . . whatever it is that happened, back there in the clearing. Tell me what's going on."

So we're back to *Callahan* now. I shake my head, holding off his questions for the moment while I slide to the ground and start toward the stairs. I want to double-check that the transmitter is okay—and maybe also stall just a little bit so I can figure out what version of the story to tell him so I can make sure he helps me. When I take a step forward, though, something crunches underfoot. The picture frame.

I pause. I pick it up, brush it off. The left side of the frame has come unglued, and I carefully push it back into its spot. I've got some superglue somewhere that can fix it, I think. The picture inside has gotten crinkled. There's no glass covering it—it was rumored that glass of all kinds might be put on the Reflectivity Index any day now, and while I'm happy to sell reflective materials to my customers, I don't want to risk spawning a Being in the middle of my office. Carefully, I straighten the picture back out.

I remember Elliott is watching me. I look up. His gaze is on the picture in my hands. Something flickers across his face—guilt.

He feels guilty because he thinks my brother's dead. Because he lied to me, and let his mother lie to everyone, about London being alive.

I slide the picture out, fold it and tuck it into my pocket. I know it's imaginary, but I still feel better with it on me.

I drop the frame back to my desk. "Okay, Ackermann," I say. "You might want to sit down for this."

And then I tell him everything.

CHAPTER SEVENTEEN

WELL, *ALMOST* EVERYTHING. I HOLD BACK A FEW key bits of information and add a tweak or two.

"Mirage forced us back into the dream," I finish, without so much as a hitch in my voice, because damn it all, even if I'm good at nothing else, I'm a fantastic liar. "He said we have to wake everyone up, and then he'll let us go."

Elliott stares at me for a long moment. I force myself to exhale instead of holding my breath while I wait for his response.

At last, he says: "Okay."

I blink, caught off guard. "What?"

"I said 'okay.'"

"Do you—you mean, okay you believe the story, or okay you'll help me wake everyone up?"

He narrows his eyes. "Now, that's an interesting way to phrase that question."

I work hard to stay still. I've made a mistake somehow. He's suspicious.

I try to deflect. "A question that you haven't yet answered," I reply.

He doesn't move, his gaze still locked on me. "Yes, I believe you—because I woke up on that ship too, and your explanation makes more sense than any guess I've been able to come up with. And yes. I'll *help you* wake everyone up."

Oh. That was the mistake.

Smelling blood in the water, he moves closer. "What exactly is it that you're getting out of this rescue attempt, Callahan? Why would you go to so much trouble for people you've been happily sacrificing to the Beings for over a year?"

"I didn't *sacrifice* anyone," I snap, stung. "I ran a business, that's all."

He presses harder. "I said I'll help you and I mean it, but not until you tell me your motive. Because we both know you're not usually big on saving people out of the goodness of your heart."

I pin my gaze to his and lift my left hand. "Do we? Is that a thing we both know?"

Guilt flits across his face again, but he refuses to budge.

"What," he says again, measuring each word, "are you getting out of this? Because the more you evade the question, the more convinced I am that you're keeping something from me."

I drop my hand. Last chance to give him some believable excuse. "When I'm not in the dream," I say, keeping eye contact, because eye contact is the most important part of a successful lie, "the Being's effects disappear. The sting disappears. What I get out of this is a *chance to live.*"

He can know that I'm doing this to save my skin. He just can't know I'm making *him* do this to save my skin. He can't know he has a choice—that he could go through a mirror right now and jet down to Earth and leave me behind. That's why I had to frame Mirage as the orchestrator of this little plan.

I'm not sure why I chose to tell Elliott that the Beings' effects disappear outside the dream instead of just saying that there's a chance Mirage *might* be able to heal me if we succeed, though. I think it's maybe because I don't want to remember I might still be a dead man no matter what we do.

Elliott is staring at me. His eyes have gone wide, and something like shock is plastered over his face. "The Beings' effects disappear on the ship? Does that mean the people who die from Being attacks . . . what, maybe they just wake up there instead of their real bodies actually dying?"

Everything in me sinks. I scramble to formulate a reply. I didn't connect the dots, didn't realize he might think Braedan could still be alive on Mirage. "I, uh, I don't know, maybe," I manage, the worst-delivered and most heartless lie of my life.

It's a good thing that he assumed Braedan might be alive. He'll be much more motivated to make the plan work this way. I tell myself I'm glad for it, but all I can see is the look on his face when we found his brother's body in the middle of the road.

Elliott stares at me. Slowly, his eyes narrow again—in thought or in suspicion, I'm not sure. Then his expression clears, smooths out, goes blank. I can't tell what he's thinking, and *that* makes me very, very nervous.

But "What's the plan, then?" is all he says when he finally speaks. "You want to use the transmitter to tell everyone the truth about the world?"

Slowly, I exhale. He took the bait. "Not exactly," I answer. "I want to use it to tell them all about the hundreds of mirrors I've planted in their shelters."

He stares at me. "You planted hundreds of mirrors . . . in the shelters."

I smile thinly. "Of course not. Even I don't have access to that many mirrors at once. But I don't need to actually plant the mirrors. I just need to make them *think* I've planted the mirrors."

Realization dawns. "And their collective belief that the mirrors are there will make mirrors actually appear." The look in his eyes says he's remembering that awful reflective forest, the way it appeared instantly when I imagined it.

"Right," I confirm. "We'll also need to give everyone the quick and dirty version of the story I just told you, so they know they need to go *through* the mirrors I've 'planted' once they start stumbling onto them in their mad dash to escape."

He spots the flaw in my plan. "No one will trust you," he says with a frown. "No one will go through the mirrors just because you say to."

"Of course not," I agree easily.

He lets his head fall back. "Which is why you need me," he says to the ceiling.

"Yep. A mirror dealer and the shadowseeker—how could they not believe us? The only way we'd ever agree on anything was if it was the truth."

He gives me a look. "What makes you think I'd lend you any credibility? I'm an exile now too."

"Don't you remember the way that crowd looked at you the night we got sent to the mainland?" I ask, with a bitter smile and an edge to my words. "Those people might've rioted to free you right then and there if you'd just had the sense to ask them to. You were their hero. A shadowseeker, willing to do whatever it took to hunt down the last mirror dealer and keep his island safe."

You didn't hunt any of us down because we put the island in danger. The words hang between us, unspoken.

"I'm willing to bet you're still their hero," I continue after a moment. "I'm willing to bet people would trust you more than the mayor, and they'd sure as hell trust you more than me."

His expression shifts the tiniest bit, but he turns away before I can interpret it, looking at the transmitter and the cavern beyond. The miners used to use that cavern as a staging area, though there's nothing down there now except ancient railcars and some broken tracks. Not that Elliott would be able to see any of that in the pitch-black.

"Even so," he says quietly, "not everyone would believe us. Not everyone would escape."

I drop my hands in my pockets, suddenly exhausted. "No," I agree. "But if you've got a better plan, I'm all ears."

I curl my hands into fists, expecting to feel the comforting bite of my key in my fingers, but there's nothing except the transmitter's little remote. The key is missing. Elliott didn't put it back after he used it to open the padlock.

It's not important. I don't need it anymore, I remind myself harshly, even as a spike of anxiety bites into me at its loss.

Elliott turns back around. He looks resigned. "What do you need me to do?" he asks.

He's in. It's what I needed, but I can't manage to dredge up any satisfaction. "Help write our speech," I tell him, pulling a hand out of my pocket to wave at the papers on the floor. "It needs to be short and believable. And we'll need to hurry—I ran into a cop right before that cave-in, and she saw the transmitter. If they figure out I plan to use it to address the city, they'll remove the radios from the shelters before we can get our message out."

"Are you sure we can even transmit from down here?"

"That thing is just a hunk of imaginary metal and wiring," I remind him, motioning at the chest. "It works because we, and everyone else who's seen it, expect it to. So expect it to transmit just fine from down here, and it will."

He scoops up a piece of paper from the ground. "I guess all we can do is try. Let's get started, then."

I pause. The anxiety is still eating at me, and I have to take care of it, one way or the other. "Do you have my key?" I ask.

He glances around, then bends over and scoops something else off the floor and tosses it to me. I catch it in my right hand: smooth silver surface, cool metallic teeth, tiny hole at the top. Familiar as breathing.

I check the door to make sure the padlock is open. Then I step to the top of the stairs, crank my arm back, and hurl the key into the darkness. It arcs away, the gleam of silver tumbling end over end and then vanishing in a split second. After a moment I hear the distant *clink* of metal on stone.

My hands are balled up so tightly they hurt. I instantly want to go down there and comb through the whole cavern until I find the key. Part of me—most of me—wishes I hadn't thrown it, but I have to deal with my OCD and I have to do it right now. I can't let it overtake me again. I can't afford to put it off until our current crisis has blown over. I'll do whatever it takes to prove to myself that I'm okay, that I've got my OCD under control. Throwing my key, which I won't need after today anyway, seems like a good place to start.

But even with it gone, I still have the urge to go check the padlock again. The ache to lock it—even though I know I wouldn't be able to unlock it, now—is almost physically painful. I've thrown the key away, and it hasn't helped at all, and I *need* it to help.

Elliott's voice startles me. "You're a very all-or-nothing guy, aren't you?" he asks.

I glance over at him and try to loosen up my shoulders, which are hunched and tight. "What?"

He's got a careful, contemplative sort of look on his face. He nods at the cavern. "Why did you throw the key?"

I hesitate—but he already knows about my OCD, and telling him might help get it off my chest. "Because I couldn't stop worrying about it. I thought if I threw it, I could prove to myself that I really do still have all my compulsions under control," I admit. "But now all I want is to go down there and find it."

He nods, more to himself than me, then searches through the desk's drawers until he finds a pen. He scribbles a few lines on the paper. I should be helping him compose the speech, but my anxiety is too high now and I can't think straight.

"Why did you say I was all-or-nothing?" I ask at last, mainly because if I don't distract myself I'm going to walk down those stairs and search for the key and we do *not* have time for that.

The pen stops. He looks up. "It's like you think you have to be either perfectly cured, if that's even possible, or else completely in the grip of your OCD. There's no in-between for you. So you throw yourself into proving that you've gotten it all under control—even at the expense of knowingly screwing up whatever life-threatening situation you're facing at the moment."

I frown and start to snap out a reply but then pause, remembering the Being that attacked us in the garage yesterday. I'd tapped the door frame, and then, because I'd wanted so desperately to prove to myself that I was still stronger than my OCD, I'd turned around to walk through the door again without tapping even though I knew we didn't have time for it. I'd meant to walk through it three times. Five times, if necessary.

Three and five. My safe numbers. I blink, stunned. I'd tried to use my counting compulsion to prove I wasn't under the control of my tapping compulsion . . . but both are my OCD. I'd gone deeper under its influence than I would have if I hadn't turned around at all.

And if I *hadn't* turned around—if I hadn't been so damned determined to prove I had my compulsions under control—I wouldn't have seen the mirror. I wouldn't have brought the Being.

"And your brother," Elliott continues, looking at the paper rather than me. "You wanted to find him, so what did you do?

You started a black-market business. You risked getting other people killed and getting yourself exiled—then you *actually* got yourself exiled—all because you threw absolutely everything you had after your goal, even when you had to know it wasn't a good idea." He lifts the pen and looks at me. "You're all, or you're nothing."

Whatever it takes. The refrain echoes in my mind, but I shake my head, rejecting the notion. Being determined isn't a bad thing. It's helping me survive long enough to get back to my brother. It helped me defeat my OCD the first time. It can do it again. In fact, I'm going to take that damned padlock off the door right now and throw it into the cavern, too. And I'm going to ignore the way that urge—the desperate need to prove that I'm not falling under the control of my OCD again—is starting to feel like a compulsion in itself.

I turn my back on Elliott. I stride over to the door. In my preoccupation, I don't hear the warning signs that I should—the creaking of the elevator floor, the quiet rattling of the padlock's chain. The scuff of a shoe against metal.

So I'm caught completely off guard when I pull the door open to find the mayor and two cops on the other side.

CHAPTER EIGHTEEN

THE PADLOCK IS IN MY HAND. I HAVE HALF A SECOND to decide what to do with it.

The cops—Ginger's older partner, along with Diaz, who's covered in mud—are raising their guns. The mayor is stepping forward, palm out, to slam the door all the way open. I backpedal, jerking in shock, then quickly turn that motion into something bigger and more distracting: My left hand flies in front of my face and I shout a warning to Elliott—all while carefully slipping the padlock off its chain and palming it in my right hand.

Diaz inhales sharply, eyes on my face. No, on the injured hand that's flung up in front of it. I can see her putting together the pieces, realizing why I was screaming in the tunnel earlier. The mayor, though, she doesn't even look at me. Her gaze scythes over the room and lands on her son.

Elliott's face freezes. His whole body reacts, reeling back a step, as if his mother's gaze is a physical force: a blow squarely aimed, unavoidable.

"How did you get back?" the mayor demands, her voice arcing through the room like lightning. She's not addressing me. She's not looking at me. Diaz still is, but the mingled shock and pity in her eyes mean—I hope—that she won't be quick to shoot. I stumble backwards, being sure to keep my right hand behind the angle of my body. I keep going until my shoes scuff against the detritus that's been knocked off the desk.

"Don't move," Diaz orders belatedly.

That's fine; I'm already where I need to be. I stop moving and let my feelings show on my face, telegraph them all over my body: panic, uncertainty, desperation. It's not an act. My heart and mind are both racing, combining to make a high thrumming that vibrates through me.

Elliott's mouth is moving. Nothing is coming out. He looks . . . broken. Something angry and almost protective rises up in me.

"He came with me," I say: a reminder to Elliott that he's not alone, and a reminder to his mother that she gave her own son no choice but to team up with a criminal to survive. My words don't arc and crackle with electricity like hers did, but they're something better: a lightning rod.

Her attention leaps to me. Her quick glance dissects and then dismisses me, and she looks back at her son, but the moment's distraction has given him a chance to recover. He still looks devastated, but no longer quite so broken.

"Mom," he greets her in that quiet, pained voice. I flash back to that moment on the boardwalk: the gun in my hand, the look on his face. *Go ahead, shoot him now.*

Out of the corner of my eye I spot a dimly glowing red light. Everyone's attention is on Elliott, so I risk a glance. The transmitter. It's still hidden in the shadows of the stair landing, waiting to broadcast our signal to the shelters above.

My heart and brain both settle into a beat that's smoother and more certain. An idea assembles itself. We're not going to get a chance to record Elliott's carefully composed speech . . . so this moment, this confrontation, will have to do.

I slip my right hand back into my pocket. Maneuvering around the padlock's bulk, I find the remote, search blindly for the button on the top right—my best guess at where an on/off button would be—and press it. Over the older cop's shoulder, a blinking green light comes on. It worked. We're transmitting live. Or at least, I have to hope we are.

Deep breath. This is it. Convince everyone, or lose Ty forever.

"You're just in time," I tell the mayor.

She doesn't even bother to look at me. "I'm not talking to you," she snaps. Her voice is edging toward sharp now. I take a moment to look her over. Her pants are wet from the knee down. She's wearing a police windbreaker and a holstered gun. Her blond hair is perfectly tied back. Her face is expressionless, but her violet-blue eyes are snapping with the same electricity as her voice.

She's pissed. That's good. Maybe she'll make a mistake. Maybe she'll believe me.

"Just in time to see what I've done with the place," I continue.

Now she looks at me. "What." It's a demand, not a question.

I sweep my left hand toward the gaping windows and the empty darkness beyond them, still carefully keeping my right hand and the padlock in it angled away. "That is my mirror warehouse," I bluff, more glad than ever that the cops never figured out my true smuggling methods—which definitely don't include a warehouse. "And it's empty."

Her eyes narrow. "What have you done?"

Elliott is looking at me now too. I feel the moment he understands. He straightens, his expression going blank. "We've placed all of Marty's mirrors around the city," he tells his mother. "Hundreds of them are hidden in every shelter."

The air in the room is something brittle and fractured, a plate of glass ready to shatter. "And why would you do that?"

the mayor asks him, her voice deadly calm.

I cut in. "Because this world—the fog, the Beings, the island—none of it's real. It's a dream, induced by alien technology. All of us have been dreaming together since the Fracture."

"But now everyone has to wake up," Elliott says. "Because if we don't, we're going to die in just a few hours, or less, now. The dream is about to end one way or the other."

The mayor's gaze is sharp enough to cut. "I don't know what you're playing at, but you need to tell me right now how you got back to the island."

"Why?" Elliott asks. I don't know if his mother can see the hope he's struggling against, but I can. He knows she's not sorry for what she did, but he can't help hoping maybe she wants him back anyway. That maybe she's finally realized his worth.

That maybe, this time, she might actually love him.

"So I can make sure," she replies, her gaze pinning him like he's a grasshopper on a display, "that you don't do it again next time." She draws her gun—and aims it at him.

Elliott doesn't react. Not externally. But I can see the ice slip into him, veins of frost crystallizing over all his hopes.

He stares at the gun. "I'll never be good enough for you," he realizes slowly. The frost spreads and cracks as he looks back up at his mother. "Will I?"

She says nothing.

I should be refocusing on the transmitter, on our message,

but I can't look away from that desolation on Elliott's face. I told him once that his blind loyalty to his mother made him just as bad as any dealer. It was true—how many people did he help exile, knowing how inhumane it was? But now I see just how much that loyalty has hurt him, too.

Because . . . he didn't drop me over that rooftop even when he had every reason to. He accepted my fears, accepted me, instead of abandoning me for being a liability. And he came back for me when we were escaping the scorpions because he couldn't make himself leave me to my fate, even though I'd attacked him, even though I'd gotten Braedan killed.

Elliott Ackermann is a good person.

Except when he's trying to be *good enough* for his mother.

He's still just standing there, staring at his mom, who's pointing a gun at him. His shoulders rise and fall with a breath. He looks defenseless. Wrecked. The same way he did when he found his brother's body.

That angry, protective thing in me rises again.

I step forward, drawing the mayor's attention. "The mirrors are exits," I say—not to her, but to my audience in the city above. "That's how you get out of the dream. Look in a mirror—because there are mirrors *everywhere* now—and wait for the rainbow sheen, then jump through. You'll wake up on a ship. There'll be escape pods. You can go home. To Earth. The *real* Earth, which is alive, with no fog and no Beings."

Elliott swallows and raises his head, struggles to focus. He knows my story needs his support. "It's true," he manages. "I've seen it. Mom," he says, and his voice breaks. "It's true. Please, trust me, just this once. Wake up. Live."

A laugh like gunfire cracks out of her. "Trust you? You've gone from failing this family to intentionally undermining it in record time, Elliott."

He flinches at his name, like it's a weapon she's flung at him, but he doesn't look away. "No," he says, his voice heavy. "I haven't failed this family. You have."

My breathing stills. He's finally confronting her. I want to hope he can get through, that we can make it out of this without bloodshed, but my cynical side—which is all of me, really— knows this isn't going to be pretty.

The mayor's eyes flash. She doesn't say anything. Even her silence is a weapon.

"You failed this family when you tried to hide my existence to win an election," Elliott goes on. He takes a step toward her.

"Don't move," snaps the older cop. No one looks at him.

"You failed this family when you exiled Braedan." Elliott takes another step. He's next to me now. "You failed us when you exiled *me*." His voice isn't heavy anymore. It's something like a black hole: burning with an impossible gravity, folded over and over on itself in an endless implosion. He takes one last step. He's in front of me now, between me and his mother, standing at the top of the stairs—framed by the darkness of the warehouse below. The transmitter blinks at his feet. It doesn't matter if the mayor notices it now. Our job is done, our message out.

Elliott covers his face with one hand and drags in a breath. When he speaks again, his words are muffled. "And you failed this entire island with the punishments you call justice. I didn't want to admit it. But it's true. It's *true*, and I helped you do it, and I'll never forgive myself." He drops his hand and pins her with a look. "But I could forgive you. I could always forgive *you*. Even when I shouldn't."

"Be quiet," the mayor snaps, but she steps forward—toward him, like she's drawn into his gravity despite herself. They're only a step or two away now.

"If you let me save you," Elliott says, "I'll do it. I'll forgive you. Not because you deserve it." He raises his hands a little, palms out, like he's surrendering. "It's because I can't help it. So, please. For once, just this once, do something for me—and let me save you."

The mayor's shoulders square. Something settles over her. "Do not," she orders, "take one more step."

She's still got her gun aimed at him, and she looks like she means what she says. Like she will stop him any way she has to, enforce her will any way she must.

My fingers curl around the padlock. I judge my moment carefully.

"Mom," Elliott says, his voice so quiet I can barely hear it. He reaches out, slowly, carefully, and wraps his fingers around the barrel of her gun. "I love you."

He waits for her to respond. She doesn't. Instead, she starts to turn her head—probably to order one of the officers behind her to cuff us.

Now. I throw the padlock hard at the mayor's head. She catches the motion, her eyes flicking from her son to me. She shifts her aim in my direction, Elliott's hand still on the barrel of the gun, as the padlock flies toward her.

She fires.

I'm already ducking out of the way before the gunshot goes off. Elliott must've been able to screw up her aim, because no bullet tears into my body, but I don't have time for gratitude. I'm grabbing for something on the floor—my emergency hand mirror, the one that got knocked off the desk earlier, the one that's lying only two inches from my foot now. I scoop it up, rip off the masking tape that covers its surface, and stand, ready to implement the next part of my plan: threatening them with the mirror. I look up to find Elliott, to yell at him to follow my lead.

He's standing in the same spot as a moment ago. No—not quite the same spot. He's on the landing now, blocking my view of the mayor completely. From this angle he's silhouetted against the darkness.

He doesn't move.

I edge toward the desk, which I plan to use as a shield. From here I can see the mayor again. She's on the ground now, both hands clutching her head. My aim with the padlock was good. It looks like Elliott managed to take her gun away after all, too. He's still holding it out in front of him, fingers wrapped around the barrel.

I lift the mirror, its deadly reflective surface facing the back wall. "Nobody move. You two, drop your guns," I order the cops.

Nobody moves. No one even looks at me. The cops are staring at the mayor, and the mayor is staring at her son.

My gaze darts back to Elliott, who's also not moving—until he sways, just a slight motion, left to right like a ship listing atop a wave. He drops his hand to his side and his fingers slowly uncurl from around his mother's gun. It falls heavily to the ground. Rust red is smeared across the matte black barrel.

Elliott is bleeding. When his mother fired at me he must've— what, blocked the shot with his hand?

He takes a step back. His heel catches on the floor and turns the step to a stumble. He twists sideways, and I get a view of his chest.

Of the ragged hole the bullet tore through it.

Elliott touches the spot. His hand comes away stained red. I feel the blood like it's on my own hands: warm, wet, sticky beneath my fingernails. My brain fills in the scent of dryer sheets even though it's not actually present.

The silence is bell-like, pealing. When he swallows everyone can hear it. "Mom," he says, but this time the word isn't a plea. It's an acknowledgment, edged in something sad and jagged. This time his mother is the one to flinch when the word hits her.

"Elliott," she replies, her voice lilting slightly upward at the end. The name isn't a weapon anymore. It doesn't arc with electricity. It's a question, one that already has an answer but can't help but be asked anyway.

Elliott exhales. He tries to take another step backwards, toward me, but his heel catches the edge of the stairs. He reaches for the railing to stabilize himself but there isn't one. He grabs for the doorway—too slow.

He starts to topple over the edge.

CHAPTER NINETEEN

THE MAYOR REACHES AFTER ELLIOTT BUT SHE'S ON the ground and too far away. Everyone is too far away. The darkness swallows his head, his chest. He's falling.

A feeling slams into me. It's . . . panic and fury and helplessness and horror. It dumps adrenaline into my veins, pumps it hard and fast.

I use it to calculate.

The drop: one hundred feet, give or take, to the cavern floor below.

The angle of Elliott's fall: slow, backwards, headfirst. He's already overbalanced, the fall inevitable, but his feet haven't quite left the stair yet.

The mirror: still in my hand. I throw it like I'm skipping a stone, face up. Can't risk breaking it, need just the right angle.

It glints, reflecting the dim yellow bulb. Everyone spots it at once. The rainbow sheen flickers over its face as it closes the space between me and Elliott. The exit is open.

Elliott's feet leave the stairs. The darkness envelops him to the knees. I can't see his head, can't see how far backwards he's tilted by now. I can only hope that my throw was a good one.

The mirror flashes as it skims the ground, its handle making its spin slightly lopsided. For a second the glass surface looks like it's still reflecting the yellow of the lightbulb, but then I realize it's the wrong color—this is more golden, and there's a slit of midnight-black running through its middle.

It's an eye. The eye of a Being, a massive one. I remember the reflective forest, the vast wing, the feathers and scales and claws. The monstrous dark. It's coming again.

But not for Elliott.

The mirror spins beneath him at exactly the right moment. It skims across his calf—and then Elliott vanishes.

I sag. It worked. I got him out. He's awake on Mirage now. He won't fall a hundred feet to his death, won't be eaten by a Being . . . but he'll still have that gunshot wound, and it looked bad.

I have to wake up. I have to find his real body. I know Mirage won't have enough energy to heal us both, but maybe I could still get Elliott to Earth in time to save him.

The mirror is almost into the dark now. One last rotation—

—and then obsidian talons erupt out of the reflective surface. Each one is as long as I am tall, covered in shadow-edged scales, with tiny, delicate feathers blooming farther up. The claws are as sharp as razors. They latch on to the top landing of the stairs with an earth-shaking blow, and the staircase shudders and groans under the weight. The scales on the massive leg ripple as the muscles beneath them flex.

The mirror continues to fall. The Being pulls itself up and out.

Another set of talons. These stab into the wall, a good seventy feet away. The whole cavern shakes, the yellow lightbulb flickering, clods of dirt shaking loose from the ceiling.

Time to make my exit. Covering my head, I run for the elevator—and then freeze.

The mayor is in front of me. She's scooped up her gun, its barrel still stained by her son's blood, and she's aiming it at me. Behind her, both Diaz and the older cop are scrambling through the elevator and back into the tunnel, but she makes no move to follow.

"What did you do to Elliott?" she demands.

We do *not* have time for this. I want to lash out at her, but I force myself to stand still. She tried to kill me a minute ago and shot her own son instead. I can't afford to try her again. "I saved him from you," I shout back. A support beam creaks and snaps, half of it hammering downward a few feet away. I jump out of its path. "Let me through! We've got to get aboveground—we've got to find another mirror!"

Something in the mayor's eyes shifts, goes shuttered and dark. "You corrupted my son," she says. "You loosed Beings on the city I swore to protect. The city I *have* protected, no matter what it cost me."

Her eyes are ice. Her aim is steady. And suddenly, there is no one, *no one*, who I hate more than I hate this woman—the mayor who lied to me about London, the woman who exiled me, the mother who might have killed her own son. She is *nothing* like him.

Because, I suddenly realize, she's too much like *me*.

Earlier Elliott said I was all or nothing. But she is too. She thinks the ends justify the means, that protecting her city is worth the price she's making everyone else pay. She'll take out whoever stands between her and what she wants. Elliott, though—he's the one who finally put himself between her and her goal. Between me, and a bullet. Because he doesn't just believe in a middle ground. He's willing to *be* the middle ground. And that is much harder, and more painful, and more right than anything either his mother or I have ever been able to do.

Outside in the cavern, the Being roars. The sound is impossibly loud with an almost metallic quality that grates in my skull. More dirt clods rain on my head. The mayor ducks.

Her second of distraction costs her. I use the same move on her that I used on her son, two days and a lifetime ago. I step inside her reach. I duck under the gun. I ram the heel of one hand into her wrist, lock my other hand around the gun, and wrench it sideways.

She pulls the trigger. The shot thunders past my ear but misses. The gun is in my hands. I step away and aim at her.

I'm not a good guy. I have done things I regret.

Killing her wouldn't be one of them.

But Elliott would regret it. Elliott would never forgive me. And somehow, even though that shouldn't matter, it does. Because I don't want to be like his mother. I don't want to make her choices anymore—don't want to make the choices I've been making anymore.

Be the middle ground.

"Run," I tell her coldly.

But she doesn't have time to move. A set of claws, so black it hurts to look at them, punches through the open-air windows. I dive away as half of my loft—the half where the elevator tunnel was, the half where the mayor was standing—caves in. She's instantly buried.

I curse as I army-crawl beneath the claws. There goes my exit. There's no other way out, not from here. I'd have to get to the tunnels that lead out of the cavern below, have to get down the stairs past the Being that's now using my loft as target practice.

The claws retract, dropping heavily downward, tearing a chunk—and the staircase landing—out of the floor and wall.

And just like that, I'm trapped.

The bulb overhead flickers again. If the loft takes another attack like that it'll kill the generator and I'll be stuck in the dark, in a cave-in, with a Being. I don't know which death would be worse: being suffocated, being torn apart by fear incarnate, or falling to my death through the darkness below.

No. That's not true—I do know which is worse. I knew it the moment I first saw those black veins crawling across my hand. The moment I realized that fear would, in the end, be the thing that finally got the better of me.

The creature roars. I drop the gun and cover my ears, unable to bear the sound. *Thud.* The whole loft, the whole cavern itself, shudders. I hear rocks hitting the ground far below. The Being is too big for the cavern. It's trying to punch its way through to the surface. I can stay here and be buried, opt for the less awful death, or . . . I can do something very stupid that might just get me out.

I crawl to the edge of the hole the Being clawed into the floor of my loft. I squint into the darkness. A massive wall of scales and feathers shifts into view, only about ten feet away. *Thud*—it crashes into the roof of the cavern again. Everything shakes, harder this time. Several of the support beams that crisscross the ceiling over my head shriek and snap.

I stand. I cross to the back wall and crouch down like a

sprinter at the starting line. My heart is thumping fast, a steady, buzzing rush of blood through my veins. I take a deep breath. I let it out. I launch myself forward.

Five steps to the ledge. Three. One. The wall of shadow-dark feathers and scales shifts in front of me as the monster slams itself into the ceiling again.

I'm at the ledge. I push off it. For a moment I'm hanging, suspended, over nothingness.

And then I crash into the Being. The shock of it jars my whole body, and my teeth snap together. Blood fills my mouth. I spit it out, grabbing for anything that'll hold as I slide down the creature's huge shoulder. Smooth scales ripple under my fingers, cool and hard like volcanic glass, same as the scorpion. The sting in my palm burns in resonance. The dim lightbulb at my back flickers off again and this time it doesn't come back on. I'm falling blindly, scrabbling at a monster, trying to save myself.

My hands close on something that holds. Feathers—massive ones, quills so big I can barely wrap my hands around them. The barbs are stiff and sharp, slicing at my fingers, but I hold on tight anyway. This Being is going to the surface, and it's taking me with it.

Thud. A shock vibrates across the Being's body, nearly shaking me off again. The ceiling of the cavern finally gives. There's a horrific rending noise and then dozens of feet of rock and earth crash down all around us. I duck my head to protect myself as the Being explodes upward, but I still get nailed in the skull with what feels like a boulder the size of my fist. The world flashes strangely bright and my grip on the feathers starts to relax. Everything feels murky and slow. I try to force myself back to alertness through sheer willpower.

Water tumbles over me—the standing water from the hurricane, gushing downward into the crater the Being has just punched through the ceiling. My loft is no longer secure in the slightest, I think with a wild laugh. The monster's front talons are latched on to the edge of the hole and it's heaving itself upward. I'm hanging off its shoulder.

The Being leaps up onto the ground. I'm a hundred feet in the air, my grip loosening more by the second, the world a strange blend of light and shadow. When the creature's wings crack open like thunder, I slide the last few feet down the feathers I was clutching—and fall.

Sky. Being. Ground. They rotate impossibly slowly.

The city is laid out at the feet of the monster. The neat rows of hundred-year-old banyan trees are snapped and splintered. The ration dispensary is already rubble, imploded by the tremors. The hurricane is screaming from not far away, the towering slate-gray eye wall looming just offshore, but here the standing water that stretches across the whole island looks almost peaceful, reflecting the yellow-gray of the sky. Maybe it wouldn't be so bad, to fall into the sky.

My pulse is a drunken stagger in my ears. Falling. I'm falling. I should be terrified. I am.

My body twists in another rotation. The Being's wings are cloaked in curling shadows, flaring impossibly wide, seeping over the sky—a spilled-ink tsunami. Fog burgeons out of the crater behind it, blooming into a mushroom cloud that towers up and out like it's the end of the world. The monster snarls a challenge to the city. I tumble past its ducked head: delicate reptilian nostrils, teeth carved of night. Eyes a violent golden contrast to the black of its body. At least I won't end my life in this thing's maw.

Another rotation. The ground is closer now. People are streaming out of the shelters like ants from a squashed hill. The water beneath them is a vast mirror, and I laugh at the irony.

Then I stop laughing.

I remember how, thirteen months ago, mirrors were the only thing that Mirage offered as an exit. Then we got rid of those and he started showing us the door through polished metal and reflective sunglasses. I remember wondering when the ocean itself would be too reflective for safety—when we would all be doomed.

Another rotation. I've got fifty feet before I hit the ground. Shadows creep across my vision as I start to lose consciousness.

I want to close my eyes but don't dare. "Mirage!" I shout, hoping he can hear me. Hoping that in the real world, I still have my Being-stung palm against the ship's rainbow floor, that

I can still communicate with him. "Use the water!" My words are slurred and sluggish. I'm not sure if he'd even be able to understand them.

One last rotation. Thirty feet left. I'm aimed right at the street in front of City Hall. The water here is dammed up, maybe knee-deep. It's not nearly enough to break my fall. But maybe, maybe, it could be enough to get me out.

The darkness closes in on me. It muffles my hearing, muffles the wind in my ears, muffles the screams of the people below. When a swarm of batlike Beings erupt from a squat building two streets over, they blend into the shadows already in my head. It's not until I spot a giant onyx sea serpent snaking through the debris of the old train station that it registers:

The plan worked. Mirrors, and Beings, are everywhere. And it won't matter at all, not to me, unless . . .

There! A vast rainbow sheen starts at one end of the island and ripples its way toward the city center. It swallows the fleeing people as it goes, body after body blinking out of existence. They'll wake up safe on the ship. Will I?

I'm racing against my death to the colorful shimmer of the exit. It's five feet away. So is the ground. But in the end, it's the shadows creeping across my vision that win the race.

I blink into unconsciousness half a second before I hit the ground.

CHAPTER TWENTY

WHEN I WAKE UP, THE WORLD IS MADE OF STARS. They roll out, horizon to horizon, shining gently like there's never been such a thing as a storm. I want to fall into them forever.

"They're still wrong," says a voice to my right.

I turn. It's Elliott. He's sitting next to me, knees drawn up to his chest, head tipped back against an iron bar. I follow the line of metal upward; about twenty feet above his head, it arrows inward and meets with other bars to support a big, blinking red light above us. It looks faintly familiar but I can't quite identify why. My thought processes are slow and muddy, and my head aches as if someone's taken a hammer to it.

I look down. We're sitting on a metal platform. I lean out to look over its edge—we're suspended above a pine forest.

Radio tower. The term for this structure finally comes to me, along with an image: a day of sunshine and honey, "Stand by Me" in the background, my brother's sideways smile. The radio tower we drove past. The promise to climb it when Ty returned.

Another image: the same tower viewed from above, the top of it scarred and twisted, snapped off like a toothpick.

I squint, trying to make my fuzzy brain work right. *They're still wrong*, Elliott said a second ago, when I was looking at the stars. "We're still . . . in the dream?" I finally manage, wondering why the radio tower is suddenly intact again, whether Elliott has fixed it with his thoughts for some reason. Although I guess I should be wondering how we got from the island—we were on the island, weren't we?—back to here in the first place.

Elliott's gaze stays on the sky. "Not exactly."

"I was falling," I remember.

The faintest trace of a humorless smile crosses Elliott's face. "Me too."

I stand up. I grab on to the iron bar and lean out, scanning the forest below us. There's no fog anywhere. This isn't right. I remember falling from the Being, I remember the rainbow sheen in the water. I should be either dead or on Mirage now. Not here.

How could I have gotten here?

Unless . . . I fell unconscious right before I hit the mirror-exit. Which has to mean that instead of waking up—because the damage that knocked out my dream self would also have happened to my real body on Mirage—I was inserted safely right back into the shared dream. Except this can't be the shared dream, because there's no fog and no hurricane.

Not exactly, Elliott said a second ago.

"Where are we?" I demand, staring down at him.

He's still not looking at me. "A mental construct," he says. "I think it's yours. I've been here about an hour, but from what I can tell, you've been here a little longer than that."

There's something off about his voice. It's too calm. He always sounds too calm when he's trying to hide something—fear, anger, vulnerability.

Pain.

I was falling.

Me too.

Something tight and fearful settles over me. I crouch down. Elliott's knees are still pulled up, his arms wrapped tightly around them. His shirt is dark gray, too dark to see any stains. I touch the spot between his shoulder and his heart. My fingers come back slick with red.

My stomach turns. "Elliott," I say helplessly.

"It doesn't hurt anymore," he says. "I'm pretty sure that's

a bad sign. Though it has been a while since I earned my first aid badge."

He shrugs, but only with his right shoulder. The way he's leaning against the iron bar starts to look less like casual stargazing and more like he's propping himself up because he doesn't have the strength to sit otherwise.

"But you got out," I protest. "I got you out."

He shifts his head in something that's almost a nod—another motion made small, made painful. "I did get out," he confirms. "Nice trick with the mirror, by the way."

"Elliott," I say again. The word is strained. He keeps dodging the obvious questions, keeps trying to distract me. Or himself.

He sighs: one last delay tactic. Then, finally, he looks at me. "I managed to stay conscious on Mirage for about an hour," he says. His eyes are tight with the pain he claimed wasn't there. "During which time I dragged you about halfway to the escape pods. Some of the other people who woke up tried to help me at first, but then Mirage started crashing, and it was everyone for themselves. Then I fell unconscious. From blood loss, probably. As soon as I passed out I was sitting up here on this tower with your body lying next to me. It's been an hour since then."

I stare at him. "You . . . tried to *drag me* to the escape pods?" I say at last.

He's been slowly bleeding to death for two hours. He was conscious for half that time—time that he'd spent trying to get me to safety. If he'd left me behind, could he have made it to the pods, made it to Earth? Made it to medical help quickly enough to save his life?

All this time I've been lying to him, thinking I needed to persuade him to help me save everyone. But he wouldn't have needed any persuading, would he? Not if he spent his last moments trying to save *me*.

I look down at my fingers, which are shining black in the moonlight. I want to wipe the blood off. I don't deserve to wipe the blood off.

"I lied to you," I tell him.

The night swallows the words. He inhales again and then, carefully, like it hurts him—because *of course* it hurts him—exhales.

Then he says: "I know that, you absolute jackass."

I blink. "What?"

He turns his head and stares me down. "I know people who die in the dream don't just wake up fine on Mirage. I knew it wasn't true about two seconds after I thought of it, because I realized it doesn't make any sense. And also, because I remembered that the very first time we woke up on Mirage, *I heard you screaming.*"

The memory flashes through my mind: waking up on the rainbow floor, my Being sting sending fire and brimstone through my veins—and me, howling like I was being burned alive.

"You were far away, but I knew it was you," Elliott says. "I came running. I could just barely see you ahead when I somehow got knocked back out and woke up in the dream again. I'm guessing that was your doing, right?"

Numbly, I nod.

He turns his gaze to the stars again. "I didn't put things together until you fed me that bullshit about how maybe Braedan wasn't really dead. I have to give you a little kudos— you at least looked guilty when you said it. That might've given me a clue even if I hadn't remembered you screaming on Mirage and realized it meant you still had the Being sting even there. Which means, I suppose, that we're both dying now."

I sit down at his back, bracing myself on the opposite side of the metal beam. He's only a few inches away but from here I could pretend I was alone, if I wanted to.

I wish I wanted to. It would hurt less.

"You were right," I tell him. "About me being all or nothing. I wanted to see Ty again so bad. I would give anything." Something catches in my voice and I stop, close my eyes. I don't want to look at the radio tower anymore. Don't want to think about what this place means to me. But, of course, now I can't *stop* thinking about it. I open my eyes. "You said this is my dream, right? Not the shared dream."

"That's my best guess."

It makes sense. I must've been reinserted back into the

shared dream as soon as I initially fell unconscious, and then when all the islanders were gone or dead and I was dreaming alone, my mind built my own personal mental construct. Just like the construct of my old house, the one with memories playing in its windows.

"This radio tower," I say. "Ty promised the two of us would climb it together when he got back from his year of studying abroad."

Elliott waits.

After a second, I sigh. "I'm sorry I lied to you. I just . . . I needed you to believe me. I needed you to think you *had* to help me wake everyone up. That it was Mirage forcing us to do it. That maybe there might be a chance Braedan was still alive, that you could see him the next time you woke up in the real world. I knew from how strongly I felt about finding Ty that it would work—that you would help me, if it was for Braedan's sake."

"I would have helped you anyway," Elliott says, "if you had just *asked*."

"I had to make sure." But that's not quite right. "I was afraid," I confess instead. "I thought there was a chance you might be like me after all. That you'd abandon me, if it came down to it."

"You think you'd abandon me, if our positions had been reversed?"

"In a heartbeat."

He breathes an almost-laugh. "Bastard," he says, more lightly than I deserve. Probably because it doesn't really matter anymore for either of us.

"Hero," I reply, striving for the same tone.

"That's not even an insult."

"Shows what you know."

We fall silent. I'm not sure if it's because it hurts him too much to talk or because there's nothing else to say. My injured hand is starting to sting again, the sign of an oncoming wave of pain. I wish Mirage would finish crashing before it hits. I'd rather die quick and brilliant than slow and painful.

"I'm guessing you've already tried to conjure up a mirror to get back out?" I ask after a moment.

"First thing," he confirms. "Didn't work—no Beings, no exit. Probably because your construct doesn't have the same rules as the shared dream. And also maybe because I've lost too much blood to wake up by now anyway." Before I can respond to that, he rolls his head to the side to look at me. "There's one thing I haven't been able to figure out. You claimed earlier that your sting went away in the real world—that that's what you were getting out of waking everyone up. But we both know that isn't true. So what *were* you trying to get out of it?"

I lift my injured hand. The skin is gray and corpselike all the way up to my shoulder now, and the black veins are spreading across my collarbone and chest. They're crawling across my skin so fast that I can almost see their growth in real time. "He was going to heal me," I say, and then pause.

Mirage said he might have enough energy to heal me once everyone was awake. It's been two hours—at this point everyone is either awake and escaped, or dead. If Mirage could heal me, he should be able to do it by now . . . if I wasn't trapped in here.

But am I trapped in here? Elliott probably is. His body is in shock, unable to wake up. There's no reason I shouldn't be able to wake up, though. I was knocked unconscious for a while but I'm fine now. And this is *my* construct, just like the memory of my old house. When I wanted to get out of there . . .

All I had to do was walk out.

Which means all I'd have to do now is walk out too. Get up, step off the side of this tower, and leave Elliott to die.

In a heartbeat, I'd told him a second ago. And it only makes sense. In the state he's in he'd never make it to Earth before he died. But me, I could live. I could go home, see Ty, finally get the things I've worked so hard for.

I can leave Elliott behind and get everything—or we can both die here, and get nothing.

I laugh out loud. The sound is harsh and brittle with irony.

"What's . . . so funny?" Elliott asks, his breathing more labored now.

I stand up. "Me. This. All of it." I step to the edge of the platform. "Thanks for everything, Elliott. I mean it. You're a good guy. And that's not an insult this time."

He lifts his head off the iron bar. He stares at me, something like alarm tugging his eyes tight. "What are you doing, Marty?" he asks carefully.

I close my eyes. "Being the middle ground," I tell him.

And then I step out over the empty air.

CHAPTER TWENTY-ONE

I JOLT UPRIGHT, GASPING. THE RAINBOW FLOOR IS flickering wildly: beeswax gold urgency, burnt umber frustration, emerald worry, and some brilliant, flaring shade of red that reminds me of a phoenix. I think it means pain.

Elliott's body is a few feet away, crumpled up like he dropped where he stood. One hand is over his chest, over his injury, like he still can't believe it's there. Like he can't believe his mother put it there. He doesn't deserve to die like this. Doesn't deserve to die at all.

I put my injured palm, which is starting to tingle with the beginnings of agony, on the floor. Instantly the colors flick to orange. I frown for a second until I understand—it's fire. Mirage is on fire. He's entering the atmosphere, burning up. Crashing.

Marty, he whispers.

"Mirage. I'm sorry," I tell him. "Is there no way you can save yourself?"

No. But I think I can heal you now. Thank you for saving the others. About two-thirds of them made it out of the dream.

Two-thirds. That means one-third of the citizens of Cisco Island—nearly a thousand people—are dead now, because of the plan I enacted.

They would have died anyway. I did the only thing I could have done. Not in the right way or for the right reasons, though.

I glance at the body by my side. "I don't want you to heal me," I tell Mirage.

A pause. *Why not? The escape pods I made, they're built to survive re-entry. You could probably make it to one before I burn up. You would be fine.*

"But Elliott wouldn't. Could you heal him?"

I . . . think so. Yes. But I only have enough energy to heal one of you.

Everything in me curls up tight, even though I'd already guessed his answer. "Do you have enough energy for healing plus a short-range teleport?" I ask. "From here to the escape pods?"

I believe so. But, Marty—

"Do it. Heal him and teleport him to a pod. Quick, before

I change my mind."

Mirage hesitates again. In my head, he's lit up bright orange with regret. *You won't change your mind*, he says.

I manage a smile. "Shows what you know," I say again, my voice shaking only a little.

What about you, then? What will you do? Won't you at least try to get to a pod yourself? I might have enough energy left to transport you, too. You might survive long enough to see your brother.

"I'd only see him for a few minutes, if at all. And you'd die alone. You were by yourself all those years, traveling through space, trying to fulfill your purpose. And then when you did fulfill it, you got shot out of the sky. You deserve at least this much. You deserve to not be alone."

Thank you, he says softly.

The floor beneath me is growing warm, getting eaten away by the orange flames. "Hurry, Mirage."

His focus turns inward. Gently, with my free hand, I roll Elliott onto his back. His hand flops limply to the ground, fingers rusted in red-brown. The wound looks wrong now—too ragged, too vulnerable—so I cover it myself. His chest is barely moving with his breaths. There's a long pause, much longer than it should be, between his inhales and exhales. His skin is cool beneath my hand.

When the wound starts to knit back together, I feel it under my fingers. First the bullet hole closes. Then his breathing eases, gets quicker, deeper. His skin takes on a healthy flush instead of that awful gray pallor. Then his forehead wrinkles like he's starting to wake up.

He must be exiting the construct. He saw me step out over the empty air and vanish just a moment ago. What would he have to lose by following me, at this point? And now that his body is no longer in shock, he'll be able to regain consciousness.

"Mirage," I say, "teleport him now."

Elliott's eyes blink open. He squints, then starts to sit up. He spots me—one hand still on his chest, the other pressed to the rainbow floor.

I smile at him. I make it look careless. "Just say hi to Ty for me when you get the chance, would you?" My voice wavers despite my resolve.

His eyes widen. He starts to open his mouth. And then he blinks out of existence, successfully teleported away.

My right hand drops back to my side, empty. I bow my head, now that he's not here to see, and let myself feel all the things that are clawing through me. Despair, fear, triumph. And pain, too. My skin is clammy under the wave of agony that's slowly building in my palm, about to explode over me, about to incinerate me.

The ship around me trembles and shrieks: a high, visceral, metallic sound. "What's that?" I ask Mirage.

I'm letting parts of me break off and burn up, he explains. *So I won't be too big when I hit the ground. I don't want to cause damage.*

I shake my head, look down at the blood that's still smudged on the floor where Elliott was. "You two are just alike, you know that? Always trying to save people you shouldn't. They shot you down. I'd leave them to burn."

No, you wouldn't.

His faith in my good nature isn't warranted, but I want to let him keep it, so I stay quiet.

Elliott is safe, he reports. *I jettisoned the pod. It'll land near the others in a few minutes.*

I nod and squeeze my eyes closed. Then I open them, because the bright orange flames are still scorching the outside of the ship, and didn't I wish for a brilliant death?

So brilliant that there can't be any darkness. So brilliant that I can't see the shadows eating me alive.

There's another trembling in the floor beneath me, more violent now, and transparent walls spring up only a dozen or so feet around me. The flames encircle me completely now, below, around, above. Mirage is letting the rest of himself burn up. I can hear him screaming. Then the wave of pain hits me and we're screaming together. My fingers curl violently inward, nails scraping against the smooth floor, splitting and tearing under the pressure.

You got my name wrong, Mirage whispers. I can feel the effort it takes for him to speak. I grit my teeth, trying to think through the pain that's still gaining strength. He's trying to distract me. Trying to distract both of us. The least I can do is let him.

"What?" I manage, the word barely a hiss of breath.

I was thinking about it more, going through all the knowledge I've gained from watching the humans, from watching you. And I don't think Mirage is the best translation of my name. It's more like . . . Refraction. The way fog scatters the lightning. The way a prism breaks sunshine apart into a rainbow. How a lens can focus light to make things seem bigger, or smaller, or distorted. That's me. And that's a better word for my abilities, too.

I think about the mirrors in the shared dream. The way we all thought the Beings were alien weapons coming through some portal when really they were just pieces of ourselves, bits of our own fears bent and reflected back to us. Or—not reflected. *Refracted.*

The way fog scatters lightning. The way a lens changes a person's perception, makes things look bigger, warped, both more and less real.

One minute to impact, Mirage reports quietly, strain fraying the words.

The pain in my hand is burning too high for me to respond now, too high for me to think. I curl up on the floor and try to brace myself. Mirage is shaking violently, screaming across the atmosphere and in my head. Scarlet agony is everywhere.

Then, suddenly, it shifts into a startling mix of emerald and cobalt blue. "Mirage?" I gasp.

The colors swirl in my head, tuck themselves around me. Emerald is worry, I remember. But cobalt—cobalt is pleasure. Mirage is *glad*. Of what?

The floor is cracking now, violent fissures spreading across it. But even though everything around me is burning up, somehow coolness is centering under my palm, calming the pain there. *I can't heal it*, Mirage says softly. *I don't have the energy. But I can minimize it. I can make you strong enough to bear it.*

The pain eases. I gulp down a breath, confused but glad. A terrible rending noise snarls through the ship around me, reminding me of the way the earth sounded when the dragon-Being punched through it. Something snaps under my hand. The fiery walls around me grow closer, closer. More of Mirage burning up. We're almost to the ground now. How long can he cocoon me, before I burn too?

Be well, Mirage says. *Tell them I meant no harm.*

I squint. "What are you—" I say, and then everything around me vanishes.

I'm standing in front of a window. It's bordered by ugly gray and pink floral curtains. They frame a view of an overgrown front lawn, and above that, Mirage. Crashing.

He's a fireball. A screaming, burning, dazzling comet. He plunges through the last bit of atmosphere and streaks toward the ground. Outside, people are yelling in the streets. Some have their phones lifted high to track his descent. Others have their hands over their ears, their heads ducked as if to protect themselves. Shattered glass is scattered all over the road—broken windows, I realize, from Mirage's sonic boom. The pane in front of me is broken too, and wind is curling through the frame and batting at the curtains.

My eyes follow the comet overhead but my brain is stalled, trying to figure out what's happening. This must be another construct. Mirage must be giving me an outside view of him as he crashes. I don't know why he wants me to see it this way, though. Maybe to distract me, or maybe so it won't seem so terrifying.

But—the *people*. They aren't flat holograms. They're running, shrieking, gasping, pointing. I thought Mirage said he couldn't replicate a sentient being in a construct?

Above their heads, the comet that is Mirage shrinks suddenly. Half of him breaks off and burns to ether. The rest is seconds away from gouging a new crater into a hill in the distance when it folds in on itself, flares brighter than ever, and then . . . crumbles into nothingness.

The last bit of Mirage burns away seconds before he hits the ground.

Something inside me twists hard at the sight of his death, and my own. I wonder if this construct is somehow protecting my consciousness, letting it live for a few more seconds after my body is already burnt up. I lift a hand to pull the curtains aside so I can get a better view of the streak of slate-gray smoke that's still emblazoned on the sky—and then I freeze, the back of my left hand hovering in front of me.

The black veins are gone.

I turn my hand over and open it. Only then do I realize I'm holding something. It's about six inches long, jagged-edged, warped and damaged but smooth on the top like it's made of glass. It's transparent, but the faintest trace of a motionless rainbow sheen is still glazed across its surface. I remember something snapping off in my hand—a piece of Mirage's floor.

Through the shard, I can make out the Being sting in my palm. The injury looks magnified, showing every detail, as if the piece of floor is a lens. The circle of white flesh is still wreathed in black veins, but they're much smaller and confined to my palm rather than streaking across my whole body. The skin on my arm and hand is a healthy tan, not gray. The wound still hurts, but it's a faint, bone-deep ache now, not a wave of unbearable agony.

What did Mirage say a second ago? *I can't heal it.*

But I can minimize it. I can make you strong enough to bear it.

And then: *Be well.* A goodbye.

I look back at the people in the street. At the curtains—the ugly floral curtains. I touch them. They feel real. They feel as familiar as they look, because they're *my* curtains, the curtains that have hung in the house my brother and I have lived in since we were kids.

Someone moves behind me.

I turn slowly. My gaze skims across the beige carpet, the chocolate-brown monstrosity of a couch, the piano. And, in the far corner with a bright red climbing harness slung around his waist and a coil of rope in his hands—my brother.

All impossibilities.

But my breath catches somewhere between my heart and my throat anyway, because it all looks so *real*. Realer even than the last hologram I saw of him. His hair is still wrong: now it's too long, too shaggy. His face looks haggard instead of smiling, and his shoulders slump when he was always chiding me for the same thing, but it all looks so alive on him. Not like a memory of my brother. More like the person my brother might be today—if he'd spent the last year mourning me.

His eyes are glossy with shock, with disbelief. He squeezes them shut, hard, then opens them again, like he's the one afraid he's in a dream. "Marty?" he says. The word arcs into me like life. I'm scared to let it in. Scared to acknowledge the possibility that this might not be a construct—that Mirage could have somehow used the last dregs of his power to teleport me to the ground while he was crashing.

I force myself to breathe. I have to step sideways. I have to know whether he's a construct, whether he folds into a flat fiction when my perspective changes. Desperation claws at me, tries to hold me in place, tries to tell me to just stand here, right here, for the rest of my life. That way I can believe he's real, no matter what.

But Ty's across the room before I can finish arguing with myself. He moves differently now too. He's quicker, lither. The studious botanist brother is gone. In his place is this person who moves with easy grace, his worn climbing harness jingling at his waist. When he reaches me, the coil of rope drops to the floor, forgotten. His hands clamp on my shoulders like he's afraid I'll dissipate.

His *hands*. His hands. Their grip is painfully tight, impossibly warm, solid and real. He didn't fold into a flat hologram when he stepped around the couch. My brother is real. My brother is alive. My brother is here—and somehow, so am I.

He holds me at arm's length. His eyes are still shining as he scans my face, like he's looking for proof I'm really me. He believes, and doesn't believe, and he's scared of both options.

"I kept thinking if I came back, if I stayed, you'd come back too," he says, his voice a hoarse whisper. "That maybe one day I would walk out of my room and you'd be here. It doesn't make any sense, you're *dead*, but—" He stops, swallows. "Marty. Tell me you're really here."

My brain is fumbling, darting from one detail to the next. I can't take it in. I can't wrap my mind around my brother, whole and alive and standing in front of me. I have to say something. I don't know what to say. I open my mouth anyway. "Why are you wearing a climbing harness?" is what comes out.

He looks down at himself like he's forgotten what he looks

like. The coil of rope is still splayed across the floor at his feet.

"I—I climb that damn radio tower every month," he says. "For you. To . . . find you. To remember you."

My brain still isn't working. I'm overwhelmed. Joy courses through my veins, brilliant and liquid like sunlight, like a jar of upended honey, like "Stand by Me" on the radio and an old Camaro humming beneath me. I can hardly speak through it. "Isn't that illegal?" I manage.

He laughs, his voice breaking. "I've been arrested three times. Someone had to fill your troublemaking quota," he says, and then he crushes me in a hug.

He smells like the woods. Like earth and grass. Like something green that wraps itself around your life, and grows through the cracks, and binds you back together.

The shard—the only remaining piece of Mirage—is still in my hand. When I lift my arms to hug my brother back I think I spot a flicker of color. Just for a second, no more than a blink. No more than a ghost.

Cobalt. Happiness.

I close my eyes and let it in.

EPILOGUE

WAIT FOR ELLIOTT NEXT TO VALKYRIE BRIDGE.

It's a ruin. The road is charred, torn apart. The statues are pulverized. The palm trees are gone. There's nothing left of the bridge itself beyond twisted chunks of metal that stab up through the waves offshore, barely visible in the dim starlight. Other things are different too.

There's no fog. The northeastern horizon no longer pulls at me.

And then, of course, there's the brand-new cluster of prefab buildings over my left shoulder. One of the researchers who works here has had their radio on full volume for the last few hours. The news station has played my interview—the now-famous one that I gave the day after I arrived back in the real world—twice during that span of time.

Tell them I meant no harm, Mirage said. I've done much more than that. I've told his story, and mine, in the hope that the next time a beautiful oval ship flies overhead, humanity won't murder it.

The radio is drowned out by the drone of an approaching helicopter. It's a sleek black one that blends in with the night sky, not the dingy white chopper that carried me to my exile, but I flinch anyway. I don't look up, don't track its progress. A sudden flood of uncertainty tingles in my gut.

The islanders were released from FBI custody today. Thirteen hundred vaguely familiar strangers, plus one Elliott Ackermann.

The helicopter lands. It's only on the ground for a moment before lifting off again, leaving a small figure staring up after it, his forearm held up to protect his face from the flying debris. I keep him in my peripheral vision as he lowers his arm. As he looks around. As he spots me, pauses for a long moment, and then walks in my direction.

I'm sitting on the edge of what used to be a bridge support. It creaks as he sits down next to me. There's a long moment of silence, and then:

"You look like shit," Elliott observes.

I let out a breath. The uncertainty settles. "I've been here three days. There's no running water," I explain.

"So that's the same, at least." He's looking at the remnants of the bridge now too.

I risk a glance at him. He's a little thinner than I remember, his cheekbones almost gaunt—with leftover grief or from his long stay at the detention center, I'm not sure—and there's a new sort of quietness about him. Not like he's hiding his emotions. More like he's learned to get along with them, maybe.

His knees are pulled up, his arms wrapped loosely around them. It makes me remember the way he looked in that last mental construct, on the radio tower. When he was dying. I flinch again, and look away.

He catches the motion but doesn't remark on it. "With all your newfound wealth, I'd think you'd be able to afford swankier accommodations," he says instead.

So he's heard the news. I just sold the movie rights to my biography for eight figures. I donated half the proceeds to a fund earmarked for the newly released islanders, so he'll be able to afford some swanky accommodations of his own soon, but I'll be damned if I'm the one to tell him that.

"Maybe I felt like slumming it," I reply—a little too lightly.

He gives me a look. "That's not why you brought me here."

"No." I hesitate. The words I want to say to him have lived in my head for so long that now they feel stuck there, rusted shut like an old door. "I'm sorry," I manage at last. "For what I did to Braedan."

His expression goes blank, impossible to read. He doesn't say anything.

I swallow and keep going. "And . . . I'm sorry for the other stuff too, for everything I did to you—for trying to shoot you in the knee, for—"

He cuts me off. "That's not why you brought me here either. You could've apologized to me in a letter." His voice is sharp now.

I fumble for words. "They wouldn't let me send you any letters" is all I can come up with.

Something in his expression eases. "Of course not," he says. He's quiet for a second, then seems to realize how tense I am—staring at the sea, waiting for him to forgive me or hate me or *something*. He raises an eyebrow and says: "Well, go on then. Finish your apology." He leans back, threads his fingers together behind his head, and waits.

I roll my eyes but finally manage to relax. He doesn't hate me. "I'm sorry I was an ass."

"Which time?"

"Just . . . you know, in general. I'm sorry for my general assery." I cross my arms. "I did save your life too, you know. Twice, if you want to get technical."

He drops his hands and turns to look at me in full, suddenly serious. "I know. I thought you died for it."

I press my lips together, my gaze flicking to the north, to the spot where the last bits of Mirage evaporated to ether after he transported me to safety. "I almost did."

"No, I mean . . . *until today*, I thought you were dead. They cut us off from everything after we landed. No news from the outside, just debriefing after debriefing. I found out you were alive when that chopper you chartered flew in to pick me up from the detention center about an hour ago."

My gaze snaps to him. He stares back. His eyes are the only thing that look exactly the same as before—they're a sharp, demanding blue. "They let you believe I was dead?" I ask, hardly able to get the words out past my anger. "For *three months?*"

That's why he was upset that I hadn't sent him letters. While I hid out with my brother until the government stopped trying to haul me in for questioning, he was stuck in a detention center along with all the other people who got pulled out of the escape pods. He had no family, no friends. He probably thought there was no one left alive who cared if he ever got out. And then he boarded a helicopter and got his first taste of the news since his arrival in the real world.

My famous interview. The protests it spawned. The demands for the islanders' freedom, for a peaceful first contact initiative, for the full crash-site findings to be released to the public. My story—and Elliott's story, which I had to tell without his permission—was the catalyst for something big, something that's still in the making. Something he didn't get to have a say in.

"I'm sorry," I tell him again.

He sighs. "I'm sorry too. Thanks for saving my life. You're still an ass." But he smiles a little as he says it, forgiving me once again.

We stare at the moonlight reflecting off the waves in silence. I wonder if he's seeing his ghosts the way I'm seeing mine.

"You could stay with us," I say eventually. "If you want. Until you figure out what you want to do." This offer is one of the main reasons I brought him here—so I could make it in person, so he would know I was serious—but I try to make it sound casual anyway, because I'm still me.

"Stay with you? Here on the island?" His tone is flat.

I make a face. "God, no. I don't *live* here."

"Then why exactly are you here?"

I stand up. I pull the shard of Mirage out of my pocket. This is the one thing I held back from the interview. If the authorities knew this existed, they'd take it away in two seconds flat. I can't let them.

"I'm here because of this," I tell Elliott.

He stands to get a better look at what I'm holding. He reaches out, takes the shard—and then grasps my hand, pulling my palm flat. The Being sting is a circle of scarred flesh now. There's no red ring around it anymore, but black veins still bolt across most of my palm.

Elliott looks at me. Some emotion flits over his face, a cross between accusation and concern. "I thought this would be gone," he says.

I sweep my thumb over the spot. "Not gone," I say. "But it's healed. Mostly."

"Does it still hurt?"

"Sometimes," I admit. "But it's okay."

And it really is. He must see it in my face, because he lets my hand drop and examines the shard. His eyes widen. "Is this a piece of the ship?"

"Yeah. No one else knows about it."

He stares at the jagged piece of glass in his hand. Then, suddenly, his breath catches and he fumbles the shard. I dive to catch it, then tuck it safely back in my pocket.

Elliott shakes his head. "Sorry. I thought I saw . . ."

"Colors?" I supply. "Flickering across its surface?"

"Yeah."

"That's why we're here. One of the researchers who lobbied to study the wreckage on the island is a consciousness expert. I want to take the shard to him, have him examine it. He and his team were supposed to get here three days ago—which is why I got here three days ago—but they got delayed till this morning. Then I found out you'd be released tonight, so I decided to wait a little longer." I start walking toward the prefab buildings behind us, motioning Elliott to follow.

After a second, he does. "You think Mirage might still be alive."

"Maybe. If he is, we have to help him."

"We?"

"Me. The researcher. You, if you'll help me. Ty."

He pauses. "So you really did find your brother?" he asks at last. There's something in his voice that wants to be glad but can't quite manage it. After all, he doesn't have a brother anymore.

I hunch my shoulders. "Yeah," I confirm.

"And . . . he's part of the 'us' you invited me to stay with earlier."

"Yes. If you want."

He doesn't answer for a second. We pick our way through the debris on the street, walk past the rubble that used to be the storm drain where I hid to watch Sam Garcia's exile. It's also the storm drain where Elliott escaped his mother, that last day at the bridge.

"I'd like that," Elliott says at last. We've come to the biggest prefab building. He reaches for the door's handle, pulls it open. "My dad is still somewhere in Miami, I think. He was always close with Braedan. I hated him, but now I think that might be mostly because my mom hated him. Maybe I'll . . . reach out. See if he wants to talk." There's only a small catch in his voice when he mentions his mother. He knows she's gone— he'll have to have seen her body next to mine when he found me on Mirage—but I know that it'll keep hurting, in one way or another, for the rest of his life.

"That's a good idea," I tell him, then pause. I'm standing at the entrance of the building, one foot on either side of the threshold. A familiar compulsion rises in me.

Elliott notices. He doesn't say anything. He waits.

I've been seeing Dr. Washburne—the same therapist I used to see pre-Fracture, who was understandably surprised to find me alive and back on his roster of patients—since I returned. He's helped me understand that flare-ups and changes in my obsessive fears are normal. We're working through some more exposure and response prevention therapy and it's helped me gain a lot of ground as well as a better understanding of myself and my OCD. It'll be a while before I'm okay, and maybe I'll never completely get there . . . but at the very least, I'm starting to be okay with *not* being okay. That's new, and actually kind of wonderful.

I step over the threshold. I tap the doorway, but only once on either side. One: an okay number, but not nearly as safe as three or five. Anxiety stirs in my gut and I let it exist.

My palm twinges. I glance down at it—at the darkness that still hurts sometimes, at the injury that will never completely heal. But that's okay. I'm learning to accept what I have. I'm learning to accept the middle ground:

An imperfect recovery.

A life that's streaked with shadows—but still brilliant.

AUTHOR'S NOTE

Although this book is a work of fiction, the obsessive-compulsive disorder (OCD) that Marty grapples with is a very real—and often very isolating and scary—experience for many teens and adults. If his struggles resonate with you, please know that you are not alone.

For more information about OCD, you can visit intrusivethoughts.org or iocdf.org (the International OCD Foundation's website). From 6 to 10 p.m. Pacific Time, teenagers can also call Teen Line at (800) TLC-TEEN ([800] 852-8336) to talk to teen volunteer listeners trained to provide support for those dealing with anxiety, depression, bullying, and a wide range of other issues.

For those who have or suspect they may have OCD, speaking with a trained mental health professional is also highly recommended, if circumstances allow.

ACKNOWLEDGMENTS

Thank you to my awesome agent, Naomi Davis, my fantastic editor, Lauren Knowles, my immensely talented designer, Rosie Stewart, and the whole team at Page Street. You all take such good care of me and my books, and I am so grateful for your hard work and investment.

Thank you to those who read drafts and/or helped me brainstorm elements of this story: Kira Watson, Sher-May Loh, Alicia Jasinski, Mark O'Brien, and Alyssa Chrisman. Thank you also to my lovely critique partners Chelsea Bobulski and Casey Lyall, whose encouragement has gotten me through so many hard times.

Thank you to Dr. Jonathan Grayson, author of *Freedom from Obsessive-Compulsive Disorder*, a book that served as an invaluable resource in my study of OCD. Thanks also to Andrea.

Thanks to the TV shows, movies, books, creators, characters, and games that inspire me: Lin-Manuel Miranda's *Hamilton*, *Thor: Ragnarok*, *Brooklyn Nine-Nine*, *Firefly*, *Doctor Who*, CW's *The Flash*, *Voltron: Legendary Defender*, *Final Fantasy XV*, BBC's *Sherlock*, Megan Whalen Turner's Queen's Thief series (read it—seriously), and *The Good Place*.

Thank you to Paige, superhero librarian and passionate champion of books.

Thank you to my family and friends. I especially want to thank my magnificent best friend, Britton, whose encouragement and take-no-prisoners boldness brings me life every day.

Thank you to my husband, Caleb, whose steadfastness (read: willingness to put up with me) often astounds me.

Thank you to my daughter—my little girl, full of fire—for lighting up my life with her zeal, curiosity, and kindness. May I someday be worthy of you.

Thank you to the God who walked me through my own shadows, even—especially?—when I didn't want to face them.

And last, thank you to my readers. The book that you hold in your hands is my soul. It was both the most fulfilling and the scariest thing that I've ever written, and part of it will always belong to you now.

ABOUT THE AUTHOR

Naomi Hughes grew up all over the United States before finally settling in the Midwest, a place she loves even though it tries to murder her with tornadoes every spring. She writes quirky young adult fiction full-time. When she's not writing, she likes to knit, travel with her husband and daughter, and geek out over British TV and Marvel superheroes.